The Liars' Gospel

NAOMI ALDERMAN

PENGUIN BOOKS

PENGUIN BOOKS

Published by the Penguin Group
Penguin Books Ltd, 80 Strand, London WC2R ORL, England
Penguin Group (USA) Inc., 375 Hudson Street, New York, New York 10014, USA
Penguin Group (Canada), 90 Eglinton Avenue East, Suite 700, Toronto, Ontario, Canada M4P 2Y3
(a division of Pearson Penguin Canada Inc.)
Penguin Ireland, 25 St Stephen's Green, Dublin 2, Ireland
(a division of Penguin Books Ltd)
Penguin Group (Australia), 707 Collins Street, Melbourne, Victoria 3008, Australia
(a division of Pearson Australia Group Pty Ltd)
Penguin Books India Pvt Ltd, 11 Community Centre,
Panchsheel Park, New Delhi – 110 017, India
Penguin Group (NZ), 67 Apollo Drive, Rosedale, Auckland 0632, New Zealand
(a division of Pearson New Zealand Ltd)
Penguin Books (South Africa) (Pty) Ltd, Block D, Rosebank Office Park,
181 Jan Smuts Avenue, Parktown North, Gauteng 2193, South Africa

Penguin Books Ltd, Registered Offices: 80 Strand, London WC2R ORL, England

www.penguin.com

First published by Viking 2012
Published in Penguin Books 2013
001

Typeset by Palimpsest Book Production Limited, Falkirk, Stirlingshire
Printed in Great Britain by Clays Ltd, St Ives plc

ISBN: 978-0-670-91991-8

www.greenpenguin.co.uk

MIX
Paper from
responsible sources
FSC
www.fsc.org   FSC® C018179

Penguin Books is committed to a sustainable
future for our business, our readers and our planet.
This book is made from Forest Stewardship
Council™ certified paper.

ALWAYS LEARNING   **PEARSON**

PENGUIN BOOKS

The Liars' Gospel

Naomi Alderman grew up in the Orthodox Jewish community in north-west London. Her first novel, *Disobedience*, was published in ten languages and won the Orange Award for New Writers and the *Sunday Times* Young Writer of the Year Prize. Like her second novel, *The Lessons*, it was broadcast as Radio 4's Book at Bedtime. She is a frequent radio broadcaster and is a regular contributor to several publications, including the *Guardian* and *Prospect*. She lives in London.

For my teachers. Especially those who taught me
Latin and Hebrew: the gift of double vision.

In Breughel's Icarus, for instance: how everything turns away
Quite leisurely from the disaster; the ploughman may
Have heard the splash, the forsaken cry,
But for him it was not an important failure

'Musée des Beaux Arts', W. H. Auden

Dramatis Personae

Jews

(anglicized versions of the names are in italics)

Yehoshuah/*Jesus*	a wandering healer and teacher
Miryam/*Mary*	the mother of Yehoshuah, and several other children, living in the village of Natzaret
Gidon of Yaffo	a fugitive
Yosef/*Joseph*	Miryam's husband, a woodworker
Shimon	
Yirmiyahu	
Iehuda	
Iov	sons and daughters of Miryam
Dina	
Michal	
Rahav	a woman of Natzaret
Ezra the Teacher	a learned man
Iehuda of Qeriot/*Judas*	a follower of Yehoshuah
Pinchas	Miryam's brother
Shmuel	Miryam's brother
Elkannah	Iehuda's wife
Caiaphas	the Cohen Gadol, the High Priest of the great Temple in

	Jerusalem
Annas	father-in-law of Caiaphas, a former High Priest
Caiaphas's wife	a well-educated woman
Darfon the Levite	a Temple administrator
Natan the Levite	the chief Temple administrator, Caiaphas's friend
Hodia's daughter	a wife in waiting
Elikan	a young priest
Bar-Avo/*Barabbas*	a rebel and a murderer
Giora	
Ya'ir	rebels, friends of Bar-Avo
Matan	
Av-Raham	a rebel leader
Ananus son of Annas	the new High Priest of the great Temple in Jerusalem

Romans, or members of other nations

Pompey	a military commander, also known as Pompey the Great
Calidorus	a wealthy merchant
Pomponius	a hanger-on of Calidorus
Tiberius Caesar	the Emperor
Pontius Pilate	the Prefect of Judea
Caligula	the new Emperor
Marullus	the new Prefect of Judea
Titus	a military commander, later Emperor

This was how it happened.

It is important to quiet the lamb, that is the first thing. A young man, learning the skills of priesthood, sometimes approaches the task with brutality. But it must be done softly, even lovingly. Lambs are trusting creatures. Touch it on the forehead just above the spot between the eyes. Breathe slowly and evenly, close enough to the creature to inhale the meaty scent of wool. It will know if you are nervous. Hold yourself steady. Whisper the sacred words. Grasp the knife as you have practised. Plunge the blade into the neck swiftly, just below the jaw. There must be no pausing. The knife must be sharp enough that almost no pressure is needed. Move it down evenly and quickly, severing the tendons and nerves as the blood begins to flow and the lamb's muscles spasm. Withdraw. The entire motion should take less than the time of one in-breath.

Hold the lamb so that the blood gushes down, that it may be caught in the sacred cup. There is a great deal of blood; the life is in the blood. It is appropriate at this point to meditate on the blood in your own body, on how quickly and easily it could be released, on how one day it will cease to flow. Sacrifice is a meditation on vulnerability. Your blood is no redder than this creature's. Your skin is no tougher. Your understanding of the events which will lead to your own death is probably no greater than this lamb's comprehension.

The smell of it is strong: iron and salt and sharpness. A priest catches the blood in the cup. The cup becomes full. The priest scatters the blood, spatters it to the four corners of the altar. The smell increases. The lamb stops twitching. The last traces of life are gone from it. This is how quickly it happens. When the blood is drained, slice open the skin and pull it from the carcass. Now the creature is meat. Every living being is meat for another. Do you think that the mosquito – one of the smallest of God's creatures – looks on us as anything other than food? Worms will one day devour you – do you imagine they will notice your intellect, your kindness, your riches, your beauty? Everything is eaten by some other thing. Do not think that because you have knives of bronze you are more than this lamb. All of us are lambs before the Almighty.

Remove the sacred organs from the flesh. Pull them, separating and cutting the sinews which hold them in place. Moments ago, they had purpose: like each man in the Temple, they had their functions to perform. Now they are objects to be burned in the holy fires. Take care not to pierce the bowel – the stench will be appalling. This is no ritual of the spirit, it is a matter of the body. Remember that your bowel too contains faeces, that the woman whom you most desire in all the world is, at this moment as at all others, full of mucus and faeces. Be humble. Remove the forbidden fats which may not be eaten: the sheet of fat across the abdomen, the fat of the kidneys.

Place the organs and the forbidden fats into the fire of the altar. As they burn, offer up praises to the Almighty, who has given us this holy duty, who has given us the wit to understand His works, who has placed us above the beasts in knowledge and in wisdom. As the fats burn, their outer membranes blackening, the soft white matter liquefying and dripping down among the burning branches, the smell will be sweet and delicious. These are the sweet savours for the Lord. Your mouth will begin to salivate, your stomach, if you have not eaten for some time, may begin to growl. You are not an angel, a disembodied spirit without desire. You are a body, like this lamb. You want to eat this flesh. You are a soul also, the more to praise your Creator. Remember what you are. Give thanks. When the fats and organs are consumed, the animal's carcass may be removed. It will be cooked for you and your fellow priests. Thus you will share the meal with God.

This is the daily sacrifice. Every day, twice a day, morning and evening, a year-old lamb, healthy and without blemish. Every time, it is a sacred thing. Every time, the animal is slain for the glory of God, not for the mere satisfaction of our hungers. Every time, as the life bleeds out, the priest should look, and notice, and give thanks for the animal whose life has returned to its Creator and whose flesh provides sweet savours for the Lord and nourishment for His servants.

They knew it would be that day. It is impossible to follow the fortunes of a battle closely without knowing when they are reaching their conclusion. Especially when that battle concerns the city in which you live.

They had fought off the army as long as they were able. They had the advantage, to begin with: the walls were high, the ramparts thick. As the army worked below, filling the ravine with boulders and felled trees, they hurled down rocks and arrows upon them. They worked in shifts, night and day, pulling the matter out of the moat by the cellar doors as quickly as it was placed there. They struggled. But they were undone by God.

The Lord commanded them to rest on the holy Sabbath. On this day, the besieging enemy was able to gain ground. Week by week, Sabbath by Sabbath, cubit by cubit, the ravine was filled in. They worked double time, but it was not enough. The invading army worked harder. They saw that soon the ravine would be so full of debris that a platform could be erected on it, that ladders could be raised and battering rams employed.

On the day that the platforms went down, they knew the end was coming. They were not afraid: fear would be a long time coming still, they had not yet seen starvation leading to cannibalism, to murder, to infanticide. Instead of fear, they were angry. They occupied a land between the river and the sea; it was a necessary foothold for anyone hoping to hold this region. They happened to stand in the way. It seemed wrong to them that the world should operate in such a manner. They raised angry cries to the Lord.

In the Temple, the High Priest heard the battering ram pounding on the city wall night and day now. Each resounding bang did little damage by itself. A small amount of dust, perhaps a tiny shift in one of the stones. Accumulating, night and day, those cedars twice as thick as the arm-span of a man would destroy the wall. The people could see the stones being bowed inward.

It was just before dawn when the first stone fell. It was towards the base of the wall, not quite at the bottom, and in the glittering early morning light the motes of dust around it seemed to shimmer as it tumbled, as it crashed to the ground. When it fell, there was a silence in the city. Outside, the soldiers whooped and shouted and redoubled their efforts. But for a moment, inside the city, there was only an astonished horror. They had known it must come and yet had not believed it until they saw. The impregnable wall was breached. Then there were cries. Bring men, bring fire, bring swords, keep the invaders back!

Inside the Temple, the young priests ran towards their master, crying out what they had heard. The High Priest watched them run, their robes flapping, their feet slipping on the blood-slick floor. He knew what they had come to tell him. Everyone in the city knew what it meant that the great banging had ceased. Were the sacrifices needed less now? Did the people no longer need to be brought close to God, to understand the shortness of their own lives?

He listened to their breathless words. One pleaded with him to leave the Temple. Another demanded that all the able-bodied young priests should take arms. A third suggested that they go out to meet the conqueror with a show of welcome. The conqueror was coming, he repeated, he was making for the Temple.

The High Priest said to them, 'Two lambs, without blemish. One in the morning, one at dusk. Together with a grain offering of fine flour mixed with oil. This is the burnt offering instituted at Sinai. An offering to the Lord.'

They became quiet. But, protested one, the conqueror is coming, he approaches. The others silenced him, stiffening their spines and pulling their robes around them. They hurried to their duties, their hands and legs knowing the ritual even as their minds blew here and there. This one began to burn the incense, that one to clean the ashes, those began to lay fresh wood.

As the sun rose above the horizon, they slew the lamb. They scattered its blood. Some of the priests were silently weeping. They could all hear the shouting outside the gates of the Temple. They continued nonetheless to separate the organs, the sacred forbidden fat. They heard the foot-beat of the army, that terrible consolidated crunch of one hundred right feet going down in unison. The lie of uniformity. As if they could become one creature. As if each of them, like this lamb, would not be utterly alone at the moment of death. No one else will save you from your own death, that is certain.

They burned the sacred portions of flesh. The High Priest felt his stomach growl as he inhaled the sweet scent of meat, because even now he was still just a man. The noise had ceased outside the Temple. The great gates were opening. Either there was no one left to defend them or they had surrendered in the face of insurmountable numbers. Well, they would find out for themselves soon enough. They began to prepare the wheat-meal offering, singing the psalm of the day. They brought the flour cake from its store. They anointed it with oil and frankincense.

And it was as they were preparing this offering that the conqueror, together with his troops, entered the Temple.

The matter was dealt with swiftly. The soldiers poured into the inner courtyard, shouting words in their own language, issuing and obeying commands at a run. They did not pause, even at the sight of the holy rituals. One or two of the priests attempted to run and were cut down. The High Priest was pleased to note that most of the younger men simply continued with their duties: burning the incense, fanning the flames, pouring the libations of wine. And if their arms trembled or their heads jerked or their mouths cried out when a sword ran them through, would not God in His infinite mercy forgive it?

The Romans swept through the sanctuary so quickly that they themselves seemed surprised, even alarmed, at how easily the thing had been done. They glanced at each other. The city had been a fortress, well defended. Was its heart to be taken without resistance? They looked around. The only man left alive was the High Priest; they had spared him to speak to their leader, the commander who was even now arriving.

The High Priest had expected a larger man, a brute with muscles of iron and a towering height. And a young man, why had he expected that? Perhaps because his way of making war had been so energetic. Pompey was forty-five, with a rather vague air, the lines on his forehead suggesting eyebrows constantly raised. He might have been powerfully muscular once, but he had run a little to fat now. He wore not the armour of battle but the toga of state, as if about to attend a meeting in the Senate.

His centurion addressed the High Priest.

'Pompey, commander of the Eastern legions and the Euxine fleet, triumphant conqueror of Hispania, consul of Rome, first man of the Roman Empire, primus inter pares, bids you . . .'

The centurion continued to speak. The High Priest looked at the meal cake in his hand. Flour, oil, water, baked to a fine flat bread. He crumbled the soft cake and placed it in the fire as was his duty. The flames flickered green and blue. He watched the cake burn.

The centurion, angry to receive no response, grabbed the High Priest's arm roughly, seemed about to strike him, when a single word from Pompey stopped him.

Pompey motioned his men to lower their weapons. Together, they watched the meal cake burn, as flour cakes and lambs and oxen burned on the altars of Rome to their own many gods. The stone floor was thick with the blood of the slain, the bodies still warm. The sweet scent of the smouldering oil and flour traced a thread of delicious aroma through the iron stench of blood. The cake was entirely consumed. Pompey uttered a word. The centurion drew his sword, grabbed the priest's chin, pulling it up and back, and slit the man's throat.

This had been the last offering made by a free man in the Temple.

Pompey was not an ungenerous man. His Hebrew spies informed him that it was a grave offence among the Jews for an outsider to enter the holy inner sanctuary. This prohibition could not, of course, be adhered to, but nonetheless he made his survey of the Temple with courtesy, examining the objects and having his scribe record them.

How many talents of gold?

Two thousand.

What golden vessels?

The lampstand, the lamps, the table, the cups.

Spices?

Yes, great chests of them, a prince's ransom.

Because he was impressed by the people whom he had conquered, because he had no wish to humiliate them further, he allowed them to keep these sacred treasures. And because he wished the people to feel the magnanimity of Rome as well as its power, he summoned the other priests, those who had not had the duty to attend the Temple that day, and bade them clean the inner courtyard of the blood and bodies of their friends and to begin the services once more. In this he was an astonishingly charitable conqueror.

The position of High Priest, of course, was a powerful one which could not simply be given to the next man in seniority. Pompey put his friend in that place, a Jewish prince who had been most cooperative during the siege and whose men had fought for Rome. It was a fitting gift for a loyal ally. This business concluded, Pompey left a garrison at Jerusalem and headed back to Rome in triumph.

This was how it happened. And everything that came afterwards followed from this.

Miryam

There is a dead boy on the hillside, they say. Or maybe just almost dead. The herder Ephrayim found him when he was seeking a lost lamb, and does not know how long he has lain in the shallow cave between the pathways. Where has he come from? They don't know. The clothes look like those made in Shomron, but the shoes are Galilean. Sturdy shoes, said Ephrayim, laying thereby his claim should the boy be lost. Sturdy, but still he should not have tried to cross the hills alone. It has been six cold nights one after another. Snow has fallen although it is nearly spring.

Still, if he is dead he must be buried, and if he is not dead they must attempt, at least, to care for him. They bring him to Natzaret thrown over the back of a mule. This is where Miryam first sees him. He is breathing, just a little, very shallow breaths, and they have wrapped him in furs. As they bring him in, a crowd comes to see – is he someone's cousin? Someone's nephew? Why did he come to Natzaret at such a time of rough travel? No one recognizes him. They push Miryam to the front in any case, to take a good look. A mother would know her own son, however changed he might be. Though they know there is no hope and he is at least a decade too young. But just in case.

Her youngest son, Iov, tugs on her skirt and says, 'Who is it, Ima? Who is it? Why does he look like that, Ima?'

She picks Iov up and passes him to her friend Rahav to hold as she stares intently at the man on the back of the mule. The half-dead man is not her son. How could he be? She notices that two fingers on his right hand are black. He'll lose them, painfully. If he's lucky.

They place him in Amala the widow's house and put him to bed with the dogs, for warmth. He sleeps the night, though they expect him to die, and in the morning begins to rouse, a little, enough to flutter his eyelids and take drips of water from a soaked rag. The pain from his blackened fingers keeps him moaning constantly, even in his sleep, a low keening wail like an abandoned newborn. He shivers and sweats and holds the injured hand like a claw. They fear a fever. They call for the blacksmith, who performs the necessary deed with kindness, that is to say: swiftly. He screams of course, a strangled, terrified howl, but that night he takes a little soup and sleeps deeply. He still has not spoken to say who he is, although he understands them when they say 'soup' or 'water'. They wonder if he is a Jew at all, and not a Syrian or a Greek.

It is four more days until he speaks. They take turns feeding him bone soup or bread soaked in milk. Among themselves, they murmur. He is not as young as the light bundle of him crumpled in the cave had suggested, but not so old as the lines on his face. His beard has not come in yet, except in mottled patches. He is perhaps fifteen or sixteen. And where are his people? There is one obvious answer. Every year, some village rebels against the Romans, refuses to pay the tax, claims they cannot pay – often it is true, they cannot pay. And the tax collectors report the rebellion, and soldiers are dispatched. Every year, some village is burned, its men put to the sword, its women and children to flight. It is not likely that a boy as young as this would have been a ringleader, would be remembered by a soldier. It is not likely that it is dangerous to have him here. Nonetheless, the old men mutter.

On the fourth day, when they come to give him his soup, they find he has woken and is patting the dog with his whole hand, keeping the injured one close to his chest. He is murmuring to the dog in good, intelligible Aramaic.

He looks up guiltily as Amala and Rahav enter the room with his soup. He knows they have heard him speaking. His good hand is twined in the dog's fur and the animal stirs and whines as it feels him tense.

Rahav puts the tray on the floor, just out of the boy's reach. Her arms are folded. She glares at him. Rahav's children are the best-behaved in the village, mostly out of fear.

'Well,' she says, 'we've fed you. Now, who are you?'

The boy glances between Amala and Rahav. He looks hungrily at the soup.

'Is this Natzaret?' he says. 'Did I reach Natzaret?'

They tell him it is. He did.

A change comes over his face. He sits up a little straighter, sets his jaw, as if facing a difficult job.

'Natzaret in the Galil?'

They tell him yes, again. And they cannot discern whether he is glad or afraid, such a shining-eyed sharpness comes over his face.

'The village of Yehoshuah the Teacher?'

And Amala and Rahav glance at each other with a sort of sad surrender. Of course, this. Out in the street, the little boy Iov is playing with some of the other children. Rahav sends him to fetch his mother, Miryam.

The rabbis say: when a loved one dies the sword is at your throat, and every way you turn your head it is there, in front of you.

So, this is how she is. When she grinds the wheat, she thinks of him. And when she soaks the cloths, she thinks of him. And when her youngest son, Iov, comes running to her, yes, it is her Iov, the foolish child who got his hand stuck in a jar because he would not unclench his fist to let go of the dried fig he'd found. But it is also that first little boy, her eldest son, the first child who ever skidded to a halt in the muddy place by the chicken enclosure shouting 'Ima, Ima!' – 'Mummy! Mummy!' She is distracted by the constant double image.

Iov is saying something. He kicks at a stone. The snow has turned to slush and the thin rain will soon wash it away entirely. He digs his toe into the hole left by the stone.

'Don't do that,' she says, 'you'll wear out the leather.'

And he looks at her sadly, because she spoke more sharply than she'd intended.

'But Ima, Ima, did you hear me? They're looking for you, at Amala's house, they're looking for you! They want you to go and see that man with half a hand!'

She asks him why, and his mouth twists and his eyes open very wide and she understands that he does not want to answer. So she has an idea, already, of what it is.

The women waiting outside Amala's home aren't waiting for her. They say nothing when she comes, most of them can't meet her eyes. One or two touch her on the back or shoulder as she passes. The rest are simply afraid. They want to know if this boy is a curse she has brought on them.

Inside the smoky, dark room, he is sitting on a heaped mattress. Someone has given him a woollen jerkin, with a thick robe on top of it. They add bulk to his thin frame. When she enters he stands, a little shakily, to greet her.

She says, 'Who are you?'

He looks into her eyes. He has an unsettling trick: that every word he says, he seems to mean with a profound depth of feeling.

'I am Gidon,' he says, 'from Yaffo.'

'And why have you come here, Gidon of Yaffo?'

His eyes are so clear and innocent that she becomes afraid. Innocence can destroy three times as quickly as guile. At least the cunning can be reasoned with or bribed.

'I have come to seek the village of Yehoshuah the Teacher, to find his friends and family here, to meet them and to befriend them.'

She breathes in and breathes out.

'He was a traitor, a rabble-leader, a rebel, a liar and a pretender to the throne. We have tried to forget him here.'

'Did you know him?' Gidon says.

She remains silent.

'Did you know him?' he repeats.

14

The fire spits. Some wet log sending a shower of sparks past the circle of stones on to the moist earth floor.

'I was his mother,' she says.

A wetness is starting in his eyes, he is shaking.

'Oh, blessings are on you,' he says, 'blessings are on you, and on your womb and breasts, because of the son you have given the world. A thousand thousand blessings from He Who is in All Places, for your son Yehoshuah.'

Her heart is a stone. Her mouth is a closed door.

'Go home.'

His eyes are shining. She thinks he might be about to embrace her or kiss her hand or fall to his knees before her.

'Go home,' she says again, before he can do any of these things. 'We do not want you here.'

And she leaves the room before he can say any more to her.

She remembers the screaming trees that night.

She thinks of them many days, and of what happens to those who challenge and fight and argue. And how little this boy seems to understand of where his words will lead.

She remembers the screaming trees and she thinks: if I can bear not to speak to him, it will be better for him. But she knows she does not have that strength.

The boy will not leave, of course. They do not understand how one simple, addle-headed, half-handed boy can be so stubborn. They offer him food for the journey. They offer him the warm clothes as a gift. When Sha'ul the merchant passes by on his way to Jerusalem, they suggest he take the boy with him as a help against bandits, and Sha'ul – whom they have known for twenty summers – is not unwilling, but the boy refuses.

He will work, he says. He will repay the kindness they have shown him. He will sleep in the stone shelter made for the goats. The weather is becoming warmer, it will not be a hardship to sleep there if he builds a small fire. His hand is mending, look, the wound has healed clean. He can work. If they will give him a bowl of food each day for his trouble, he will tend their crops and mind their animals and mend their gap-toothed walls. They shrug their shoulders at last. If he wants to be the madman of their village, so be it.

All of them know which house he will choose to settle by. Which byre will be his dwelling place. Whose fields he will clear of stones. Miryam is unsurprised when, one morning, she awakes to find him sitting patiently on a rock by her door.

He watches her stumble, morning-stiffened, to the well. She lowers the bucket and twists the rope just so, to make it dip under the water and fill, but when she tries to pull it up he is by her elbow.

'Let me do it.'

And she is old and tired and her knuckles and wrists ache. It is easy to let him. If he wants to, why not let him? He hauls the full bucket up. He is a little clumsy with his half-hand, but he is adapting quickly, as children do. As she watches, he tests out different ways of gripping the rope, settling at last on using the arm with the injured hand to trap the rope close to his body and secure it, while the other hand works to bring up more. He reminds her of a blind man she saw once, reading his way along a wall with a light and interested touch, as though his fingers were eyes.

He carries the bucket for her, a little unsteadily, slopping out more than she would like. He brings it into the room where Iov and Michal are still sleeping, wrapped around each other. They do not stir. Gidon puts the bucket by the fire. Looks at her. Like a sheep, she thinks, looking for its flock.

'If you pour it into the pot,' she says, 'and put the pot on the fire, we can make hyssop tea.' She nods at the bundle of dried leaves hanging from the ceiling beam. 'There is bread from yesterday still.'

Favouring his good hand, he hoists the bucket again, pours the water into the pot. Lifts the pot on to the raised stones over the fire. She pokes at the logs with a stick of wood.

'You do not want to talk to me.'

His voice is not accusing. He is calm.

'No,' she says.

'But you let me help you.'

There is no trace of bitterness.

She shrugs.

'Do we not read: "The Lord will recompense you for the work you have done?" – and so is it not good to work?'

He starts, and stares at her. It is true, a woman of learning is not a common thing, but neither is it entirely unknown. All the people of the village know their letters; one or two of the other women could best her in quoting Torah passages. She knows it is not this which interests him.

'Tell me again,' he says, 'or again another thing.'

She shakes her head.

'If you want to learn, there are better teachers than me. Go and seek out a teacher.'

And he says, 'I have already done so. My teacher cannot teach me any more.'

The water begins to boil. She dips in a jug, breaks dry leaves into the water and pours some into a small clay bowl for him, and for her. The well water is good, thank God. It is clean and pure and tastes of old stones.

'If you are willing to work then you are from the Lord. If you work then I will feed you, until the spring, when you should go back to your people.'

There is such happiness in him when she says this that she knows what she has done.

There is a thing she often remembers. It was a little thing. When her first son was only a baby, and she was a new wife, and her husband was so young and strong that he lifted great boulders to make the walls of their sheep pen. In that part of their lives, she remembers, they passed evenings gazing at their little son sleeping. Every first baby seems like a miracle. The old women laugh and say: by number six she'll forget what name she gave the new one.

But this was their first child. Yosef, her husband, made the baby a cradle of woven branches. Yehoshuah was snug in there, on a bed of fur with a lambs-wool blanket.

The thing she remembers is that there was a scorpion. It happened between one moment of looking and the next. The baby was sleeping, she looked away, and then there was a small yellow scorpion in his cradle. Poised over his heart. Yellow scorpions are the most dangerous. When she was a child, a man in the village was stung by a yellow scorpion like that, its tail dripping venom. He died of it, shaking and sweating and crying out for his mother. He was a man of forty and strong in himself.

She looked at the scorpion, sitting on the chest of her sleeping child, and there was not a thought in her head. Every mother knows how it is. There is no thinking or weighing one thing against another. She reached her hand into the cradle, plucked out the scorpion, threw it to the ground and crushed it beneath her shoe to oozing yellow muck.

She had been fast, but scorpions are also fast. It had grazed the skin of her hand with its sting, leaving a faint red score on her flesh. As the day passed, her hand grew hot and heavy, her limbs ached. Her heart pounded, her knees buckled. She thought: I shall die like that man in the village, but it is better that I should die than my baby. When Yosef came home from the fields in the evening, expecting his supper, he found her lying on the straw-filled mattress with hot dry skin and glassy eyes and the baby crying in her arms.

It was three days like that. Yosef brought her well water and she drank a little, and vomited, and the baby would not cease from crying though Yosef fed him goat's milk from a skin bag. But at the end of three days the fever broke. Yosef had to bring her a pot to piss in because she could not walk to the stone outhouse. Her right arm and right leg, the side the scorpion had stung, were numb like a fallen branch.

She recovered slowly. It was hard, with a small baby, but she was young and strong then and with God's help she grew well. Her right hand never regained all its cunning. Still it is slower than its fellow, still it will not close into a tight fist only a loose one. She cannot use a needle with the right finger and thumb and had to teach herself to use the left. And she never regretted her action, not as she saw him grow tall and wise and strong. When he was a grown man of twenty she would thank her own hand sometimes for his life. Her hand, and the guidance of God.

But this past year, she thinks: what was it for? What was the point of all the thousand thousand acts of work and love that go to raise a child? What was the point of any of it, seeing what has happened, and that he has not left even a grandchild from his body to comfort her?

The boy Gidon works hard, there is that at least. Her own grown sons will help her if she is ill, but they have their families now, and Iov, the littlest one, is too small to be much use lifting and carrying. He minds the sheep, but he can scarcely keep his thoughts even on that. Gidon has the single-mindedness that impressed and frightened her the first time they met. He has cleared the back field, which has lain untended since her husband, Yosef, was with them. They will be able to plant wheat in it, or barley, in a month's time.

He has not asked her more questions. She has not mentioned Yehoshuah. Whenever she speaks of her sons, she says 'my son Yirmiyahu, the second one' or 'my son Iehuda, the fourth'. So that he will know, and not think she is inviting conversation. He asks her, sometimes, questions about the Torah. She has taught him, a little. It is hard not to, when his yearning is so open within him.

He sees her once giving food to one of the beggars who pass through even an out-of-the-way village like this. A blind woman, making her way with a stick and a bundle of little dolls whittled from wood in her backpack. Miryam slips a few extra apples into the woman's pack before she walks on with some other travellers.

After she leaves, Gidon says, 'My teacher said that the poor will always be with us.'

And she cannot help herself.

'If he wasn't a fool, he meant that each of us can find someone who has less than us. Don't you know that every Jew is obliged to give charity? Even the beggars must give.'

'Tell more,' he says.

And she teaches him what she had learned when her parents took her to hear the great Rabbi Hillel speak, that our duty to love each other is the highest of all the commandments of God. That our duty of charity extends even to our own bodies, and we must care for them because our souls are guests in them.

He wants a mother, this boy, she can read it in the lines of him as he sits in the dust by her feet listening to her teach, until it is time for supper and the children come in bustling and hungry. He wants a mother to notice that he is there, and to teach him.

Later, Iov and Michal are sleeping and she tends the fire, banking it high so that it will burn slowly through the night. Gidon is still in the house, leaning his long, thin frame against the wall, whittling a wooden stick to a sharp point with his knife.

She says, 'Who are your people?'

He says, 'My family are those who believe what I believe.'

She has heard of such groups. The Essenes are one – they live together and follow the same customs although they are not kin – and there are other small groups, those who follow the same principles or who gather around a teacher.

'And where are they?' she says, because she thinks he will say that it is a group who live in the caves, or in the desert, or in the wooded hills near Jerusalem.

'We are scattered,' he says. 'Now we who followed your son Yehoshuah are wandering. Teaching. We are spreading his words.'

She looks at him. He is leaning forward on his haunches now, observing her. He moves towards her. Not to touch, but closer to her body.

'Become one of us,' he says to her, softly. 'Mother Miryam, listen to the teachings of your blessed son and tell us what you know of him. There must be stories –' his voice is low, so as not to wake the children, but he is speaking more quickly, with a dreadful urgency – 'you must know the holy stories of his birth, his childhood. No one sent me to ask this, but I had a dream. It was as the winter came on. In my dream, the clouds parted and a voice spoke from heaven telling me to find you. It said that I must come and help you and work with you, to learn the stories you could teach me.'

She is tired now. Not angry any more, barely afraid. He's a good worker and a kind lad, but she is tired.

'There are no stories,' she says.

He reaches out towards her.

'There are no stories. He was a baby and then he was a child and then he was a man and then he was killed. That is the story.'

'But,' he says, 'what kind of baby was he? How was his birth? What manner of child? How did his great wisdom first show itself? And where did he get his learning?'

She sighs.

'Gidon,' she says, 'you are a good boy. And you have no mother. Let me be a mother to you.'

He toys with his pointed stick, saying nothing.

'If I were your mother, I would tell you this: take a wife. I know you have only eight of your fingers, but there are many girls who would have you willingly.'

The daughter of Nechemiah for one, her mother has mentioned this to Miryam casually more than once now, has happened to ask if she knows whether Gidon has a wife somewhere.

'Learn a trade. You are skilful with your hands even still. Then take a wife. Fill her belly with sons and with daughters.'

He blushes a little at this, his face becomes bashful.

'Then you will think of your wife and your craft and your sons and your daughters, and forget that you came here for any other reason. That is a good life.'

But she sees from his face that this business is not over.

He had been, she admits it to herself now, a distant child. Not always distant. Often helpful, often sweet. But a child given to entertaining himself for hours. Yehoshuah could sit staring at the waving barley and when Yosef said, 'What are you doing there, boy, sitting idle?' he would reply strangely, with an odd question, 'Why did God make the locusts?' or simply say, 'I am thinking, father.' But for all that, he seemed happy. He made friends easily. He had a way with him that was charming.

She remembers a small boy, Ze'ev, the child of Batchamsa from the village. Yehoshuah and Ze'ev played together, some game of catching a ball and counting the throws. They were eight or nine. Yehoshuah threw the ball too far, Ze'ev made a lunge for it and fell in the mud. It was funny. Miryam, half watching while sifting the dried lentils for stones, laughed. The boy was covered in mud, brown streaks over his clothes and in his hair. Yehoshuah didn't laugh, he simply looked.

Later, when he was settling down to sleep, he asked her, 'What did it mean, Ima, that Ze'ev fell down?'

'It didn't mean anything, sweet. He just fell.'

'But what did it mean?'

He returned to this thought again and again. What did it mean that the rain fell? What did it mean that the dog died? As if the world were a book and each person and event in it had been carefully chosen, and their meanings could be understood if one only read aright.

She and Yosef argued about him.

'He's always hanging around your skirts,' said Yosef, when he came in from his workshop and found Yehoshuah reading, or thinking, or whittling some wood by the fire when the other children were out playing in the orchards.

'He's different to other boys,' said Miryam. 'He doesn't like their rough-and-tumble games.'

'You're making him weak,' said Yosef. 'You give in too easily.'

'Give in what? I should throw him out of the house and force him to play?'

'Yes! Or give him work! He's nine, he's old enough to work! Give him some of your jobs, working your fingers to the bone. Set him to chop the wood, or carry the water. If he wants to be a woman, let him pluck the goose!'

'A woman? He should be like you?' said Miryam, and this was the start of their troubles.

'Like me? What do you mean like me?'

'Like you, never studying any more as you did when you were young, never going to learn with the rabbi.'

And so it went on. And Yehoshuah sat by the fire, and although he must have heard every word he said nothing, did nothing.

As he grew to adulthood she feared, for a time, that she had done something wrong. Her fears were only calmed when she saw that her younger sons were normal. Yirmiyahu was married at seventeen. Iehuda went to the wedding canopy at twenty. Shimon, the quiet one, developed such an ardent passion for a girl from the next village that no one could hold him back and the wedding was arranged when he was barely fifteen. But although they suggested girls to Yehoshuah, he would not meet them, and though they tried to persuade him, he did not hear their words.

As a young man, when he and Yosef could no longer be in the same home together, he began to travel. He stayed for a time among the Essenes, those men who live without women and refuse to defecate upon the Sabbath day. He took, for a year, more difficult vows. She had grandsons and granddaughters from her younger boys and the oldest was still unwed.

He came back home for a time when he was twenty-seven. Still no woman with him, though she had hoped that after his wandering he might return with a sweet bride and surprise them all with

. . . what? With normality at last. But no. He was odder than ever, more distant and strange. He would not meet anyone's gaze, seemed always to be staring at something just out of view. He and Yosef argued. When would he found a family of his own? Build a house? There was that far field, if he wanted he could build himself a place there, but he could not live with them any more, it wasn't right, a fully grown man living like a child, waited on hand and foot by his mother.

Yehoshuah was different now, though. Not quiet but angry, suddenly, with a violent rage that swept over his body and made him go stiff and white-faced.

'You know nothing,' he said quietly, 'old man.' And then, his voice rising to a shriek, 'You know nothing, you know nothing. You. Know. Nothing!' and he picked up a pot from the table and smashed it on the ground.

The other children were not there. They did not see what happened. Yosef and Miryam looked at the broken shards. Yehoshuah stared, with flared nostrils and rolling eyes, at his father and then darted for the door. It was three days, that time, before he returned.

He spoke to himself. Or he heard voices. Or demons. Only sometimes – not all the time, she told her other children when they complained. He does not do it all the time. He is engaged in his studies, she said. He is reciting the words of the Torah, to keep them pure and complete in his heart, is it not praiseworthy? Yosef looked at him like a stranger at their table. Not a son, an odd, fullgrown man, whom they had taken in for no reason.

The arguments grew worse. There came a day, if she was honest she had known it was coming, when Yehoshuah hit Yosef in a rage. Yosef had provoked it, probably. With a critical tone, angry words. And Yehoshuah rose up from his place by the fire and with the heel of his hand whacked his father hard on the temple. Yosef was a man nearing fifty and Yehoshuah was young and strong. Yosef stumbled, almost fell. Yehoshuah looked at his hand in disbelief. And Miryam found that she was saying, 'Yosef! Why did you speak to him like that?' Because what will a mother not do for her son?

After that, Yehoshuah wandered further from their village, into the desert, for days sometimes. He had not founded a family, he had no crops to tend or harvest to reap. When he returned from the wilderness he would not say who he had seen there or what he had done. And she remembered the charming child he had been, the one who would reach his little hand out for hers and show her a lizard he had seen, or a new fern, and she wondered when she had lost him.

Then one day, a week had passed, then two, and he did not return. For a month or two she thought he had died out there. In her dreams the scorpion returned, or its parent to exact vengeance on her son for her murder of its offspring. Her hand ached in its old wound and she thought perhaps it was a sign.

She and Yosef quarrelled about it.

'Why were you always so hard with him?' she would say, and although she knew in her heart that there was no answer here, she could not stop. 'Why could you never show him kindness?'

'He needed less kindness from you, woman! He needed to be taught to be a man, instead of you constantly keeping him near, mothering him!'

'I am his mother. What else should I have done?'

And Yosef made that disgusted noise he kept specially for arguments he knew he could not win with her.

She saw Yosef one day talking closely with the daughter of Ramatel, the blacksmith, a tall, well-built girl, but at that time she thought little of it. Her mind was occupied with chewing over Yehoshuah and what had become of him and when she would ever hear from him or see him again, or if he had died somewhere out there in the desert and the wolves had had his bones.

And then she heard a tale from a merchant that he had been seen in Kfar Nachum, and he was preaching and working wonders like a holy man. And they said another thing. They said he was out of his mind.

And it is evening, and it is morning. And it is time to prepare for the Sabbath. She washes herself and the children. She bakes bread for today and for tomorrow. Just before sunset, she lights the oil lamps which will burn through the night and makes the blessing. And it is Friday morning, and it is Friday evening. The Sabbath day.

The boy Gidon goes to pray with the men in Ephrayim's field. She and the small children go to sit in the long barn and sing the women's songs welcoming the Sabbath. They share out bread and wine and make the blessings on it. They drink the sweet wine made in years when they were young, the jars sealed with wax by their fathers, keeping in those long-ago summers until this day.

Some of the women ask about Gidon. Not just, like Nechemiah's wife, because they have a daughter who has taken an interest in him. They have heard something. The news has come that there was a small rising in Yaffo several months ago, in the autumn. A man appeared claiming to be the rightful king of Judea, the son of the king the Romans slew. He had followers, only two or three hundred, but they tried to break into the armoury. The soldiers quashed the rebellion easily enough, but the man himself, along with several of his most important followers, had escaped.

Does she think ... Gidon was from Yaffo, they knew, does she think that he might be one of those men?

She shakes her head.

'He is what he says he is: a fool, not a liar.'

Rahav puts a thin arm around her shoulder and hugs her.

'We still mourn with you.'

Rahav kisses the side of Miryam's head. She's a kind soul, especially with a glass of warm fragrant wine in her.

It's Batchamsa who introduces a note of caution.

'They're looking, though,' she says. 'They've sent out armed men as far as S'de Raphael.'

'They won't come this far north,' says Rahav, 'not for a fugitive from Yaffo.'

'They might,' says Batchamsa. 'They just keep looking.'

Rahav shakes her head. 'One of his own people will betray him. They always do when they get scared or hungry and want to come home. In a month they'll have found him in a cave near Yaffo and that'll be the end of it.'

Rahav does not say the part in the middle, Miryam notes. She does not say, 'They'll find him and then they'll kill him and that'll be the end of it.' Miryam supposes that this is Rahav's kindness.

She finds she feels a little protective of Gidon.

In the evening, they eat with her brother Shmuel's family. His wife has made soup and roast goat-leg with wild garlic. Gidon eats with them. The village's decision to treat him as an imbecile has faded. He has done good work on Miryam's land. Those who work deserve to eat.

Shmuel sets in on him again, saying,

'But you will return to Yaffo in the spring, yes? Before Passover?'

Gidon shifts his shoulders awkwardly. He is less comfortable here than he is with her alone. He does not talk so readily.

'I might stay here,' he says, and then seems about to say something more, but falls silent.

'He has been useful with the goats,' she says. 'Iov can never bring them all in. We lost two over the winter. Gidon gathers them safely in.'

Shmuel nods and takes more bread and goat covered in the thick paste of herbs and olive oil. Her brother is the patriarch now, the one who makes the decisions since her husband has gone. But he's not an unkind man. He dips his bread into the green oil and swallows it, leaving a few emerald flecks in his beard.

'But you'll tell me when you get tired of him, yes?' he says, then grins widely, 'so we can send him on his way with courtesy, of course.'

They said he was out of his mind. This, they came to tell her. The sympathetic women from the villages nearby came, when they passed through for market day. 'Passing through' was what they said, though Natzaret was a mile or more out of their way. People who had not visited her for five years came to tell her that her son was mad. Just as a kindness.

He had desecrated the Temple, they said, and she could not believe it. He had loved going to the Temple as a boy, buying the cake for a meal offering in the outer courtyard and accompanying the sacrifice.

He had done work on the Sabbath, they said, and she laughed and said, 'Yehoshuah? Who never did a stick of work the other six days of the week?' And they laughed too, because nothing is funnier than a mother mocking her own son, and agreed that perhaps on this point she was right.

Yosef, she noticed, did not laugh at this joke.

As they were getting ready for sleep, he said to her, 'It's not enough that he's run away? Now he brings disgrace on the family?'

She did not bother to argue. He wanted to lie with her that night, but she refused him, and he made that special noise again, of unconquerable exasperation.

Those friends who loved her best told her simply that Yehoshuah was changed. That he seemed frightening sometimes, or frightened himself. Those who loved her best told her that it had been hard to recognize him, that something in him had begun to work differently, that his face even was changed. One said she heard he had been questioned by the Roman guard but they had not held him.

'You should go to talk to him,' she said to Yosef one night.

He looked at her.

'It's your job,' she said, because this sometimes called him to his duty. 'You are his father. You should go and see that all is well with him. I'm worried about him.'

'You've always worried about him over the wrong things.'

'Rahav said she'd heard that the guard questioned him. You should go there. Talk to him. Bring him home. Please.'

He stared at her levelly. His beard was all grey now, and his eyes wrinkled and his skin burnished, and where now was the young strong husband who had lifted her up with one hand? And had loved her? She had thought that he had loved her.

'No,' he said, 'he will have no more from me.'

'Then I will go myself.'

He breathed in and out. She saw in his face the same lines as Yehoshuah's face. The same angry stiff mouth, the same twitching brow. They had the same anger, that was the problem.

'I forbid it. Do you understand? You are not to bring disgrace upon us. I forbid it.'

She looked at him. Whatever he had been, he was not it any more.

'I understand,' she said.

It was around two weeks after that when Yosef went north to take a look at some lumber and to trade. And she called her grown sons to tell them what she intended, and they agreed to it.

She will not go with her family to Jerusalem this Passover. Her brother Shmuel will make a sacrifice for her. She and her sister and Shmuel's wife will stay behind, as they did when they were young women with many small children to care for. But still, although she will not eat the sacrificed lamb with them in Jerusalem, there are duties to be performed. The house must be cleaned, every jar that has held flour must be emptied and scoured.

Gidon helps her, carrying the wool blankets back from the stream when they are heavy and sodden and throwing them over the rope she has tied between two trees. He climbs into the back of the clay-and-reed flour store and washes the stone floor, bent double, inhaling the flour dust, so that when he comes out his eyes are red and his back cracks as he stands up. They do not speak of the anniversary that is fast approaching until the very eve of Passover.

The day before Passover is time to bake the matzot – the flat unrisen bread that they will eat for the next week. The flour cakes will last overnight, she will wrap them in cloth and put them in a stone jar to keep off insects and mould. She puts the flat stone into the fire to heat, takes three measures of flour from the jar and pulls up a bucket of cold clear water from the well. She begins to mix the water into the flour – swiftly, because her mother taught her that matzot should be made as quickly as possible – pulling it into a dough, forming round flat cakes, pummelling them out with the heel of her hand, stretching the dough to thinness. She makes dots in the surface of each cake with a wooden point, then quickly tosses them on to the heated stone, where they immediately begin to bubble and crisp, becoming fragrant with wood smoke and with flakes of burnt flour on the surface.

When she looks up, she sees that Gidon is watching her. She does not know how long he has been there. He watches her so tenderly. He must have seen his own mother perform this task.

'We ate them, the last meal with Yehoshuah,' he says at last.

Her blood is chilled and her bones are old ash. She does not want to know what they did. She wants to know everything. Her mouth tries to say, 'Don't tell me.' Her breath longs to beg him for every detail. She is thirsty for every moment she missed. She wants to ask if there was a crumb in his beard from the unrisen bread. Did he remember to change his clothes before the festival started? Would anyone but a mother notice? The desire, always coiled in her, always ready to pounce, springs now: the desire to wail and say why was I not there at his last meal, why did I not force him to come home?

All this rises up in her. She throws another flat round matzo cake on to the hot stone. She looks at Gidon.

'I miss him too,' the boy says.

30

And she cannot help herself. There are always tears in her now. Her voice cracks and she says, 'You do not know what it means to miss him.'

She picks raw dough from her fingertips and lifts the flat matzo from the stone.

Gidon's eyes, too, are filled with tears.

He says, 'I have not your right.'

She finishes the baking, wraps the flatbreads in a cloth. Her sister will arrive soon with the lamb, so she banks the fire up high, with the hyssop grass and herbs she has dried for the occasion. Gidon gathers armfuls of green branches to make a smoky fire, separating out the dry logs which will burn long and evenly.

She says, 'Did he ever speak of me?'

Gidon pauses and thinks. She can see that he wants to be kind to her.

'He spoke about his father,' he says, 'or he told stories about a good father, and that father I think is God, who reigns above. There are many stories and sayings he told about fathers.'

'But not mothers?' she says.

He shakes his head slowly, and she can see the thought is only now occurring to him.

'He told a story of a widow,' he says. 'Perhaps that widow called you to mind?'

'Perhaps,' she says.

She believes Gidon that her son didn't talk of her, or ask for her, or even think of her. He had distanced himself from her deliberately a long time before.

People said he was out of his mind.

They agreed to journey to see him speak. Word came that he had circled round in a wide loop, through Hoshaya and Cana towards Emek. It was a long trek – a quarter of a day or a little more. Yosef would be away for several days longer and they need never tell him where they'd been. It was a bad business, to lie to him, but the brothers all agreed, and if the younger ones blurted something out, they could say that they had imagined it, dreamed it. Yehoshuah was their oldest brother and they wanted to see him.

They took the donkey, loaded it with water skins, bread and cheese and walked. At S'de Nachal, they met a woman on the way, her hair uncovered, carrying a baby at her breast wrapped in a woollen blanket.

She said, 'Are you going to see the teacher?'

Iov opened his mouth to answer but Miryam interrupted him.

'What teacher is that?' she said.

The woman checked on the baby, fussing and pawing, its little hand waving as it struggled to latch on to the nipple. Though her breast was covered, the older boys looked away, disgusted or embarrassed.

She shrugged. 'Some teacher. I saw one last winter who cast a live snake out of Rakhel who had the pain in her gut. She vomited, and it came up and crawled into the grass covered in her blood and slime. Rakhel was better for a while after that, and after that she was worse and then she died.'

'Is that the same teacher as this one?'

The woman shook her head. 'We wouldn't have him again in Emek. No, but this one will do cures, I expect, the same as the rest. Are you sick, any of you?'

She ran her eye appraisingly over the children. They had all come, leaving their families some of them. Yirmiyahu, tall and broad-shouldered, had a wife, Chana, with two months to go in her fourth pregnancy. Iehuda had two little boys with him. Shimon's wife had not yet borne a child and there were fears . . . well, it was too early to fear that yet. Dina was becoming a woman – time to think of finding a husband for her – while Michal and Iov were still children, she older, he younger, tracing patterns in the dirt while they waited for the grown-ups to finish their conversation. They were a healthy family, may the Evil Eye stay far off. Miryam did not like the look the woman gave them – a jealous look, as a poor man might give a rich man's flock.

'Thank God,' she said, 'we're well. We're bored, that's all. The harvest is in and the sun is shining and we thought to entertain ourselves – perhaps we'll see this teacher.'

The woman nodded. She knew Miryam was lying but could not quite tell why, or what. She sniffed, moved her shoulders uneasily and the baby began to wail.

'He'll be working his wonders at the synagogue on the hill.' She jerked her head towards the structure at the opposite side of the valley.

'May you be blessed in your going,' said Miryam.

'And you in yours,' said the woman, without a great deal of sincerity.

As soon as she passed out of sight, Iov tugged on her skirt and began:

'Why didn't you tell her, Ima? Why didn't you tell her we were going to see Yehoshuah? Why didn't you tell her he's our brother? He's my brother –' this last addressed to Michal, as if Yehoshuah weren't her brother too.

Yirmiyahu hoisted Iov on to his shoulders and said, 'Not everything needs to be told, pipsqueak. Maybe Ima didn't want to make the woman jealous.'

And this answer appeared to satisfy Iov for the time being.

They would not have needed directions. As they approached Emek, a great swarm of people became obvious, walking from every direction to the synagogue on the hill. Perhaps three or four hundred were here! A greater number than Miryam had seen anywhere outside Jerusalem. They pressed forward, towards the synagogue. Were all these come to see her son? His name must be larger than she thought. He had no such name in Natzaret, where the people remembered him as a stumbling infant, a complaining child, a petulant boy-man. The synagogue was full, the people had spilled out on to the street. At one side, a man was selling hot flour cakes to those waiting for the wonders.

Miryam did not see him at first, through the crowd – she, a woman with children, was kept to the back with the other women. But Iov wormed his way forward, tugging on her hand, until they were almost at the door of the synagogue. And two heads parted suddenly and there he was, speaking. Her body turned cold and then very warm. As if she were in love. Ridiculous! For her own son? The little boy she had washed and clothed and fed from her breast? She ought to have gone to him and washed his face off, where his forehead was always dirty because he would sit on the ground and sift the dirt and then rub his brow. She could see that little dirty smear even from where she stood. She ought to have strode over to him and said, 'I am this child's mother – give me the seat of honour.'

And she knew now why she had not done so, but she hadn't known it then. Only in the seat of her soul, she had faltered. She thought it was the way the other men looked at him. He was the kind of man her own father would have uncovered his head for, stood up in the house of learning for, told her to call 'teacher'. Yehoshuah looked so comfortable there.

He was debating with an older wise man – she heard others in the crowd call him Ezra the Teacher, his beard was as white as a lamb's fleece. There was a jar of wine on the floor and a table before them. Ezra dipped a cup in the jar and placed it with a sharp slam in front of Yehoshuah. He dipped a cup for himself, took a mouthful, swirled it around. He pulled on his beard. The crowd became silent. This was the debate they'd come to hear.

Ezra said, 'I've heard it said that you work wonders and make cures in the name of God.'

Yehoshuah nodded. Ezra smiled.

'Well, this is no crime. God gives great power to those who trust in him. When I was a child I saw Khoni the Circle Drawer bring down rain by his prayers from a cloudless sky. Those who are as old as me remember it.'

Ezra looked around the room, indicating a few grey-bearded men with his finger who murmur, 'Yes' and 'I saw it.'

'And many a man has come to this village to perform cures. And many of them found some success. Now tell me, is it true that you make your cures on the holy Sabbath day?'

Yehoshuah said, 'It is true.'

Ezra banged the table so violently that the cups of wine jumped and spattered.

'Then you make yourself greater than God!'

There was a low rumble from the crowd, a murmur of agreement from the people of the village, a mutter of discontent from Yehoshuah's friends.

Ezra turned to the crowd, bringing them with him as he spoke:

'Wasn't it enough for the Lord Almighty, God of Hosts, to have six days to create the world? And didn't he make man with one gesture of his finger –' Ezra flicked the little finger of his right hand – 'on the very last hour before the Sabbath, along with all the diseases that plague us and, it must follow because God knows the end of all things, all the cures for those diseases?'

Yehoshuah stared directly ahead of him, neither agreeing nor disagreeing. Miryam had seen that look on his face many times before, a way of staring that made her think he wasn't listening. Ezra evidently thought that Yehoshuah's lack of response meant that he was winning the debate.

Ezra raised his voice so that even those standing outside could hear him with perfect clarity: 'And if He Who is in All Places could create the cures for all diseases in six days and rest on the seventh, who are you to challenge him? Who are you to do away with the commandment to rest on the Sabbath?'

He lowered his voice again and brought a chuckle to it – he was a skilled orator, taking the crowd with him as he spoke: 'Now, I don't say it's wrong to heal the sick, of course not. But you couldn't do it on the other six days? Why make these unfortunate people wait till the Sabbath? Can't you heal them on a Friday, so they can be home to enjoy their soup with the family like everyone else?'

The crowd laughed. Miryam heard people whispering, 'That's a good point,' and 'If even God could make the world in six days . . .' to each other.

'But of course –' Ezra was coming to a conclusion – 'there is an explanation, isn't there?' His voice became hard again, low and firm and solid. 'We know that our God rests on the Sabbath like all his creatures. And so if you heal the sick on that day, where does your power come from? Not from God.' He banged the table again and shouted, 'Not from God! We've seen you jerking and crying out as you heal, and we know what it means. If not from our God, the God of our forefathers Abraham, Isaac and Jacob, your power comes from a foreign god like Ba'al Zvuv!'

His voice was loud and strong, and as he finished speaking the crowd erupted into foot-stamping and shouts of agreement.

And then Miryam's son rose to speak. He spoke softly, rocking all the time on the spot and looking not at the crowd, as Ezra had done, but above their heads, as though reading from letters written in the air like a prophet.

He said, 'Tell me, is it permitted to save a life on the Sabbath day?'

And one of his followers shouted out, 'It is permitted!'

He said, 'And is it permitted to do anything which might save a life? Even if the outcome is uncertain, is it permitted?'

One of the other men in the crowd, not one of Yehoshuah's friends, called out, 'It is permitted!'

'Well then –' he turned his whole body round to Ezra in a jerking unsteady motion – 'who are you to say that I should not perform a cure! For if I left them one more day, perhaps there would be no cure at all? And tell me –' now he spread his arms wide to the crowd, but still spoke quietly – 'is it permitted to circumcise on the Sabbath, revered Ezra?'

Ezra, a little puzzled, but gracious, nodded to acknowledge the truth.

'It is permitted, of course. If the eighth day after the boy is born is a Sabbath, we circumcise on the Sabbath.'

36

'Well then!' Yehoshuah turned to the crowd, 'If we can put right one part of the body – and not even a part that is broken or hurting – all the more so we should be able to make right other parts!'

Emek was a pious village. But this argument made sense. There were some unwilling nods in the crowd.

Ezra stood up and, with all the appearance of good humour, said, 'But God has told us to circumcise on the Sabbath! He has not told you to heal. Where is it written or handed down in the law? The Lord Himself rests on the Sabbath – this is how we know your power does not come from Him!'

Yehoshuah became angry now. It was swift and frightening to see him flash to sudden wrath.

'You say my power comes from Ba'al Zvuv, whom the Philistines call the prince of demons,' he said, 'but I drive out demons from sick men and women! You've seen me!'

He appealed to the section of the room containing his friends, but Miryam saw several others nodding.

'And can a demon drive out demons? Can the prince of devils drive out devils? A house divided against itself cannot stand!'

He thumped the table now and looked down for a moment breathing deeply. When he looked up, his face was dark.

'Listen,' he said, 'Rabbi Ezra, you're committing a grave sin. Because you're slandering God. Now, we all know –' he stared around the room – 'that if you tell a lie about your friend and you ask forgiveness, if he forgives you God will also forgive it. But if you tell a lie about God,' he was shouting now, 'if you tell a lie about God there is no forgiveness for you! God will not forgive you, Rabbi Ezra, for lying that my power is not from Him!'

The arguments continued. At times Ezra seemed to hold the crowd's approval and at times they favoured Yehoshuah. At one moment, when the crowd were shouting to Yehoshuah, 'Praise God!' and 'You speak the truth!' one woman called out, louder than the rest: 'Blessed is the mother who gave birth to you, Yehoshuah, and blessed are the breasts that nursed you!'

Miryam saw which woman it was who said this. She was young, neatly dressed, no children with her. She thought: this woman does not even know me and yet she loves me. And she almost spoke up and said: it is me. I am here.

But Yehoshuah replied angrily, 'No. Blessed are those who hear the word of God and obey it.'

And she said nothing. And the debate went on.

There was a raving quality to Yehoshuah. As he spoke, spittle flew from his mouth, his face became red, his eyes looked wildly, angrily around the room. He quoted from the Torah and from words he'd heard listening to the sages. And she thought: is this my son? How did this man come from me? Every parent will think this about their child some day – all children become strangers to those who gave them birth. This was what she told herself.

When they finished speaking it was dark. Their arguments had twisted and turned, each of them had become angry and dissatisfied with the reasoning of the other. At last when it was evening Ezra called a halt and they embraced as friends, as was right. Ezra said: come, eat meat with us and bread and drink wine. And most of the crowd began to disperse. They had meals to eat in their own homes, or long walks to make. Only Yehoshuah's little band of friends, thirty or forty of them, and Ezra and the elders of the village remained while Ezra's wife and daughters brought roast lamb and bread and olives and fresh figs.

Miryam waited longer than she should, she supposed. She could have rushed through while the crowd was dispersing and touched Yehoshuah's arm, and perhaps he would have turned around and smiled and said, 'Mother!' She sometimes occupies herself for hours imagining that that is what happened, imagining the smile on his face and her own swelling heart.

But by the time she had gathered the family and given the little children the last of the bread and cheese and straightened her robes and her head-covering the men were already in the smaller back room of the synagogue, eating. She walked around to the back of the building, holding Iov and Michal by the hand, the other brothers walking behind her. There was a sound of loud debate, noisy laughter from behind the old wooden door. She wormed her hand out of Iov's sticky grip and knocked.

A man opened the door a crack. She recognized him. It was a friend of Yehoshuah's. She had heard someone in the crowd point him out, Iehuda from Qeriot, a man with a curling beard and an anxious look. He frowned, as if she had said something entirely inappropriate before she even spoke.

'You are . . . Iehuda?' she said, trying to smile. 'I'm . . . we are the family of Yehoshuah, your teacher. We are here to see him.'

His frown deepened. 'I'll ask if he wants to see you.'

'If he . . .'

But he had closed the door already. They waited there. Her older sons met her glance and then looked away. The anger rose from their shoulders like the steam-wreathed breath off cattle in the early mornings.

He came back. He had the grace, at least, to look embarrassed now.

He shook his head.

'He doesn't want to see you,' said Iehuda from Qeriot.

He stood there for a moment in silence.

'What did he say?' said Yirmiyahu, the anger hard in his voice.

Iehuda from Queriot moved his shoulders uneasily.

'It doesn't . . .' He paused, breathed out through his nose, like a bull. 'We are a family now,' he said, 'we who follow his teachings, we are like his family.'

Through the open door she could hear her son's voice. The other guests had become quiet and he was teaching. It was his voice, the consonants of that little boy she had taught to feed himself with a spoon, and if she shouted out now he would hear her. She wondered for a moment if Iehuda from Qeriot was lying. But she knew he wasn't. She'd known as soon as she left for Emek, as soon as she'd heard that he was here, but not because he'd sent word.

She turned around to look at her children. Yirmiyahu would have been willing to start a fight with Iehuda from Qeriot, she thought. She hoisted Iov up on to her shoulders.

'Come on,' she said, 'come on.'

When she came back to the village, she could not be bothered to hide that she had seen him. The people in the village asked where they'd gone, the whole family altogether, and she said: we went to see my son, Yehoshuah, preaching. We ate meat and drank wine with him but we were tired and preferred not to travel further. She knew this would find its way to her husband. She did not care any longer. Neither could she care what was true and what a lie. She found that she was waiting for Yosef's return not with fear but with a dull emptiness. She had sons and daughters but not one can fill the place of another, and she would never have another firstborn. She wanted to mingle truth with lies, and to have Yosef be angry with her for speaking to Yehoshuah, because that was better than remembering that he had not spoken to her at all.

She should have done it then, turned her heart into a stone. She should have said to herself, 'My son is dead,' and begun to mourn him. As if it were possible. As if we can begin to mourn for a death a moment before it comes, as if we can grieve for any destruction before it arises. Even if we have known for a hundred years that it must be so. Nothing can be anticipated in grief – for if we could bring our sorrow forward, would we not mourn for a baby on the day of its nativity? She should have mourned for him then, on the day he was born.

It is the first day of Passover. This is the day, of course. She knows it down to her fingers' ends. She has wondered how she would feel, but like the impact of an anticipated blow, contemplating it in advance cannot reduce the pain. Pinchas her younger brother, knows it too. He has walked from S'de Raphael for the Passover feast. When he sees her, he makes a grimace at her and rises from blowing the embers of the fire. He puts his arm around her shoulders. His wool jerkin is damp, moss-scented. He pulls her close and says, 'May your other sons live, Miryam! May they make you proud and bring you more grandchildren and great-grandchildren.' He kisses the top of her head and she nestles against his shoulder, pressing her nose into that mushroomy fabric. It feels safe here. Safe like family.

She sniffs and pulls away.

'Better get that fire going.'

He lets his hands fall to his sides.

'I still think about the ones we lost,' he says at last.

And she does too, and she understands. The two that died, the little ones – lost at the pinnacle of their sweetness and grace to a cough and a chill and the simple fact that she could not keep them here. And those that never quickened, or that quickened but did not hold. But this particular thing is different. Perhaps it is only different because there is anger in it too.

'It'll be like this all day,' she says. 'The cousins and the aunts and the nephews and their wives.'

Pinchas shakes his head.

'Never. Some of them will forget.'

'The others will tell them.' Then, 'Iov will remind them.'

'Has he still got that gossiping tongue? Like a woman at the market.'

She smiles. 'Still.'

'So he'll tell them, and they'll wish you that your other sons live.'

This is how life continues. Learning to bear the unbearable.

Through the family feast Gidon watches and is mindful and says nothing. The family ask about him. She says, 'He was lost in the mountains when the snow fell. He is staying here until he is well enough to make the journey home.' And they glance at him, looking his rangy form up and down, seeing that he appears quite well, and they say nothing. It is Passover, when it is especially meritorious

41

to take in the stranger and the wanderer. Some of them remind her of what happened this time last year, and some say nothing. She finds they cannot make it harder for her either way. At least they do not ask about her husband. They are mostly concerned with tales of the soldiers still scouring the country for the last of the rebels from Yaffo. They are coming nearer to Galilee because their search has not been fruitful further south. The family shake their heads and worry. They eat the unleavened bread and drink wine.

When she wakes the next morning, Gidon has completed his chores and has a soup bubbling on the fire. He is cutting some vegetables for it – onions and leeks.

He smiles. 'One who helps a widow,' he quotes, 'isn't his portion doubled or tripled under heaven? And she who gives succour to an orphan will find herself blessed, and God will turn His face to her.'

She frowns. She thinks – I could tell him, and then he will know all my sorrow.

'I am not a widow,' she says. 'As far as I know.'

Gidon's hands stop working.

'He was angry with me. I disobeyed him too often. I was a stubborn wife, and people told him that I had disobeyed his wishes in . . . a certain matter. He put me away,' she speaks quickly and quietly, 'he took another wife and moved her to another village. He gave me the *keritut*, the contract of divorce, and told me I was permitted to other men.'

She is not sorry he's gone. Apart from the strength in his shoulders, she barely misses him. She wants her children close to her and she wants her son back, and Yosef and his new young wife seem the least of her concerns.

Gidon says nothing. He knows she has told him a sad and lonely thing. Most women in her position would lie and say that the husband was dead.

She heard that Yehoshuah preached a teaching which had never been heard before. Many of his teachings were not new. He told them well, and with a force and skill that impressed the listeners, but the teachings themselves were as familiar to her as her own skin.

She herself had taught him the famous story of Rabbi Hillel. A man came to the two great rabbis, Rabbi Hillel and Rabbi Shammai, and made of each of them the same request: 'Teach me the whole of the Torah while I stand on one leg.' Rabbi Shammai chased him off with a broom. But Rabbi Hillel said: 'Stand on one leg and I will teach you.' And the man stood on one leg. And Rabbi Hillel said: 'That which is hateful to you, do not do to other people. That is the whole of the law: all the rest is commentary. Go and learn.'

When Yehoshuah said, 'Treat others as you hope they'd treat you,' it was not a new teaching. Rabbi Hillel was an old man when Yehoshuah was born.

But he taught a new thing, one of the women from Kfar Nachum told her. He said that if a man divorces his wife and takes another, it is the same as adultery. This saying was popular among women. They passed it one to another. Every village had some woman whose husband had put her away, scraping a living in her old age on the goats and land their marriage contract made him give her, with no rest for her aching bones even though she had borne him sons and daughters.

She wondered if this was a secret message for her, a sign that he thought of her still. But he did not send word to her. He did not speak about Yosef. He talked of having another father, spoke of God as his father. And she thought: he wants me to go to him again. Surely this means he wants to see me.

It is a curious thing, the growth of trust between two people. When two strangers meet, there is no trust. They may fear one another. They do not know if one is a spy, or a traitor, or a thief. There is no dramatic moment which marks the transition from mistrust to trust. Like the approach of summer, it walks a little further on every day, so that when we come to notice it, it has already occurred. Suddenly one notices that, yes, this is a person whom I would have watch over my flocks, my children, my secrets.

She is moved by the softness of Gidon's features. His beard has hardly begun to come in, just a few patches of fuzz like a mountain dog in moult. His eyelashes are long, and his smell is the sweet thick scent of a young man in whom the sap is just rising. His elbows and knees are sharp, his shoulders are stiff. There is a wanting in him, and not yet an understanding of what he wants. Her son was just so when he was twenty. His tender eyes were just so. The way he holds the cup of warm liquid, cradling it close to him, rubbing his knuckles in the cold, he was just like this boy.

She says nothing more of her husband. Her heart comes close to him. For a long time, he says nothing more of her son. He works. They bank the fire down after the evening meal and talk of what could be done with the western field next year.

She went to Yehoshuah the winter before Gidon arrived in Natzaret. It was not such a harsh winter, there was no snow. She had heard that he had a mighty crowd of followers with him, perhaps five hundred people travelling in a great convoy. They were circling near to Natzaret, not half a day's journey, and she left the littlest children with Shimon's wife and wrapped woollen robes around her and borrowed a mule from Rahav and went to see her son.

It had been many a year, she thought, since she had last made such a journey alone. A young woman would never travel so unprotected. But there was a fierce freedom to it. Who could rob her now? What would they take from her? She had water, and hard bread, and a bag of apples. She kept to the main roads. She told her sons where she had gone and when to expect her return.

She ruminated as she rode. There was such an anger in her heart, she hadn't known it was there until she was alone on her mule, riding the iron-hard miles. She had never been a bad mother, never truly a bad wife. She'd cared for her children – she flexed her stiff fingers, reminding herself how much it had cost her to care – had made loaves of bread and meal cakes and soups and roasted meat and dried fruits, had washed the children and kept them free from disease, had lain with her husband even when she was tired or unwilling because these are the duties of a wife and a mother. She had vanished into it and not accounted it a loss. This is who she was: a mother.

And this child could not pay her the duties of a son? Not to visit her in glory with his mighty crowd of men? Not to give her a place at his table? Not to write to her or send word to her after all she had done? From the first red scored line that had popped open across her belly when she grew big with him to the last bowl of soup she had made for him before he vanished, was all of this nothing?

Her soul grew bitter as the miles passed and when she arrived at the encampment – there was no mistaking it, five hundred travellers make smell and noise and smoke – she felt as tough and unyielding as the frozen earth.

'Where is the tent of Yehoshuah of Natzaret?' she said to a Roman hanger-on with fine clothes.

'Who are you to ask?'

'I am his mother,' she said.

The first they know of it is that the long barn is on fire. The barn at the edge of the village, the first one you come to if you're walking from the south. There are cries in the street of 'fire, fire' and Miryam runs out like everyone else, carrying her bucket, ready to be part of a chain down to the river. It has been dry these past few weeks – a stray cinder from a careless fire could have set the barn ablaze.

They begin to run down the hill to the barn, barefooted mostly on the chalk-dry baked earth. Calling to one another that they should make for the river to bring water. And they see the crested plumes and the glittering spears and they hear the sound of the phalanx. And they are afraid.

It is only a scouting party, ten men with a guide who speaks the native language. Rome does not send its finest and best to seek out a small village sixty-five miles from Jerusalem. But even a scouting party brings with it the authority of those who sent it, the invisible chain stretching back from these ten to the centurions garrisoned at the capital, and from there to the Prefect, and from there to the Emperor himself. If these men are not satisfied, others will come. If those are not satisfied, further men will come. Eventually Rome will have its answer, or the place will be reduced to a bloody smear upon smouldering earth.

This is why they have burned the barn. It is not your barn, they are saying. It is ours. Rome owns you.

They come to a halt in the town square. The people gather there too. There is nothing to do now about the barn or the stores that will be lost.

The leader of the soldiers makes a brief statement. The people of the village do not understand the language. Some of them, those who go to the larger cities to trade, have learned a few words, but this speech is fast and complex.

They know the translator. He is a man who works for the tax overseer in Galilee. They have seen him often. He never brings good news. It is no surprise to see him now with the Roman soldiers; he has come before with mercenaries to exact his payments.

This time, he attempts to pretend that he is their friend. The Romans do not understand what he is saying, the people do not understand what the Romans have said. There is no way to be sure that he is even communicating the true message.

'They've brought me here,' he says, 'because they're looking for people who fled Yaffo. In the uprising a few months ago, I know you heard about it. Now, I've tried to reason with them, tried to persuade them. You're good people, you pay your taxes on time, you don't make trouble. But they've heard the rumour that a boy from Yaffo is living in the village now. A new boy. And I'm sure you don't want to harbour known criminals, not in a quiet place like Natzaret! So my best advice is, hand him over. They'll take him away and ask him questions and leave you alone. You might even have time to save some of the –' he inclines his head faintly towards the barn – 'some of it, perhaps.'

They look around at one another. Gidon is not there, he is in the hills with the new lambs, he will be there for a day or two probably. Miryam wonders if any of them will speak.

'He is living with me,' she says, loudly and suddenly, surprising even herself a little. 'But he is not the man you're seeking.'

The tax collector smiles. The gold ring glitters on his thumb.

'Mother Miryam, I would never have thought it of you! Well, hand him over and we'll be on our way.'

Miryam sees her brother Shmuel shift in the crowd. He would go and get the boy now, she realizes. He would mount a pony and gallop into the hills to find him and give him to the Romans.

'No,' she says, 'he is not the man you want.'

Shmuel's body stiffens. He tries to catch her eye, to mouth something to her.

'We'll have to judge that ourselves, Mother Miryam.'

'No,' she says.

And something in the atmosphere turns. Perhaps it is that one of the soldiers fingers his spear, not understanding the conversation but hearing something in her tone.

The lead soldier bends to whisper a word or two in the tax collector's ear. The man nods.

'If you can't produce him, Mother Miryam,' he says, and his voice is hard now, 'we will take you instead. For questioning.'

She tightens the muscles in her stomach. She will need to lie.

When she came in to see him, she found she was singing a song under her breath. It was a psalm, set to a tune the goat-herders sing. She used to sing it to Yehoshuah when he was a tiny baby and perhaps some part of her thought that it would turn him back to the child he was, and he would remember how he used to need her.

He was sitting with three of his men, and when he saw her he

47

frowned and she realized that for a moment he did not recognize her. Oh, this was heavy and cold. But at last, within a heartbeat, his face broke into a smile.

'Mother,' he said.

They walked together, to soothe her sore legs, stiff from the ride. She told him at first all the news of the family, the nieces and nephews and the doings of the village. He listened but he seemed distant. He replied, 'That is good,' to news of a good harvest or 'Those are sad tidings,' to a death in childbed.

'And what of you?' she said at last. 'Here you are, a mighty man with many followers.'

She took his arm in hers and hugged it. 'Are you going to set up a great school and be a teacher? I would be so proud to tell the people at home that you had founded a college, taken a wife . . .' She lets her voice trail off.

He paused his walking. She stopped too. He bent down so his face was level with hers.

'Mother,' he said, 'God has called me. He has told me to go to Jerusalem at Passover, because it is time for a new heaven and a new earth.'

His eyes were unblinking. His face shone like the moon. There was a smudge of dirt in the centre of his forehead.

She felt suddenly impatient.

'Jerusalem, yes, very well. A good place to find new followers, but then what? Will you wander like this forever? Like a tent-dweller, with no place to find rest?'

'God will show me. God Himself and no other.'

She frowned.

'You should come back to Galilee. We have fine pastures, the fishing is good. Bring your people there. Settle. Be a great man in Galilee. Yes!'

'It is not mine to decide. I follow the will only of God.'

And this enraged her. Thinking of all she had done for him and how he was as stupid as a stone.

'Grow up,' she said. 'The will of God is all very well, but we must also plan for ourselves. Be a man.'

'Like my father?'

'I will bring your father!' She could not control herself now, she took any weapon to throw at him. 'He will come here with your brothers and they will bring you back home and stop all this nonsense!'

Yehoshuah looked at her benignly. She felt afraid of him. What a foolishness, to be afraid of her own small boy.

'I love my father,' he said.

'That is not what you used to say,' she snapped back.

'I have learned a great many things,' he said.

'And you have not learned to send for your mother, or send her word that you are well, or write to her, or give her the honoured place at your table.'

He drew her to him and kissed her on the top of her head. 'Ima,' he said, 'you will see such things, you will be amazed.'

But he would not come home.

'Gidon is my grandson,' she says.

The tax collector knows her, and all her children and grandchildren. He does not believe her. She can see his disbelief in his face. She will have to try harder.

'He is my grandson, son of my son Yehoshuah, who died. He got her on a whore in Yaffo many years ago and I did not know it till last year, when he came –' here she makes her voice waver like an old, grieving woman – 'when he came and found me and told me signs and I saw in his face that he must be that child.'

The tax collector laughs. He mutters something to the soldiers and they chuckle too. The mood has changed again. She does not know what they are joking about. That she has taken in the son of a whore, who could be any man's? That she boasts of it? That she has been deceived by an obvious fraudster looking for an easy home and meals provided? Perhaps among all this they will not notice another lie.

'He came last year, you say? About when?'

'In the summer,' she says quickly, 'between the Feast of Seven Weeks and New Year.'

Around the square, there are looks from one to another, another to a third. It is a hard thing she is asking of them. If none of them contradict her, they will all be accomplices. If Rome finds out they have lied, the whole village will burn.

The tax collector looks at them suspiciously, waiting to see if any will break. No one speaks.

'Well,' he chuckles, 'if you have a whore's son in your home, don't let us detain you! Perhaps you find him as skilful as his mother!' He chuckles to himself, then, evidently disappointed by the lack of laughter from the crowd, translates his joke for the soldiers, who are as amused by it as he.

No one speaks to her after the soldiers leave. Rahav and Amala and Batchamsa are all there, but they do not embrace her or comfort her. Their looks are wary.

At last, Rahav says, 'You have put us in danger, Miryam.'

It's true. She will have to set it right.

Gidon comes down from the mountain after two days. He has heard what she's done before he sees her, she can read it in his solemn face.

He looks different now from the way he was when he first came to Natzaret. Working outdoors has weathered and darkened his skin. He is not so thin, that's her good stews and bread. The place where they took off his fingers has healed to a fine silver scar across the end of his right hand. The way he works now you'd think he'd been born like that. He will be all right, she tells herself, when he has to leave.

She gives him lentil soup with flatbread and he eats it greedily. A thin dribble of the sunny liquid drips down the scraggly beard on his chin. He finishes, and she tries to take the bowl from him to wash, but he holds on to it with his maimed right hand, the three fingers stronger than both her arms.

He says, 'Why didn't you tell them where I was?'

She lets go of the bowl. She sits down opposite him.

He says, 'I didn't come here to bring danger to you all. That isn't what I wanted, I didn't . . .'

He slams his good hand down on the table. The earthenware pot jumps. He reminds her of her son at that moment. The memory makes her sickened, and the sickness makes her angry.

'Why did you come, then? What was it for? To stir up an old woman in her grief? To plague me with your love for a dead man?'

He looks as if he is about to say something, but stops.

She says, 'There is no reason, except that you wanted a place to hide and knew that telling me your stories would make me take you in.'

He stares down at his hand. At the place where his fingers were. He traces the line of the scar with his left thumbnail.

He says, 'I came to bring you good news.'

She says, 'There is no good news. My son is dead. That is all the news there can be.'

He says to her, so softly that she can barely hear the words, 'He is risen.'

She does not know what to say, does not think she has understood, so she says nothing.

He looks at her, to see if she has grasped the heart of his words.

There is such a wild hope in her.

She has had dreams like this. Dreams in which the men came to her and said, 'It was a mistake! He has not died, he was rescued. He is still alive.' And dreams, more painful yet, in which she knows that she has one day, one hour to speak to him, that he has returned so she could cradle his head against her body and smell the scent of him and hear the sound of his voice. She has lost the sound of his voice.

Gidon says, 'He died and rose again. A miracle made by God. He showed himself to Shimon from Even, and to Miryam from Migdala, and to some others of his friends. He is alive, Mother Miryam.'

His voice cracks and his eyes burn and water and his face glows with a fervent intensity and she finds a feeling rising up inside her so strong and so immediate that at first she cannot identify it until suddenly she finds that she is laughing.

She laughs as if she were vomiting, it is from the stomach not from a glad heart.

He is hurt by her laughter. He thinks she is mocking him, although this is not what is happening.

He says, affronted, 'So laughed Sara our foremother, when God told her she would give birth to a child at ninety years old, and yet it came to pass.'

And she stops laughing, although she cannot help a smile from creeping to her lips, as if she were merry.

She says, 'You are too old, Gidon, to believe this.'

He feels a flush across his cheeks.

He says, 'They came to the tomb, Mother Miryam, the tomb where he had been laid, and the body was gone. He had risen.'

And she laughs again. 'Are you so foolish? Are you so unwise? Gidon, I sent my sons for his body as soon as the Sabbath was over. So that he would not lie in a stranger's cold chamber when he could be buried in the warm earth, like his forefathers.'

He looks at her, puzzled and aggrieved, and mumbles, 'Yet he is risen. He has been seen.'

She says, 'Did you come here for this? To convince an old woman that her dead son yet lives?'

He says nothing. She is angry now.

'If he lives, if they did not kill him, if he revived in the burial chamber, if God returned him to me, why is he not here, Gidon? Whom should he see more than his mother? Why would he show himself to Shimon and to Miryam from Migdala and not to me?'

And even as she says it she hears the voice in her head of Iehuda from Qeriot saying, 'We are his family now, we who follow his teachings.' She sees his face, the last time she spoke to him, when she felt afraid and did not know why. She knows he had relinquished his family a long time before his death. If this child's story were true, it would not be her he would have come to. And this is too much to bear. She stands up quickly, her knees cracking and her back aching at the strain, and without knowing that she is going to do so she raises her right hand and hits Gidon across his left cheek.

The sound is loud. Her hand stings. She stares at him because she is an old woman and he a young man and if he responded in kind he could easily kill her.

He does not respond with a blow. He does not move or try to flee. He looks at her levelly and turns his face so that the opposite side is towards her. He waits. It is a kind of invitation.

Her hand falls to her side.

'I would have known from across the world if he were still in it.'

The first year she was a woman, her father had taken her to Jerusalem for Shavuot, the festival at the end of the seven weeks from Passover. It is a joyous festival, a simple one, a celebration of the harvest that is just beginning. Farmers bring the first fruits of their fields to the altar, to thank God for blessing their trees and their ripening vines and the swaying golden seas of their wheat. They stayed with her father's younger brother, Elihu, who lived so close to the Temple that they could see its walls from the roof of his house. The early summer light was golden, but the days blew with a sweet breeze so that the heat did not thicken or the air become still. She sat at the window on the first day, watching the never-ending procession of oxen-pulled carts filled with ripe pink pomegranates and furry yellow dates heading for the Temple, and her heart was glad.

It was a good time to come to Jerusalem – especially for a girl who had become a woman, her mother said. The people had come from all corners of the land. A young man might notice her, or she might notice a young man. There were many nervous, eager, excited girls like her, walking to the Temple with their fathers, and many young men too. In the courtyard, her father gave her the coins to buy the lamb for the offering. She examined the creatures closely, chose one tied to the back of the stall, not the largest but with the purest white wool.

There were soldiers outside the Temple, of course, auxiliaries employed by Rome. She heard another man tell her father there had been a skirmish, swiftly quashed, earlier in the day when three farmers had attacked a soldier. Miryam's father said nothing, though in the past she had heard him rail against the Romans, wishing that the people would rise up and drive them from the land. He put his arm around her shoulders as they entered the Temple and whispered, 'If you see something like that while we are here, Miryam, run. The Romans cannot tell the guilty from the innocent. If there is a squabble, run to your uncle's house, you will be safe there.'

They made their offering in peace. Seven baskets of the fruits of the land they brought to the priests: figs and barley, wheat and pomegranates, olives and dates and grapes dropping heavy on the vine. The pure white lamb was slaughtered, its blood scattered, its forbidden fats burned on the altar for the Lord. And they heard murmurings again as they left the Temple. The men gave one another secret signs, making a hand-shape like a dagger and whispering low and confusing words.

Miryam's father kept a tight arm around her and brought his lips close to her ear. 'You see nothing,' he said, 'you hear nothing. We feast with your uncle tonight and tomorrow we go home.'

When it happened, it was swift. They were walking past the spice market, homebound, and as they came in sight of the Hippodrome, with its tall colonnades and its fluttering flags, she knew something was wrong. Her father's grip tightened on her shoulder. He stood still. Behind them, back the way they'd come, there was a tight knot of men, walking slowly but at a steady pace. The shutters on the buildings nearest the Hippodrome were shut and closed tight with wooden pegs. To the right, up the narrow alleyway, another small group of men. Burly farmers with corded muscular arms, each with a long bag on his back.

The soldiers on the steps of the Hippodrome were laughing.

Two of them were throwing dice. The others had wagered money on the outcome. Some were on lookout, most were watching the game. Miryam's father's grip was like iron tongs on her shoulder. They were in a thin crowd – some other parents with children, or whole families, each looking as frightened as they. They walked into the Hippodrome square, moving as quickly as they could without breaking into a run. Passing an open doorway, she saw that the dark room beyond was full. She had the impression of watchful black eyes, of shifting flesh, of the dull sheen of metal. Men had come to Jerusalem from all over the country for this festival. The thing had been planned.

The day had grown over-warm and clouded, the sky off-white. The breeze faded away, the air was soft and moist as damp cloth. A splash of rain fell on to the cream marble plaza. A heavy, ripe drop-let which burst on the dusty stone. And then another drop, and another. And as if the rain had been a signal they had agreed on long before, the men came.

Screaming, they ran. Dark-skinned and red-mouthed, letting every rasping breath go from their lungs with a cutting edge like their metal blades. Wild shouting, anger howling, swinging their iron arms like free men whose home was overrun by vermin, they pelted up the steps of the Hippodrome and began the slaughter. The first guards, shocked by the sudden inrush, legs trembling, died before they had unsheathed their swords. Miryam saw one split from stomach to throat – a quiet smiling man who had unloosened his breastplate with the hotness of the day. Another soldier went down screaming, calling to the garrison.

There were arms around her, suddenly. Strong arms around her waist and under her shoulders, lifting her up off the ground though she kicked and wrestled, pulling her back, gripping her close, and in her confusion it was several moments before she realized that the voice shouting in her ear 'Be still! Be still!' was her own father's.

He ran with her, as the rain fell more strongly and the men screamed, ran back through the crowd. Charged at them with his shoulder, held her pressed close into his chest so that she could only inch her face to the side to breathe and, with one eye open, see glimpses of those who pushed forward. They were smiling hot, blood-grins. It was those soldiers who had taken their land, it was this man, and this, who had stolen their harvest, their women, their God. Miryam did not see where her father was running to, only that he was striving against the sea, pushing away from the place of blood.

When at last they came to rest and the noise was more distant, she saw at once that her father had taken two gashes, one across his shoulder, through the fabric of his robe, and one to his ear, which was half gone, the top sliced off, and oozing dark blood. He had collapsed, with her still grasped firmly by one of his arms, on a pile of sacks. They were in a dark room across the courtyard from the Hippodrome. She tried to stand up, but her father pulled her back.

'Be still,' he whispered, and fell back on to the sacks.

Clasped against his chest, Miryam could feel his breathing, rapid and shallow. His grip loosened, and she crawled out from under his arm, staying low. The shouting and the dreadful cries from the square were increasing. She saw a long trickle of blood run down her father's neck and, feeling with her fingers in the gloom, found a wet patch on his skull. He was still breathing though. She put a palm in the centre of his chest to reassure herself of that. Still, yes.

She looked about. They must be in a stable, probably for a priest's family so close to the Temple. It had that clean smell of horseflesh and dry straw. They were just beneath the window, which was shuttered, but she pressed her eye up against a chink in the wood. Arrows were flying in the square – one thudded into the thick shutter, and she thought: what if one were to hit my eye? – but she could not look away.

The slaughter was endless. The soldiers at the Hippodrome had lowered the metal gate to keep the attackers out. They had the upper ground now, looking down the steps on the mass of Jews running up towards them. They fired arrows through the grille and she saw twenty men brought down as she watched, pierced through the stomach, the chest, the groin. Near to her hiding place a man slumped with an arrow sticking out of his thigh. He tried to pull it out and screamed. He was young, she thought, maybe eighteen or nineteen There was a sheen of sweat on his brow. He looked around for a safe place to shelter. What if he came here? What if he opened the door and they were discovered? And if the soldiers came, what then? Another arrow found his neck with a crunching snapping sound and he fell back, dead. God forgive her, she was grateful.

As she watched, the Jews, unable to sustain the heavy losses from the archers, fell back into the surrounding streets. The square in front of the Hippodrome was dark with bodies, and running red – Roman blood and Jewish blood, she thought. One of the soldiers was still moving, moaning. She wondered how long his comrades would leave him there. Her father was still breathing. She moistened his lips from her water skin. He licked them. It was a good sign. It would be dark in two or three hours – perhaps he would be able to move then.

She heard cheering from the street outside. Were the Romans celebrating their victory? But the noise intensified. Not a cheering. A rising again of the raging voices. The clash of arms. She put her eye to the shutter a second time. From the roofs of nearby houses, the Jews had raised ladders and ropes, and had hoisted themselves to the upper levels of the colonnade. From there, they had the upper ground and were throwing down rocks, bricks pulled from the structure itself. There were boys with their slingshots, hurling down missiles – the more the Roman soldiers looked up, the greater the danger to them. She saw one man smashed in the mouth with a brick, his upper lip gone, his teeth out and the whole centre of his face pouring blood and gouts of flesh. The Romans tried to fight back at first – they sent their arrows upwards and even pulled some of the men down bodily, and set on them with swords, cleaving their limbs and heads from their torsos.

But the advantage of holding the higher ground was too great. The Romans withdrew, sheltering in the back of the colonnade. The centre of the Hippodrome, Miryam could see, was piled with the bodies of the fallen. There was a great cheering from the Jews on top of the Hippodrome, a victory cry. Miryam could not see what the Romans were doing. The Jews atop the colonnade could not see either.

She turned back to her father. His lips were moving. She wet the sleeve of her dress in her water skin and dripped a few drops into his mouth. He swallowed. The stable was dark and cool. She leaned close to his lips.

He was whispering, 'Run, Miryam, run to your uncle Elihu's house. Run now.'

She looked outside again. The square was quiet. She saw a weeping woman walking at the edge find a particular corpse and kneel, cradling a head in her arms. If she were to run, this would be the time for it. But if she ran, and soldiers retreating from the Hippodrome found her father here, they would kill him. At least if she were here, a young girl, she could plead for him. She could not leave.

'The danger has passed, father,' she said, 'the square is quiet. Rest, and when you are able to walk we will go together.'

'Run,' he kept saying, 'run now.'

His fingers and his legs were cold. He was shivering. Crawling on the floor, she brought more sacks and covered him. The shivering diminished. He moved on to his side and began to breathe more slowly and evenly. He was sleeping – a true sleep, not a faint.

There was a sound from the square like the sound of trees being felled. A great cracking sound. She wondered if the Romans had brought battering rams. There was a low, rumbling roar, like the sea heard from far off. She put her eye to the shutter again.

The Romans had set the Hippodrome on fire. The bottom part of the structure was stone, but the upper floors and galleries, the parts where the Jews had climbed, were wood. And the wood was crackling flame, like the altar of the Temple, like the smell of the burning sacrifices, the wood was on fire.

She saw that a great host of men had retreated to the very roof of the Hippodrome, where the clay tiles were not yet aflame. But there was no way down. The ladders had burned and no building was near enough the Hippodrome to jump. They were going to burn to death there, on the flat roof of the building. Some of the men were clinging to each other and some were on their knees praying and some were shaking and tearing their clothes and hair. She saw one man take five paces back from the edge of the roof and run forward, as if trying to jump to the next, but it was too far and he fell to the stone floor and did not move again.

There were others who joined him soon enough, jumping from the roof to escape a death by flames. She saw some as the fire crept up the wooden structure draw their swords and fall on them. And some did not jump and did not take a blade to end their lives but waited or tried to climb down through the flames and their cries were the loudest and most anguished of all. She had heard it said that a man who died as a martyr to Rome would be rewarded by heaven. The growling, unquenchable fire sent bright sparks up to the skies and she remembered how the life of a lamb goes back to its maker while the flesh remains here on earth, but the cries were so loud that after a time she could not think of anything else.

The square between the stables and the Hippodrome was stone and marble. The flames did not extend across them. She watched through the night, ready to drag her father behind her if he could not move himself and the flames jumped to the buildings nearby. But they did not. The soldiers had made a neat job of it. And the rain, coming and going, helped a little. The fire burned out while it was still night, leaving just blackened stumps of wood poking up into the sky from the stone base. Before dawn the next morning, Miryam shook her father until he woke and, stumbling, dizzy, crawling sometimes, he came with her to the house of his brother Elihu.

They stayed in her uncle's house then seventeen days, not daring to leave even to find food or to hear the news of what had passed in Jerusalem. They had the well, and wheat flour and dried fruit enough to live on, and her father grew stronger every day. He and her uncle agreed they must not go into the country – the Romans would be looking for anyone who fled Jerusalem, guilty or innocent. Anyone trying to leave the city would be branded a criminal and a traitor. Especially a man with fresh wounds showing.

When at last her father was well enough to attempt the long journey, and Elihu had heard and understood what had happened in the city, they left. They went in the early morning. The soldiers at the Double Gate asked them what business they had and Miryam replied, as her father and uncle had schooled her, that they were citizens of Jerusalem, and she was betrothed to a boy from the north and they must attend the wedding or the dowry would be lost. The soldiers joshed among themselves and made bawdy jokes to her about her wedding night. She cast her eyes down and, tiring of the game at last, they let them go. It was only then that she saw what was to be seen.

Along the roads to Jerusalem, the Romans had erected wooden frames – two planks crossed, one over the other, a long upright and short crosspiece – making a shape like the letter *zayin*. There were thousands. They lined the road on either side as far as she could see, down the hill and curving around. And to each frame, they had nailed a man.

The day was warm. The sun was bright as if it knew not what it shone on. As if the Lord God Almighty, the Infinite One, He Who is Everywhere had forgotten this place.

There was the smell of blood. And the buzzing sound of flies. They gathered at the soft places – the ears, the nose, the eyes. And the beating wings and low tearing rip of the vultures and the crows. The blood had trickled down the frames, had pooled at the bases, had dried in brown drips. And there was the stench of rotting flesh, like a taste in her mouth. And there was the sound.

They walked along the rocky path. The men nearest the city had been nailed up first. They were already dead, their bodies contorted, their faces and flesh already eaten away by the carrion birds. As they went further from the city, though, they came to the more recently captured rebels. These men had been there three days, four, five at most. It was they who were making the sound.

The soldiers, she knew, were still watching from the parapets of the walls of Jerusalem. No man could be cut down until the Prefect gave leave, and these men would rot here and the flesh would be eaten from their bones by the birds and the swarming things of the air. For all that, those who still had tongues in their heads pleaded for mercy, for a sponge to their brows or a swift sword to their throats. They cried for their mothers, she remembers. This was where she learned that all dying men call out for a mother. No matter what they said or thought before.

'Do not look up,' her father whispered to her, 'do not stop, do not hesitate. Look down. Walk on.'

So she walked through the valley beshaded by the screaming trees.

This was the message of Rome to the people of Israel.

There are things which are too painful to think of. And she tries, she struggles constantly not to think of it. But she cannot make a day pass without remembering those men calling for their mothers. She knows what a man calls out when he is nailed to a cross-beam. She should have forced him to come home.

He sits on a rock a little way from her house. The wind brings news that summer will come soon.

She watches his sitting. This boy who is so very alive.

'Were you there,' she says, 'in the uprising in Yaffo? Were you one of the rebels with the pretender king? Was your hand injured before you ever came here, injured in the fighting?'

He says, 'I was there.'

'Following another master, Gidon? Another king of the Jews?'

He shrugs. Says what she has known to be true for a long time.

'They killed my family. My mother, my brothers, my father, my cousins and uncles. For a long time I followed anyone who promised to destroy them.'

She nods. They are silent for a long while.

'I am different now,' he says. 'I did not lie that God told me to seek you out. It was after the rising in Yaffo, after we had been defeated, I was sleeping in the mountains waiting for spring and in a dream a voice as clear as a sword told me to come and find you.'

She believes him.

'You cannot stay here now.'

He nods.

'I'll leave tomorrow.'

'No,' she says, 'too soon will raise suspicion. Wait another week or two. Start travelling with the early pilgrims for the next festival.'

He nods again.

She sits next to him, on the rock. The place is warm where the sun has been. A lizard is heating its blood an arm's length away from them on another flat stone. She can feel his body next to hers as if they were touching. She sighs. He places his hand over hers. He clasps her hand. His thumb moves, feeling her fingers, absorbing them. She does not know whether he even sees her any longer or simply the man he hopes to reach through her. But he is so soft with her that her heart cracks open, she cannot help it.

She says, quietly, 'You believe what you told me? You hold it in your heart?'

He says, 'I do.'

She says, 'Then my son Yehoshuah lives in your heart.'

He says, 'And in the heart of all who believe it.'

She nods. That is where the dead live. In the heart.

He begins to hum a little melody. It is the melody the goat-herders often sing when they are moving the brindled flock to summer pastures. She joins in, letting her voice run alongside his, sometimes choosing the notes which harmonize, sometimes singing the same tune. It feels as though they are one person, singing like this.

And she will not, she will not. Her son is dead, he is gone, but when she closes her eyes she can believe that he is here now, that he has come back to her in the long notes and the tune and the piping warble at the back of the throat. He has not let go of her hand. He is so young, younger than her son was when she saw him last. His skin is soft, his hands uncalloused. She does not want to be moved but she cannot help herself. She is swept away.

The song ends. He looks at her, those eyes so full of longing. She knows what he wants from her, this young and beautiful man.

She says, 'Shall I tell you a story?'

He sits perfectly calm, with those shining eyes.

'It is a story from long ago,' she says, 'when I first became pregnant with my child Yehoshuah.'

She sees him mutter something under his breath as she says her son's name.

'Now I think of it,' she says, and her voice has taken on the sing-song quality of a child's storyteller, 'now that I think of it, there were signs that his birth would be special.' A chaffinch begins to sing in the thorn tree; a song of joy that the winter has, at last, receded. 'There were birds,' she says, 'the birds seemed to follow me wherever I went, singing to the child in my womb. And once, there was a stranger . . .'

She pauses. Anyone who has read the Torah knows what a stranger is. A stranger could be anyone. A stranger could be the angel of the Lord come with a test of kindness or hospitality, and if you passed that test the angel might bless you. A stranger could be the Lord walking among you.

'There was a stranger in the village who saw my belly swollen with the child and began suddenly to speak, saying, "Blessed are you, and blessed is that child whom you carry within you!"'

She continues to tell this story. She thinks of how all the stories she has ever heard must have come to be. There are only three ways: either they were true, or someone was mistaken, or someone lied. She knows that the story she is telling is a lie, but she says it anyway.

Not in fear, and not in anger, and not even in hope of anything that is to come, but because it brings her comfort to see that he believes it. Even such a simple, foolish thing as this. It brings her son back here, for a moment, back to her side and his small head under her hand and his life again unfolding. It is too good a gift to turn down, this opportunity to return him to life. And she knows it is a sin, and that God holds special punishments in store for such sins, but she cannot imagine worse than she has already seen.

She had been in Jerusalem that last spring. After he was gone, after the first day of Passover, which is sacred and on which no work can be done, she heard that he had not hung long on that wooden frame. Her son brought her the news. One of Yehoshuah's friends, a wealthy man, had bribed the guards and taken him down and placed him in a tomb.

She thought on it for a day and a night. She remembered what he had said: they were not his family. They were not the ones he had called for, they were not the ones he had spent his last days with. But was it possible that he had died without thinking of her? He had no wife to mourn for him or children to carry on his name. If he had belonged to these friends in life, perhaps he was his family's again in death.

So she told her sons to go to the tomb and fetch his body to take it into the hills and bury him in the ground. She thought: at least the crows will not have him. He will be buried in the same warm soil that will take my bones one day and until then I will know where he lies, and this thought was a comfort to her.

Shimon, who was always the kindest, tried to lie to her.

'We found a shady spot for him, by an olive grove,' he said, when they returned.

But when she asked him exactly where, when she asked them to take her there now so she could mark the spot in her mind, their story didn't hold.

They had not found him. The body was gone. Taken, they supposed, by his friends to some special burial place.

Even in death they would not give him back to her. She did not want to tell her sons her worst fear – that the Romans had the body, that she would see him again on the ramparts of the walls of Jerusalem, black and bloody and gouged by beaks and rotted away.

She left Jerusalem that day and did not look to see if there were bodies on the walls, and did not ask, and told herself that her sons must be right and his friends had surely buried him in honour.

It was as if he had never been now. As if that first son had been a curious dream, leaving behind no trace. Not a ploughed field, not a grieving wife, not a grandson or granddaughter. No one in the village spoke of him. Her own children had tried to forget him. It had been as if she had never borne that first son, until Gidon came to Natzaret.

He leaves as they had planned, when it is coming close to the Feast of Seven Weeks and the farmers are making their way to Jerusalem with carts filled with first fruits. He'll be invisible among so many travellers.

She has filled him full of stories. Some have a measure of truth to them, with Yehoshuah's childhood curiosity and his interest in learning and the way he would sometimes say things that made the adults surprised. And some are things she hoped had happened, she wished had happened. She gives him hard cheeses and bread and dried fruit so that his knapsack is bursting and she imagines another bag on his back full of the tales he'll tell, the stories he'll take to his friends in Jerusalem and across the nation.

'I'll come back,' he says, 'when things are less dangerous for you.'

She does not say that she is an old woman now, and does not expect to live to see the day when things are less dangerous.

She embraces him like a son, and he turns and begins to walk.

She watches him until he is out of sight. If the soldiers come back, she will say: he deceived me. He lied. A broken-hearted mother, he had no pity.

And perhaps they will listen, and perhaps they won't. It is like the scorpion, she thinks, rubbing her right hand with her left. Once a child is born, the mother's previous life is gone, all that matters is how she cares for the child, protects the child. Even that tiny part which is left when they are gone.

She turns. The children will be waking soon, little Iov demanding his breakfast. It is nearly the fourth hour since dawn and she has still not made bread. She goes to begin her work.

Iehuda from Qeriot

In the marketplace, during Passover, he hears two strangers saying that he is dead.

He is examining some clay oil lamps decorated with a blue inlay from Tarshish. At a stall nearby selling ripe melons, two women, their hair modestly covered, are discussing the rising in Jerusalem last Passover. It is not much discussed any longer, but the return of the season and the festival have brought it to mind. One woman, wearing a yellow scarf trimmed with fringes, knows more than the other. When he looks at her closely he thinks he remembers that she is the sister of the wife of one of the rabble who joined them in the last few weeks. Perhaps.

'It is sad,' she is saying, 'so many of them fled. Or took on other names.' She lists several of his former friends whose faces he never expects to see again in this world. Mattisyahu the former tax collector fled south to Africa, young Yirmiyahu to Egypt, Taddai to Syria. Others she has not heard about, or has heard only vague rumours. He stops to listen. This is more news than he has had of his former friends for months.

The woman seems well informed. At one point she implies that some of her friends here in Caesarea send and receive letters from the dispersed disciples. He has heard that there are rebels here, still – Caesarea is a Roman town, the capital of the region, a waypoint for trade, so a good place for all kinds of conspiracy. But it is a mark of how little they accomplished that it is not dangerous for her to mention Yehoshuah in the market square. No one is now afraid of those who followed him.

The woman shakes her head: 'There are still so many mothers who do not know what became of their sons. And Iehuda from

Qeriot died, of course. He threw himself from a rocky cliff on to a field of stones. Or I heard someone else say that some of the others threw him off.' She shrugs.

'Where did you hear that?' he asks, before he has thought whether this is wise.

The women look at him curiously. He is dressed in a fine toga, his face is beardless, his hair neatly clipped. He is not a man who should pay them attention. They look modestly to the floor.

'I . . .' he says, 'I was rather interested in the fellow at the time. Such amusing teachings.'

He has learned the lines well. They come easily to him.

The woman who was just now so full of gossip opens and closes her mouth but no sound emerges.

At last she says, 'Just rumours, sir. My brother is a sailor, he tells us tales. We have no common cause with traitors against Caesar.'

Her tone is pleading.

He nods and smiles, allows his gaze to drift from them. He has no interest in scaring them.

The other woman has decided which melon she wants and buys it hurriedly. They move on, mumbling a goodbye, their eyes cast down. He wonders how many of their other snippets of news were outright lies or strange misheard half-tales.

He turns the clay lamp over in his hand. He imagines throwing it to the floor, how the oil would spill forth, staining the hard earth with fragrance. It is a little time before he realizes that he is remembering the perfume bottle smashed on the ground, the room choking with its scent.

He wants to think about what he's heard. None of what the woman said might be true, or a portion of it, but if this is the tale being told among those who knew his friends, perhaps it is time to leave his hiding place. Perhaps he should find them, tell them he is still alive, try to explain what he did.

He walks home slowly, taking the long route around, west

towards the harbour. Here the boats are constantly working. Even on the Sabbath, even on the festivals, men from fifty nations load and unload cargo. There are baskets of fresh fish, figs from the orchards in the north, oil and perfume from across the ocean, bolts of expensively dyed cloth, pretty stones and jewels for women, even silver mirrors and ivory combs for those who can afford such things. Caesarea is rich.

The harbour too is one of the wonders of the world. Herod's men slung it across the bay in seven years. They worked on the Sabbath, and in the seventh year, the year of rest. If he were still in Jerusalem, some preacher would even now be shouting to a crowd of followers that the harbour was cursed, that all who traded in it had earned God's eternal anger. But this is not Jerusalem and the work goes on.

He wonders if this is the freedom he had sought all along. To be in a place where one could decide to care or not to care about the laws for oneself. The Romans had brought that freedom, together with their statues of their little arguing gods, and he had never noticed.

It is a kind of freedom, he thinks, to be dead. If he is dead, he smiles at the thought, perhaps even God has ceased to care what he does.

And as he thinks this, he finds that his feet have taken him wandering past the small Syrian temple to one of their goddesses. From inside the squat marble building comes the sound of laryngeal chanting, the soft cries of the worshippers in response.

He has never visited before, but he is suddenly curious to see what the nations do with their many gods. And he is not ready to go home quite yet – not to face the crowd of Calidorus's perfumed friends with the smiling ironic face of a dead man. He picks up the hem of his cloak, ascends the dusty steps and, ducking under the curtain, enters the temple.

It is dark inside, and the smell of fragrant wood and oil is thick. Well-trimmed oil lamps are positioned in alcoves, but there are not enough of them to cast more than a glow. The people are tightly packed, crowding towards the altar, and for a while all he can see is an indistinguishable mass of humanity. But his eyes become accustomed to the gloom. At the front of the temple, on a raised marble platform, lit by the brightest lamps to draw the eye, the service is taking place.

It is not so different. They slaughter a pigeon and pour its blood on to the stone. Libations of wine are poured on the altar, prayers are uttered in Greek. The priests are women, of course, that is different. They are clad in white – he thinks he has heard that this symbolizes the fact that no man has had them. It's been a long time since Iehuda last had a woman – nearly a year now – and his body often aches to hold soft, yielding flesh again. He is sure that the other men must feel the same rushing in their loins when the soft virgins bend to pour the oil – does it make the moment more sacred for them? He has heard that they believe their gods are pleased with sexual congress.

And there is the idol, of course, that is different to Temple services in Jerusalem. She is the best lit of all: a dozen lamps carefully placed on hand-shaped ledges jutting out from the wall surround her. She is a naked woman, large breasts, broad hips, round belly, beads around her neck – is this worship nothing but sex? They pour the oil on the feet of the statue as if it could feel, they waft the incense around its head as if it could smell.

At a certain point, some of the worshippers surge forward and ecstatically plant kisses on the feet of the statue, grabbing her ankles, mumbling prayers, placing pieces of clay with messages scratched on them and small coins into the sacred pool in front of her. As if, he thinks scornfully, this object they had made themselves could grant their wishes. He is unimpressed. All these years he had thought something terrible, even monstrous, went on in these temples. Like most Jews, he had never set foot inside a place of wicked idolatry and had imagined something much worse than children playing with a doll, pretending it could grant favours.

And then there is something else. There is a screaming ululation from the front of the crowd, where the people are pushing close to the statue. Something changes in the mood, he can feel it around him, the way that one can feel the change in the dry air of the desert when a sudden rainstorm approaches. People around him are breathing more rapidly, pressing closer and closer. He feels a hand at his back and a woman's arm around his waist. He cannot see her properly – it is dark and her head is turned away – but he guesses she is about thirty, with pale skin and hair oiled and scented with pine resin. She is dressed like a respectable married woman and yet her fingers are clutching at his robe. He begins to wonder whether this will end with an orgy – he had heard rumours of something like this in Jerusalem. He finds he is both horrified and excited, half hard already at the thought.

But when the crowd parts momentarily, allowing him a clear view of the brightly lit area in front of the statue, he sees that it is something else. A woman with unbound hair, with eyes rolling back in her head, is dancing in front of the statue. Her skirts are hiked up past her thighs. She goes down into a crouch repeatedly and thrusts herself up. She is making guttural cries. She has pulled her robe off her shoulders and arms, it is slipping from her breasts, but what is happening is no love-dance.

She has a small silver knife and she is cutting herself, across her arms, across her chest. Other women are singing with her, clicking with their tongues, slapping their arms against their bodies in rhythm, and as he watches she presses the tip of the knife into her own breast by the nipple, cutting a bright blue vein. She leans forward and allows the blood to gush over the feet of the statue, like milk from the breast of a woman giving suck. She squats and thrusts her pudenda towards the statue. She slices at her own thigh, completing the impression that she is bleeding from her places of sex.

The woman next to Iehuda is still holding on to him, her fingers convulsively scrabbling at the fabric and the flesh of his side. He can smell her sweat. He is certain that some sexual rite is about to begin, or something more than that, something even more appalling than what he has already seen. He is afraid now of what may happen. But no one is moving. Only the bleeding woman at the front of the room continues to dance, to smear her blood on to the statue, to dip and sway until, suddenly, with a wild cry, she drops and falls across the idol's feet, quivering, spent.

The woman standing next to Iehuda lets her arm fall away from his body. He catches her eye. She looks dazed, her lips half-parted. She reaches for him again, fumbling at his robes. Her hand finds the warm flesh of his back, under his clothing. It moves lower, grasping his buttock, squeezing. At the back of the room, through the curtains, a few people are stumbling out into the light, but he sees that two or three couples are already pushed up against the walls of the temple. The woman's skin is covered in a sheen of sweat. He can smell her; through the incense and the odour of two hundred bodies pressed tight against each other, he can smell the thick willing scent of her. He puts his arm around her waist and half lifts her from her feet, pushing men and women aside to gain the temple wall. She is already gasping as, between a pillar and rough stone, he lifts her up, presses her against the wall where her feet can find the pillar, swings her skirts aside and enters her. She is wet and hot and ready and she cries out and bares her teeth and her hands scrabble at his back as he thrusts. It does not take long. He has not even uncovered her breast before he is done and, shuddering, lowers her to the floor.

He wants to take her again. He feels already that it will not be long before he is ready to do so. He grabs at her waist. But she squeezes his hand, lets it go, and is now drifting towards the doorway. He follows as they exit, blinking, into the early-evening sun. He sees, with surprise, that her hair is red: it had looked dark, brown, in the dim light of the temple. He realizes in the same moment that she may be surprised to see his features, his own red-brown curls. He tries to speak to her.

'What is your name?' he says.

But she looks away, apparently faintly embarrassed, and says nothing.

He thinks: woman, I have felt the grip of your cunt.

But before he can find something else to say – something more uncomprehending, perhaps, or the thing he wants to say that she would not understand: did you know that you have just fucked a dead man? – she pulls her scarf over her head and hurries away.

At the top of the marble steps leading back into the street, a maiden is holding a wide flat dish. Her arms soon struggle with the heavy heaping of coins that worshippers place there as they leave. Iehuda finds a small coin for her and steps back down into the street.

Two older women pass him as they leave.

'She was Assyrian,' mutters one to the other, 'the one who cut herself. I've heard about their rites.'

The other woman, dressed neatly and with the hairstyle of a respectable matron, sniffs and frowns. 'A lot of fuss,' she says. 'What's wrong with a pigeon?'

He smells the banquet before he sees it: the sweet sticky smell of spilled wine. The smell of pomades, too, of the fragrant oils with which Calidorus and his friends anoint themselves before a feast. It is the smell of money, copiously spent.

He is late for the party. This is a mistake. He had not realized how long the temple service had gone on, he had stumbled back home dazed and would be grateful for a bath and a sleep. But although no one chides him, the anxiety of the slaves shows that he has made a bad error. One of the men hurriedly washes him with a wet cloth, another dresses him in a fresh robe and tries to touch his hair with the perfume. He grabs the man's wrist as he approaches with the stone vial.

'No,' he says.

The slave, who has tended to him a hundred times, looks puzzled but places the perfume vial back on the table. 'My master is waiting,' he says.

'Waiting' is something of an exaggeration. The feast had begun without Iehuda. In the dining room, six men are reclining on upholstered couches arranged around a low table. The table is well furnished. The men have silver cups of wine mixed with honey. There are dates, olives, bread, white cheese with herbs, dishes of lentils with fruit and in the centre a huge ocean-fish with sliced citrons, dill and parsley. The men are drunk already and the meal is not even halfway over.

'Ah, Judas –' Calidorus pronounces his name in the Greek fashion – 'we were beginning to think you had forgotten about us entirely.'

There is acid in his tone.

'Never,' says Iehuda. 'I was detained by some business in the market, that is all. My apologies, gentlemen.'

Calidorus eyes him suspiciously.

'Business? I thought –' he puts on a laugh – 'that all the business you would ever have is been and gone.'

'My apologies,' says Iehuda.

It is time for him to perform.

He is not exactly a guest at the banquet, just as he has not exactly been a guest in Calidorus's house these past months. Not a slave, no certainly not that, but neither precisely a friend. He has been treated well, allowed to roam as he pleases, fed and supplied generously with wine, given clothes and two rooms of his own and even writing instruments and certain books. But there have been these parties. His presence has been requested in a way which is slightly firmer than an invitation. He has begun to wonder what might happen if he refused one of these generous offers of 'an evening with some friends'.

He takes a stance in the centre of the room. The other men hush each other loudly, one spitting into the fish with an excessively enthusiastic 'shhhhh'. In a dark corner of the room, Iehuda notices, two slaves are standing almost motionless.

Calidorus introduces him with the usual flourish.

'Behold the man before you,' he says, 'once a follower and close confidant of a man some called the King of the Jews, but now a guest in my house. Since the subject of debate tonight is the gods, whether they are wise or foolish, to be loved or to be feared –' Calidorus had produced a series of such topics for debate at his symposia since Iehuda came to stay – 'his assistance will be invaluable!' He beckons a slave to fill his wine glass again. 'Come, tell us, Judas of Cariot, tell us about the God of the Jews and how your master was very nearly mistaken for him!'

'We have heard,' says one of the men, his face flushed with drunkenness, 'that you Jews believe that your God lives in only one house in Jerusalem! Is he not as wealthy as our gods, then, who can afford to keep up many homes?'

The others find this hilarious. One laughs so long and loudly that he begins to choke, and the slave to his right has to help him to some wine.

Iehuda sighs inwardly. It is one of the things that every gentile has heard about the Jews. Like the lie that Jews worship the pig and that is why they do not eat it. Like the lie that at the centre of the Temple in Jerusalem, in the most sacred place, there is a donkey and its shit is piled up around it. Like the lie that Jews hate their bodies and their wives so much that they only make love through a hole in a sheet. How do these things begin? Which debased mind invented them? Who chose to pass them on, unthinking?

He has learned to play along with such tales rather than challenge them. Or to circumnavigate them, like a boatswain foreseeing choppy waters. He tries to tell the truth jokingly.

'Ah,' he replies to the drunken fool, 'perhaps it is that our God is more loyal to us. Like a loving husband, he stays close to home. While we all know how Jupiter spreads his . . . favours.' He mimes the thrusting motion of the body, the bunching of his thighs reminding him suddenly, overwhelmingly, of the musk scent of the red-haired woman in the temple.

But the trick works. The other men laugh. One punches the drunken questioner gently on the arm.

'You'd do well to learn from them, hey, Pomponius? Stay a little closer to home and maybe your wife wouldn't stray so much!'

The others laugh and Pomponius, a jowly man in his fifties, though still with a fine head of thick black hair, reddens and scowls and drinks more wine.

Calidorus, Iehuda notes, looks nervous. Rein it in, Iehuda says to himself, don't embarrass important guests.

'Ah –' he fakes a little laugh – 'perhaps it is just that our God, like a wise husband, knows he cannot trust us, as no man can trust a woman! If he left us for a moment, we would start rutting with some other god.'

He does a comical little mime of a woman peering through the curtain of her house, seeing her husband leave, and immediately grabbing the nearest slave and mounting him. The men laugh uproariously, toasting each other with wine, spilling more than they manage to get in their mouths. He has them now.

'Yes,' rumbles Pomponius, relaxing a little, 'you can't trust women.'

Calidorus gives Iehuda a small smile.

'But now,' says Iehuda, 'to my own small role in the downfall of a god. It is hard now even to recall how different I was back then. If you can believe it, I had a full beard.' He cups his two hands upwards at his waist, to indicate a beard so long that these clean-shaven Romans grimace.

'Not only that, I was a virtuous and honourable man. I prayed every day, I observed the festivals and the Sabbath, I kept to the old ways of cleanliness in foods and in washing my body and in making sure I fucked only my own wife, and not anyone else's.'

He winks broadly, as if to say that he is exaggerating slightly here. The men chuckle. Iehuda has read Ovid, with the stories of gods fucking women, women fucking animals, animals turned into human beings so that they can rut and grunt and screw. He understands what these people are like. They would not really believe that any healthy young man could have been a virgin at twenty-eight when he took a wife, that it would never have occurred to him to be

78

unfaithful to her. Perhaps they would not even believe that he had never eaten the flesh of a pig.

So he tells them the story they want to hear. It is an hilarious tale, he has rehearsed it many times at many such dinners. He knows exactly where to pause, where to emphasize a joke, where to undercut a tragic moment turning it to ridicule. In the version he tells, he is the impudent puck, the fool who dares to challenge the king. In this story, Yehoshuah – his friend, the man he loved best in all the world – becomes a puffed-up little prince who waved his needle-like sword at Roman rule. Iehuda becomes the naïve innocent who says, 'If you irritate their skin, they will swat at us all.' He paints himself as foolish, giving his friend up and believing that Pilate would do no more than scold him. The men laugh. They drink more wine. Calidorus is pleased.

And while he tells this liar's tale, Iehuda reminds himself of how it really was. He does this every time, although it pains him, because he must know it, if only in his heart.

He had been so holy and abstemious that no Roman would believe it. His father had died when he was a boy. He had worked the farm, and attended the Temple on holy days, and cared for his mother and his two younger sisters, and only when they were fed, and wed, did he think of himself. He was a boy who loved the Lord too much, if such there is. Loved Him too much and thought of Him too much, and wanted only to do His will and know His words. The days in Jerusalem for the three festivals were his only respite from work, and they were joyous indeed, for then he was close to the place where God lived. And when he married – yes, at twenty-eight, and yes, a virgin, and yes, this had not seemed a special hardship to him – a thoughtful and hard-working and quiet man – when he lay with his wife that first time he thought of the deed as much as a joining with God as with the shrewd and lusty woman, Elkannah, who had consented to marry him.

She worked in the fields by his side and spun wool and wove cloth and baked bread, and he felt lucky past imagining – though he was too serious a man ever to be freely joyful. His beard was long and full, though Elkannah used to sit astride him on the bed and trim it with the knife when he let her. He still remembers the curve of her behind and how neatly it fitted into his two cupped palms, and how his cock would rise to meet her while she wriggled on his lap and laughed and told him to hold still or she would end by stabbing him with this knife and who then would provide for her and the children they would surely have, would he think about that?

But when he was twenty-nine a hard fever passed through the village of Qeriot. It had been a long hot spring when they were taken down and water was short in the mountain streams. Only the well gave a good supply and some days they were too weak to lift and turn the bucket. It was a blinding fever, putting black spots in front of the eyes and then making it too painful to look out in full sunlight. But it was his fault, he knew, even though he had been as sick as her. He should have found a way to get water.

On the third day, he managed to leave his bed to walk to the well. He tottered like a newborn lamb all the way there and all the way back, with the black spots hovering at the edges of his sight, but when he brought back the water Elkannah was dead. Quiet in the bed, as if she had slipped out between one breath and the next. As if she had simply forgotten to take that next breath and might remember in a moment, wipe her hands on her apron, chide herself for her foolishness. But she was gone.

And then something else was gone, suddenly and without his consent.

It was not the sweet soft scent of his wife in bed in the mornings that he missed the most – though he missed her beyond enduring. He missed the most the God who he had always felt watching over him, who in quiet moments he would speak to and imagine that he heard a comforting response. Who he had wept to on long nights after his father had died and who had placed a hand upon his neck and said, 'I am your Father in heaven, and I shall give you strength.' He felt that the line joining him to heaven – like the cord that connects a baby to its mother – had been severed. Perhaps the Father was still there, but Iehuda's face was turned so far away that he could not tell any longer.

He thinks now that it may have been a crime to feel as he did. To mourn for a God more than for a wife? But it is so.

Some time passed, but he did not measure it. A handful of seasons, and he worked still just the same, because what else was there to do, and the people of the village – who had themselves lost parents and children, spouses and siblings – said to themselves, 'Before long he will take another wife, he will have sons and daughters and forget this first one.' They did not know that his heart was as cold as the earth and as empty as a dry wheat husk.

And then the man came to the village. Iehuda had heard nothing of him. The decision to go and listen to him speak was merely the choice between a long night alone in his home and sitting with the people to hear whatever foolishness they would hear. He had seen dozens of such preachers over the years, he and Elkannah had gone to listen to them sometimes and joked over their prattle or, occasionally, debated their wisdom.

This man had not been so much different, at first. Telling tales to illustrate his messages, talking about God's love. At a certain point, he fell silent. Sifted the earth with his hand. Rubbed his forehead. Looked up, as if searching through the crowd, and with his eyes found Iehuda, and he held the gaze, and held it, and Iehuda could not look away.

'You are looking for God,' said the preacher, 'but God is also looking for you. And He will find you. He has found you tonight.'

And Iehuda felt tears starting in his eyes.

'You have lost much.' The man spoke in a level tone, neither emphasizing nor attempting to persuade. He spoke as if he were hearing the simple truth from heaven.

'God has felt your loss,' he said, 'and He has not forgotten you, although you have turned your face away from Him. He speaks to you today as a Father. Tell me whom you have lost.'

This was no secret. Any child in the street could have told him that Qeriot had been struck by the sickness. Every person had lost something.

Iehuda said, 'My wife.' It was defiant, the way he said it. Challenging the man to impress him.

'And your father?'

It was a lucky guess, Iehuda told himself, nothing more, a guess from a preacher. How many men of thirty have not lost their fathers? He could not have known that he had lost him especially young, that he had taken it especially hard.

But still he said, 'Yes.'

And the man, whose name was Yehoshuah, unfolded his long limbs and stood up from the earth and walked over to Iehuda and gave him a hand to lift him up. He put his hands on Iehuda's shoulders and said, 'You think that your Father in heaven has forgotten you. But your Father in heaven is here. Now. Guiding me to you today. Listen,' he said, 'this story is for you.'

And he told a story to the crowd.

There was once a man who had two sons. And because he had business both near and far, he sent one of his sons to do all his commerce in the city and kept one by him to learn the ways of the farm. That son who was sent away burned with rage, for he was kept from those he loved, and from his father. He sent angry letters back to his father, begging him to let him return, but the father left him there for ten long years, while his brother raised a family, and lived at home, and tended the fields. At last, after many years, the father brought the son home from the city.

'Father,' said the son, 'why did you keep me away so long?'

And the father said, 'My beloved son, you were always on my business, every moment you were away. And now that you have come to understand all my doings, this farm and all that is in it is yours.'

'So it is,' said Yehoshuah, 'with men. It is those who suffer who will inherit the kingdom of heaven, and our Father in heaven has already picked out a golden seat for you, my friend. He loves you best of all.'

The man moved on with his talking and preaching. But it was as though Iehuda had been struck by lightning through the top of his head and into the ground, because he wanted it so much to be true. Not like Job's suffering, a test. But as this man had said, a gift.

That night the man made camp near to the brook, with a small fire and some gifts of food for his trouble and three of his friends, for few men followed him then. Iehuda, with about eight or nine others from the village, sat with them in their camp and listened to them talk.

There were things the man said that filled Iehuda with fire, as if his blood had turned to flame.

There was a beggar among the group, and when the rest of them opened up their packs and ate their barley cakes and olives or dried fish, he had no food to eat. They each gave him a little of their own to make up a meal and he ate ravenously, gratefully.

Yehoshuah sifted the dirt under his hands and said, 'Why do we give charity?'

Iehuda replied quickly, 'It's written in the Torah: "When your brother becomes poor, extend your hand to him, and strengthen him – even the convert and the settler." God commanded it.'

Yehoshuah nodded slowly. 'Now answer me this. Why is it written in the Torah? Why did God command it?'

Iehuda blinked. This is not a question a man can hope to answer. To ask, 'Why did God do so?' is as much as to say, 'I can understand the infinite mind of God.'

'For our highest good,' piped up one of the others. 'All God's commandments are for our good.'

'But why?' pressed Yehoshuah. 'Why is it good for us? Why did God lay this down for us?'

There was silence around the fire. The three men who had arrived with Yehoshuah must already know the answer, or the special point he was making. The others were dumb, afraid that they would give the wrong response. Iehuda, suddenly tired of the game and of this man trying to make them feel stupid, replied.

'It's not given to us to know why God does anything,' he said. 'Our job is to listen to His commands and obey them.'

The other men nodded. This is what it means to be a pious Jew: to learn the law and to obey it.

'Like the soldiers of Caesar?' said Yehoshuah, a smile on his lips. 'Like a man bought for hire? To do without knowing the reason for what you do? Our God is not a tyrant. He would not have given us sharp minds if we were not meant to use them. Think. Why did God tell us to give charity?'

At this, two of the men quietly began to pack up their things to go. Yehoshuah did not try to detain them. He had compared their belief to the blind obedience of the soldiers; he must have known this would be intolerable to some.

Iehuda felt his mind stretch after the question, though. It was a good question. If he had to make a guess at the reasoning of God – and even the thought was faintly sickening, like looking down a long drop – if he had to guess, he might say . . .

'Perhaps God has commanded us to help the poor because He loves them.'

Yehoshuah clapped him on the back: 'This is a good answer, my friend! See, we have been reasoning for but a few moments and already we have puzzled out who God loves! And from His commandments, who else does He love?'

'The blind and the crippled . . .' Iehuda began, thinking of the commandment not to put a stumbling block before the blind. 'The widow and the orphan? For it says in the Torah, "Do not mistreat widows and orphans. If you mistreat them, I will hear their cries."'

'Yes,' said Yehoshuah, 'God has a special love for women without husbands, sons without fathers. Think more. Why does God say, "Love your neighbour"?'

Iehuda had it now. 'Because God loves . . .' He paused. 'He loves those who are near to us?'

'Has he not taught us all to love our neighbours? Is not every person the near neighbour of some other person? Even soldiers, are they not –'

'No,' said Iehuda, extremely irritated, 'soldiers are not neighbours. If you go on this way you will have us sharing our food with the men who come to burn our crops and marrying our daughters to the men who raped our wives.' He paused.

Yehoshuah looked at him, interested.

Encouraged, he went on, 'You cannot know what God had in mind for us. He told us to love our neighbours, that is enough. If we start adding to the law where will we be? Like the Romans, making little gods to tell us everything we want to do is right.'

'How if I say this?' said Yehoshuah. 'The Torah says, "Love your neighbour." But since everyone is someone's neighbour, I say, "Love your enemy."'

'That's nonsense. We could love them, but it would not make them love us.'

'But imagine if everyone did so. Imagine if we spread that word. Love your enemy. From village to village and town to town. What would happen? Imagine it.'

Trying to grasp it made Iehuda's mind stutter.

'I cannot imagine,' he said at last. And then, because he yearned to understand, 'Explain it to me, teacher.'

Yehoshuah put his rough palm on the back of Iehuda's hand.

'If the world were filled with people who listened to these few words, only these words, we would build the kingdom of heaven on earth. That is why I travel from village to village. That is the work of my life. To teach people to look into the words of God until they see the heart of everything. Imagine it: the Romans and the Greeks and the Syrians and the Babylonians and the Persians, imagine if we all learned, together, to love one another.'

Iehuda allowed his mind to follow, across the map of the wide world, across the empires and kingdoms that fought and tried to rule and subdue each other. And he imagined what might happen if these words travelled from mouth to mouth, from mind to mind, from one city to the next to the next, if this simple message – love your enemy – were the accepted creed of all the world. He did not see how it could happen.

'If one man went against it,' he said at last, 'the whole thing would be broken. In a world like that, a world of peace, a world of soft people with no knives, one man could destroy everything.'

'Then we cannot rest until every man has heard it. Think,' said Yehoshuah softly, 'what shall we use up our lives for? More war, like our fathers and their fathers, more of that? Or shall we use ourselves for a better purpose? Is this not worth your life?'

And Iehuda saw it, just for a moment. In this instant, the whole world was new to him.

He could not stop thinking after that. His mind was rattling like a cart on a rock-strewn road, picking up speed, heading downhill helter-skelter, jerking and bouncing. He wondered if he were going mad.

When the other men went home, past midnight, he stayed and talked with Yehoshuah, asking each question as it came to him, sometimes sitting silently for a long time.

'What about people who come to harm you? What shall we do if they try to hurt us?'

Yehoshuah stretched out his long body on the bedding roll over the stones. He put his hands behind his head, leaned back and looked at the dark, coruscant sky.

'What do you think, Iehuda,' he said, 'what does your heart tell you?'

Yehoshuah had folded one leg over another. His simple brown travelling robe was stained with dust and sweat. The skin of his face and arms and legs was sun-worn and weathered. He was still so young, though. How had he come to know so much?

'I am trying . . .' he said, and came to a halt. He tried to think afresh, to imagine a world entirely new, with no certainties, but he could not make himself bend. 'If we must love our enemies, and our enemy is the empire of Rome, would we not have to become their slaves?'

Again and again, all he could come back to was the single alternative he knew.

'Would we be like the priests in the Temple,' he said at last, knowing it was a kind of capitulation, angry with himself for not being able to think further, 'bowing and scraping to Rome? Trying to please them?'

Yehoshuah sat up a little. 'Come and lie by me,' he said.

He shifted position to make room for Iehuda.

Iehuda came and lay beside him.

'Look up at the heavens,' said Yehoshuah, 'look at the stars.'

Iehuda looked. The sky was crammed with stars as a pomegranate is filled with honey-sweet seeds.

'We know that God is in the heavens,' said Yehoshuah. 'He looks down on us all from there as from the top of a mountain.'

Iehuda felt it. God looking down on him. He had forgotten.

'God doesn't choose his dwelling place by accident,' said Yehoshuah. 'Look at the stars. Is any one of them raised a single cubit above his fellows? Has God placed a crown upon one of them? Do they rule one another?'

Iehuda shook his head.

'So, think.'

'If we cannot fight Rome, we must become their slaves . . .' he began.

'Must we?'

Iehuda thought about it. His mind was so clear now, it was as if he had removed the top of his head and the starlit sky was pouring through him, into his heart.

'Could we somehow love them and continue to live as we always lived before they came . . .? But they would kill us.'

'Do you think so? A whole country?'

Yehoshuah moved his arm slightly, so his fingers touched Iehuda's. Iehuda felt the touch as a burst of warmth starting in his hand

and radiating up through his arm, across his chest, blooming in great sunbursts along his body.

Yehoshuah said, 'It is possible to love with dignity. Listen. If a man hits you on the cheek, give him your other cheek to hit. That is what he wants – give it to him freely. If a soldier commands you to carry something for him for one mile, carry it two miles. That is love – to show you are giving it by choice as a free man, not because of a command. If they demand you give them your coat, give them your shirt too.'

Iehuda imagined it. A rainstorm. A soldier demanding he give up his coat – such things happen. And him taking off his shirt too and standing bare-chested in the rain for this ideal of love.

'They will take us for madmen.'

'Seeing such love will change them. This is how we will bring the message.'

'You are talking about a new earth,' he said, 'and then what?'

Yehoshuah smiled.

'I do not know. But I believe my Father in heaven will find an answer for us.'

'And what are we to do?'

'Now?' Yehoshuah's voice dropped very low. 'God came to me in the desert and He told me to spread this word. It is my holy duty. And you, Iehuda, He has told me that you will come with me and help me and be my friend.'

Yehoshuah patted Iehuda's flank, like a man thanking a loyal and obedient horse, pulled his robe around him and rolled over on the blanket to sleep.

Iehuda lay down but his whole body was vibrating like the plucked string of a harp. He knew he had to join them. When they walked on from Qeriot, over the dusty yellow hills north to Hevron, he would go with them. This man, he thought, this angry righteous man, would change the whole world.

There were more of them soon. And more, and more. They walked from town to town and in each place there would be some men –

and once or twice a woman – to whom Yehoshuah was especially drawn, for whom he seemed to have a particular message, a new parable or saying. And they would sit talking until the fire died low and in the morning one or two or three men would walk on with them.

They became something, and it was not clear precisely how it had happened. In Iehuda's memory, one day they were walking dusty-footed into a town and the old women were spitting out their chewed-up leaves as they passed and people were only coming to hear Yehoshuah because at least he was a new thing, like a pedlar or travelling musicians. And then suddenly, arriving at a new village, people came out to meet them. Young men and women, and children, tugging on their robes and saying, 'Is that him, is that him?'

But when he thinks of it, it is not so strange. Because of course, there were also the cures.

He had not made any cures in Qeriot. He did not always do it. Only when there was a certain kind of person or, Iehuda noticed, an especially large crowd. He felt unkind and unworthy for noticing this, but he could not put it out of his mind once he had seen it.

In Remez, where there were five children gone blind with the same pox that had afflicted Iehuda's wife, Yehoshuah touched them on the head and whispered that God would comfort them and make them strong, but made no cure. In Chidyon, where a girl who had lost both legs and pulled herself on a little wheeled tray by her arms begged Yehoshuah to help her, he wept tears at her suffering, and prayed with her for courage and for the blessings of God, but no new limbs sprouted where the old ones had been.

But in Kfar Nachum there was a great crowd, about two hundred people, and several had brought members of their family who had been unwell for years. From among them, Yehoshuah picked out a man who was wailing and shouting and ripping at his own hair and garments. He was possessed by a demon, they could all see it, the kind who attacks the innocent and the guilty, who will jump into a child if they can.

Iehuda had seen demons like these rip a man slowly apart, cause him to dash his own head against a wall, or to attack his wife and children or to throw himself from a high place and make an end of his life. There had been a man in Qeriot like this, so tormented by the things the demons shouted to him in his own head that he bit chunks of flesh from his arms and the wounds began to stink and so he died.

This man in Kfar Nachum was snarling like a dog when they brought him to Yehoshuah, pulling off his cloak to show his bum to the women standing in a half-circle beneath the tree. He snapped and howled and made to grab the women and tear at them with his teeth, and many ran from him and Iehuda was not surprised.

But Yehoshuah was not afraid. Two of the man's brothers held him steady. They offered to sit on his chest to keep him still, but Yehoshuah looked into the man's eyes and said, 'You will be peaceful for me. For you know I am your master.'

And the man stared at him like a frightened dog finally finding the leader of his pack. There was fear in his eyes but also relief and a quality of begging.

'Let his arms and legs go,' said Yehoshuah.

'But master,' said the brothers, 'he will run wild and attack the women, he has done it before.'

'Let him go,' said Yehoshuah, in the same level tone, still looking into the man's eyes.

They let go and the man did not move.

'Tell me your name,' said Yehoshuah. 'Demon in this man's soul, tell me your name.'

The man rolled his eyes back in his head, and whined and howled and gnashed his teeth, but he did not move.

'Tell me your name,' said Yehoshuah again, 'in the name of God our Father I command it.'

And then the demon in the man spoke. Its voice was a growl like a wolf and a low hiss like a lizard and it said, 'I am Ba'al Nakash, the Lord of Snakes, and this man is mine.'

The people were amazed, because this demon had never told them its name before, and everyone knew that a demon can be commanded by its name.

So Yehoshuah put his hand on the man's forehead, and even though his eyes rolled and his teeth gnashed he remained still.

Yehoshuah said, 'Ba'al Nakash, in the name of God our Father I command you to come out of this man!'

The man fell to the floor with a great gasp and a choking sound. His body began to shake and the people muttered to each other, 'That is the demon, trying to hold on.'

Yehoshuah knelt down and put his hands on the man's chest and shouted, 'Ba'al Nakash, I command you to come out of this man!'

The man writhed and hissed and bit through his own tongue so that blood and spittle foamed from his mouth. He clawed at the ground until his fingernails broke and bled on the stones, and he writhed and threw himself against the rocks until great bruises began to show on his body. Yehoshuah took a deep breath, let it out slowly and then, with one hand on the man's chest, he gave his order.

'By the name of Yahaveh!' said Yehoshuah, and the people gasped, because this is the true name of God, which is never to be spoken aloud, except by the High Priest in the holiest place in the Temple in Jerusalem on Yom Kippur, the holiest day of the year, but Yehoshuah spoke it in this backwater village for the curing of one demon-infested man. 'By the name of Yahaveh, come out of him!'

And hearing this forbidden name of power, the man's whole body stiffened, his back arched and he let out a wild scream. The people said afterwards that they had never been more sure they heard a demon in all their days. In neighbouring villages, they said they had heard that scream, five miles distant.

It lasted for the time of ten breaths, and everyone heard that it was the sound of the demon leaving the man's body. Some said they saw black smoke rise up from his mouth, but Iehuda did not see it, only the clouds of dust he raised from his thrashing. But when the scream ended the man was still and it was obvious that the demon had left him.

A boy at the back of the crowd suddenly called out, 'A snake!'

And they turned, terrified, expecting a giant snake, a demon the size of a man. But it was just a mottled viper, lazily coiled behind some rocks.

'The demon has gone into it!' shouted someone, and another boy picked up a stone and threw it at the snake. Then more and more pelted it, and though it arched its back and bared its fangs just like the demon-haunted man had done, it could not win against so many and soon enough it was dead.

They brought the limp, crushed snake to the man, dangling it by its tail. He was sitting up now and blinking, probing his bitten tongue with one finger as the bloody saliva spilled from his mouth. Though the demon was gone from him, he was not as a normal man – no one could expect it – he seemed dazed, and frowned and muttered, but he did not growl or hiss any longer. He blinked at the snake as they laid it beside him.

'That was your demon,' said one of them. 'Burn it and you will be free forever.'

But Yehoshuah smiled and clasped the man's hand.

'Your faith in God and in His holy name has set you free,' he said.

That night the village killed three yearling goats to feed them. And the next morning, when they walked on, more than ten men and women of the village came with them.

There had been others travelling with Yehoshuah before Iehuda arrived, but Iehuda knew that he was special to him. Yehoshuah could tell him things the others could not understand.

After Yehoshuah had taken the snake demon out of the man in Kfar Nachum, they sat up talking long after the others were sleeping the sleep of those whose bellies are filled with roasted goat.

'How does God tell you,' said Iehuda, 'which to cure?'

Yehoshuah thumbed the edge of his sleeping blanket.

'I can see,' he said, 'which demons will listen to me.'

Iehuda lay back on his own blanket.

'I knew a man in Qeriot ran mad with a demon,' he said. 'He would dash his head against walls.'

'Demons make men do such things,' said Yehoshuah.

'But when his mother spoke to him,' said Iehuda, 'he became calm. For a while. It was only after she died that the demon would not let him be. He died of that demon, but while his mother was alive he could hearken to her voice and not the demon's.'

Yehoshuah stirred the embers of the fire with a stick.

'Is it like that with you?' said Iehuda.

Yehoshuah shrugged. 'I do not understand what you are asking me.'

'If a demon listens to a man's mother,' Iehuda said, 'it is not because the mother has power over the demon. The mother has power over the man. The name you spoke today has power over all men. Not just demons, but men as well.'

Yehoshuah threw back his head and laughed.

'This questioning is the wisdom I taught you,' he said. 'Use it always with me. You are right. I do not know how I do what I do. When I speak, the demons may listen, but what happens next is in God's hands.'

They walked on and their host became bigger. Mighty. A multitude. There started to be another group too, among those who came to hear Yehoshuah speak, or watch him doing his cures and casting out demons. They were the other rabbis. They were only to be expected. They came to wrestle with him.

Some met him boldly. In Emek, Ezra the Teacher challenged him to debate and after they had finished calling one another fools Ezra held Yehoshuah close to his breast and brought them all in for supper. In Me'etz, they set up two great piles of stones and had Yehoshuah and their own teacher, Nechemiah, preach atop them. In Refek, the people asked Yehoshuah questions in turn until his patience was utterly exhausted and he cried out that no man could bear such an assault without a cask of wine.

They tried to trip him up, and find the flaw, and winkle out his hidden assumptions and specious reasoning. For Iehuda, these were the most glorious days. Everyone knew that the debates were the 'arguments for the sake of heaven' of which the sages speak with praise.

The more a man argues with you, the more he respects you. The more he tries to pick holes in your argument, the gladder is the Holy One Who is in All Places. The great rabbis Hillel and Shammai argued with each other so fiercely that their followers attacked one another bodily – several of their students were killed in these fights. And though this is to be regretted, their ardour for debate is commendable. For how are we to hear the infinitely stranded voice of God except in the grappling voices of those who care about the Torah and seek out its never fully graspable truth?

Some rabbis were merely angry, of course. Lesser men and weak men. Every part of the world contains men who cannot bear to hear their words questioned. They are people who believe that only their purple robe or their silver chain gives them power over others. They forget that Moses had only a staff of wood and stuttered when he spoke. And there were such men in Yehoshuah's camp too – some of his followers could not bear to hear him questioned, just as some of the rabbis could not bear to hear his criticism.

But the best men on each side rejoiced in the fight, chewing on the muscle of it, crunching at the bones of it. And when the arguments were done, in the light of early dawn, more men and more women walked on with them to the next village, and the next.

It was about this time that there started to be twelve of them. The closest ones, the inner circle. Iehuda would not have imagined that the group could grow so large as to need an inner circle, but it had done so. They needed to exclude the provocateurs in their midst sowing dissent or spying for Rome. There were spies, of course. Yehoshuah needed trusted men.

He came to each of them separately, whispering that he had need of their counsel, their eyes and ears. It took Iehuda a little time to work out who the other trusted men were. He noticed that, although there had been many questioners in the outer circle, he was the only one in that inner group who had been known to argue back, to challenge in open meeting.

There had been a time when they made no distinctions. At Beit Saida, when everyone had shared a single meal, Yehoshuah had seemed to be saying that all distinctions would be swept away. But now Iehuda was the only speck of dissent left in the inner circle. He could not speak to the others.

'Do you know what they are saying of you?' he asked.

Yehoshuah frowned, but said nothing. They were alone, by the fire. It was late at night and the others were asleep. It was like it had been at the start. There were not enough such nights now.

'They are saying that you are the Messiah. The one we wait for. The true son of David. The one who will end all disease and suffering. The one whose arrival we will know because there will be no more war and all the dead will rise from the grave.'

He wanted to carry on, to list all the different kinds of magic that the Messiah would do, to make Yehoshuah laugh. He wanted so much for him to laugh. If Yehoshuah laughed, then Iehuda could laugh too, and they could go back to talking about remaking the world through their work and struggle and not waiting for God to bless them with miracles when the true son of David was on the throne.

He did not laugh.

'Are you going to make a lion lie down with a lamb?' said Iehuda, and there was accusation in his voice. 'Are you going to rebuild all the cities that have been destroyed?'

Yehoshuah spoke very low and quietly: 'Who knows what may happen through God's will?'

There was no argument against this. But still Iehuda knew what he knew in his heart.

'I think some of them already believe it,' he said. 'You should tell them to stop saying it, even among themselves.'

Yehoshuah stirred the embers of the fire.

'It is not for me to stop them. They must speak the truth as they find it.'

And Iehuda wanted to shake him by the shoulders, to slap his face, to say: for God's sake, man, all that we have worked for, all that we have talked about. But he saw that it was too late for that.

'You have begun to believe it yourself, haven't you?' and his voice was angry and he could not stop it. 'You've listened to what they've said about you. Like Herod, who could only hear the flattery of his sycophants, you have listened to it too much.'

Yehoshuah became pale and still. His nostrils flared, his eyes reflecting the dying fire, and he said, 'Do you think that you know the will of God better than I?'

And Iehuda remembered the man who had taught him to listen to the knowledge of his own heart, and to think out each precept like a Greek, testing it for the signs of truth and for what could be learned from it.

'I think,' he said, very slowly, 'that if God has chosen you, He will tell us in his own time, and until then we should not think of it.'

Yehoshuah smiled at that. His old, easy smile.

'Is this my own wisdom you are handing back to me?'

'Yes.' Iehuda smiled too. 'If you cannot tell them "I am not he," then at least do not think of it until God makes it all very clear. Or' and he laughed, 'until the hour of your death. For if you die without becoming the king, we will know you were not the Messiah.'

'I shall have to repent of my folly on my deathbed, then,' said Yehoshuah, and chuckled, and leaned back on the heels of his hands.

It was a little time after that that he sent them out across the land to spread his words and to heal the sick. It did not matter that they said, 'I cannot heal as you heal, I do not have the power as you have it'; he touched them on the brow and murmured, 'Do what you can.' And they went to try to do what they could. They would meet again in three weeks and bring with them new followers or not as God willed it.

It was clever, also, to disband at this time. The group had grown too large. There had begun to be spies from the local authorities at the edges of the gatherings. A quiet cluster of them sometimes, listening to the words, watching the mood of the people. Any man who can lead a rabble is a threat to an empire. To love their enemies did not mean to submit to them. Rome was interested in anything that stirred people up. So they broke apart, for Rome would have broken them otherwise.

Iehuda set off in high excitement. Most of the other men had gone in pairs but he, and some others, had decided each to go alone. To see what God meant for him to do. And so he came to the place.

It was a village in the east. He does not remember the name now, and he will never go there again. A small place, perhaps eight or nine homes with fields all on hillsides, so that it was with effort that the seed was sown and with pain it was reaped. A place where the living was hard. He arrived in the evening, a preacher in the name of Yehoshuah, whom two or three of them had seen before in Galilee. They fed him soup of lentils and hard bread and he knew it was more than they could afford. When he was left alone in one of the shacks by the field he looked into an earthenware grain store. It was empty, save for two dead wasps at the bottom of the jar.

And there they brought him a boy. The child was perhaps ten years old and crippled. He had a misshapen leg: the bone of it was bent and the knee joint swollen and the skin sore and the whole leg crushed by the weight of his body, so that he had to support himself on a stick. His armpit was blistered from the place where the stick rested. His whole body was overturned by that leg.

Iehuda's heart leapt out of his body when he saw that boy, and his spirit flew over to him and touched the boy's heart. He felt it. This poor crippled child needed the love and mercy of God more than anyone he had ever seen. He felt the sore places as if they were on his own leg, and the crooked bone as if it were his bone, and the stiff, aching, oozing joint as if it were his own body crying out in pain.

He prayed to God as he had learned as a child, calling him 'Father'. Father, he said, heal this child, take his suffering from him, make him whole as I am whole. Do not refuse, as a father would never withhold water from his thirsty child if he had it. Father, you have the healing of this child in your hands. He felt the power in him, the tingling in his fingertips, the heat in the palm of his hand, and he knew that when he touched the boy the power would flow out of him, and as he lowered his hand he was already saying, 'Thank you, thank you, thank you.'

He thought of the men and women he had seen Yehoshuah heal with his touch, how the demons of pain fled from their bodies, how their backs unbent and their flesh became whole. And the boy on his mother's knee, both of them looking at him with such trust because everyone had seen the power of God working through Yehoshuah to cure any affliction.

'Thank you,' said Iehuda under his breath as he lowered his hands on to the twisted limb, 'thank you, Father, for making me your conduit to do this holy work.' And he grasped the leg with his hands so full of warmth, as if his arm were the outstretched arm of the Almighty, as if his fingers were the mighty hand of God.

Later, when they gathered again as Yehoshuah had told them, the disciples sat around the campfire and told their tales. Mattisyahu told how he had cured the boils of a man afflicted for ten years with this horrible skin disease. A good storyteller, he made them all imagine the suppurating wounds, the pus flowing out from every sore place, the stench of rot on the man's clothes and the contortion of his face every time he moved and the cloth rubbed against one of his agonizing pustules. Mattisyahu said that he had called upon the name of God, that he had prayed as he had been taught, and when one of the women bathed the man's legs they found that the sores came off as they washed and that the flesh underneath was new and whole and without pain. 'Like the skin of a new-shorn lamb,' said Mattisyahu.

There were other stories like this. Netan'el had cast out seven demons from a woman in Be'er Sheva who had previously spat like a camel and cursed and screeched at anyone who tried to approach her. He had seen the demons rise from her like smoke, he said, like white ash flying up from a fire made of very old dry wood. The demons rose into a tree and went into a flock of birds nesting there, who shat mightily upon the people gathered to watch. But the people were handy with their slingshots and stones and brought the birds down, so then the demons were no more.

Yehoshuah listened to these tales calmly, nodding when one of the disciples mentioned a prayer he had used, or a way he had found to bring greater faith to the people watching.

When it came to Iehuda's turn, he told his story quickly. He had none of Mattisyahu's gift with a yarn.

'There was a boy,' he said, 'he had a bandy leg, and I called on God by name as my father and the boy's leg was healed.'

The others clapped him on the back and thanked God for the great miracle.

Yehoshuah looked at him shrewdly and said nothing.

Iehuda wondered how many of them had lied as he'd done. Was Mattisyahu's tale, full of incident and detail, just an elaborate deception? Was Philip's simple story of a blind woman given sight a sign that he, like Iehuda, was too embarrassed to say more than a few words?

Iehuda had laid his hands on the boy's leg. He felt the power in him, in his heart and his hands, a warm tingling rush inside his whole body, the spirit of God moving him, so that he understood why God is called a terror as well as a love. He felt the power go into the boy, and praised the name of God, the one who is and was and will be.

And the boy smiled, and shivered, a shudder going through him. And the leg twitched. And the boy said, 'It is so warm!' And he moved his leg and said, 'It moves more easily.' But it was not healed. They could all see it. It was still bent, and the sore place in the skin was still raw and he could not put his weight on it.

The boy's mother looked at Iehuda.

'You may be a man of God,' she said, 'but there is no power in you.'

The boy's father shushed her, and the boy protested that the pain was a little easier, that it would surely mend. But the mother, who knew her son's body better than her own, knew that nothing had changed.

They offered him a bed for the night still, a place by the fire and a meal for his trouble. And in the morning, when he woke by the ashes of the fire in the lean-to, he saw the boy limping across the yard, dragging his leg. When the boy saw Iehuda, he tried to straighten himself, to smile.

'It is easier already!' he cried, and Iehuda gave a sickened smile in return.

But the mother looked at them both from the door of the house with dark and angry eyes. And Iehuda left, not stopping to break his fast.

He thought, on the slow, dragging walk back, of what Yehoshuah would have done. Had he been there he would have said, 'The cure is not in me but in God,' or he would have said, 'God has not chosen to bless you in this way, I am sorry for it,' and he would have told them a tale that proved that those who suffered were the most beloved, that God had them close in his heart. Yehoshuah would have told him that the power was not for him to command.

And if Yehoshuah had said those things to him, he still would have known that his faith had been weak, and that was why the boy was not healed. He had seen Yehoshuah do it. The other disciples said they had done it. And the worm chewed at his heart, because he knew that God had not favoured him.

He could not sit with the others that night as they shared bread and oil and talked of the great miracles that God surely had in store for them in the future. He wandered down to the camp of the foreigners, where the non-Jewish people interested in the teachings of

Yehoshuah slept. It was an accident that he happened to speak to Calidorus. It could as well have been another as him. He did not even know what he was looking for. Maybe only someone to whom he would not have to lie.

Calidorus and some of his friends were playing a dice game by a low-burning fire. When they saw Iehuda approaching, they stood up and offered him the place of honour, but he refused it, preferring to sit and watch them play for a time. 'Venus!' called one, when he had thrown a specially lucky set of numbers, and the others cursed him good-humouredly and poured more wine from a leather flask.

As the evening wore on, more of the friends took their bedrolls and made camp, until only Calidorus and Iehuda were left by the last embers of the fire. And Calidorus spoke of his travels and the interesting people he had encountered. He was a scholar of the writings of the Greeks, spoke highly of the Roman Republic – this dream of government by the people had died when Julius Caesar took imperial power, and even to speak of it was to show a measure of trust. So Iehuda, in the end, told him his troubles.

'Ah,' said Calidorus, 'I have seen this trick performed. By a man in Shfat, who seemed to plunge his hand into the centre of a boy's chest and pull out a piece of black sticky stuff which a demon had placed inside him. I paid him all the gold in my purse to show me how he did it and the coat on my back to sell me the mechanism.'

He said it matter-of-factly, so that Iehuda showed no surprise on his face. They were men of the world, discussing something everyone knew.

'Would you like to see how it was done?' said Calidorus.

Iehuda nodded slowly.

Calidorus sent a slave to fetch something from a leather bag in the back of his tent and had Iehuda turn away while he prepared. When Iehuda turned back, he showed him the trick. Calidorus concealed a sheep's bladder in the sleeve of his robe, near the wrist. When he pressed it, a red liquid spurted across his arm and up to his hand.

'It is dyed water,' said Calidorus. 'It is better if you use fresh sheep's blood, though. And a piece of burnt wood resin – it goes sticky and black like this – concealed in the palm.'

He showed Iehuda the piece of tacky material. It looked like the sort of evil a demon might place in a man.

Calidorus shrugged. 'If you're willing to pay enough money, you will discover how a thing was done. I expect your friends did some trick like this, if they did anything at all.'

Iehuda felt afraid, suddenly, in the centre of his chest. How many times can a man lose his faith before he ceases to believe in faith itself?

'I saw a holy man once bring a swarm of frogs out of a girl who suffered from the palsy,' he said.

Calidorus smiled.

'Did he lean very close into her?'

Iehuda thought on it. He had been only a child when that grey-bearded preacher came to Qeriot, but now he remembered it, yes, the man had embraced the girl, caught her up from her bed, and then when he let her fall the frogs had begun to swarm, seeming to come from every part of her.

'He had a bag of frogs concealed in his robe,' said Calidorus. 'When he pulled her close he emptied that bag into her clothes, so the frogs seemed to come from her when he released her.' Calidorus looked at Iehuda's face and made a wry half-smile. 'I was young once too,' he said, 'don't be ashamed. Children believe the stories.' He frowned. 'Surely you must have thought this yourself already?'

Iehuda thought: I am entirely alone. Anyone like Calidorus who sought this knowledge out already disbelieved. Why else would one look to learn the truth, except to be proved right in unbelief?

'It hurts me,' he said.

Calidorus's mouth twisted a little. He clapped a hand on Iehuda's shoulder, but the gesture was immediately awkward and he withdrew it.

'Ah well,' Calidorus said, 'he makes a fine spectacle, your friend.'

He laughed. 'I am certainly enjoying his story. And some of the things he says are fascinating.'

Iehuda felt a pain rising in the centre of his chest. His heart was heavy and he thought: could I be like this man? Could I take it all as an entertainment, a pantomime? There were five hundred people in Yehoshuah's encampment, some of them talking as if he was the promised Messiah, some of them debating his teachings and some, like Calidorus, simply enjoying the performance. Calidorus's way seemed easiest – the man's presence was like a cool spring of fresh water in the fires of Iehuda's mind. He knew he could not be like Calidorus, but he also knew he could not now unknow the things he knew or unsee the things he had seen.

He shifted his weight from one foot to the other.

'What am I now?' he said.

And Calidorus seemed uncomfortable.

'Come and stay with me,' he said, 'when you grow tired of following your prophet through this wilderness, come and be my guest in Caesarea. Ask anyone there for my house and they will tell you. When all this is done, come to me.'

He came back to the inner circle changed. He found that he listened differently. He watched differently. He noticed, again and again now, Rome. And how Yehoshuah's words, and the words of his friends, were a provocation to Rome.

There was an angry tone to him now. Had it always been there? Had Iehuda only just begun to notice it?

On the road to Shomron, men and women ran out of their homes and across the fields to see Yehoshuah. In one place – a rich and fertile land, where the soil was tilled in great soft waves and the barley was growing high and strong – a man was kneeling by the side of the road, waiting for them. He was a prosperous farmer, one could tell immediately by the quality of his boots and the thick wool coat around his shoulders. But he was kneeling at the roadside, tears falling from his cheeks, mumbling.

Yehoshuah bent down to talk to the man. And Iehuda saw that old Yehoshuah, the one whose very presence soothed the heart.

Yehoshuah shook his head softly.

'Do not weep my friend,' he said. 'God has told me that He has chosen you to walk with us. Come now.'

This was a great deal to ask. The farm behind them was good. On the hills, a flock of brindled sheep grazed, guarded by a shepherd boy. The boy was probably the man's son, the sheep probably his flock.

'My father has died,' said the man, the tears still falling silently. 'He died this morning, just as you approached. Teacher, give me a blessing.'

Yehoshuah placed his hands on the man's shoulders.

'You are already blessed,' he said. 'Our Father has blessed you with this call. Come and walk with me. We are travelling to Jerusalem. Come now and do not look back.'

The man stared Yehoshuah full in the face. A man who has lost his father is like a man felled by a mighty blow. The death of a mother is the loss of love, but the death of a father is the loss of certainty. The tallest tree that will ever stand in the forest is fallen.

'I must bury my father,' he said. He spoke, Iehuda thought, without hearing his own words. It was not an answer, it was a realization. He said it again. 'I cannot walk with you now, for I must bury my father. Let me go and bury my father first.'

Iehuda heard one of the other men – he thought it was Jeremiah – whisper to his fellow, 'Is this how he speaks to the son of David?'

If he could, Iehuda would have hit that man in the face, but he realized suddenly that if he did that, it would be dangerous. How had he not known that they had come to this pass, where dissent was dangerous? If he hit the man, the others would say that he did not believe that Yehoshuah was the son of David – that is, the rightful heir to the throne in Jerusalem. And then . . . he did not know what might happen.

There had been a fight, a week earlier, between some of those different factions. A man had been stabbed with a knife and they had left him in Rafa'at for his wound to mend. Iehuda had not thought of it after that day. But he found himself thinking of it now. What would happen if he argued with this crowd of angry men? He felt afraid. And ashamed of his own fear.

Yehoshuah knelt down and clasped the farmer's hands.

'Are you dead?' he whispered softly.

The man, pulling one rough paw from Yehoshuah's grasp to wipe away the tears from his eyes, looked bemused.

'I say again,' said Yehoshuah, 'are you dead? For you say you must bury your father,' and then he turned to the crowd behind him, all straining to catch his words, 'but I say,' and he raised his voice to a shout, 'let the dead bury their dead. You must come with us to announce that the kingdom of God is here!'

The men standing behind Iehuda cheered, for they understood this to mean 'nothing is important but our own work', and the people far back in the throng who could not see what was happening cheered. The tender-hearted women did not cheer, for their hearts went out to the farmer, from whose eyes tears were falling like ripe fruit. And Iehuda did not cheer.

Yehoshuah stood up and walked on. Iehuda looked back at the man in the mud and dust at the side of the road, who would have to bury his father that afternoon.

There grew to be an inner circle within the inner circle. Iehuda was not part of that group. It was Shimon, and Jeremiah, and Jona. They had not been the first to join the wandering rabble, but they were zealous. Jona saw signs and wonders in every speck of dust. Jeremiah muttered darkly about the days that are surely to come when the Lord will destroy all those who do not hearken to his holy name. Shimon was a steady man: he was not enraged by doubters but filled with sorrow and pity for them.

There was a day when Yehoshuah took those three alone up into the hills to pray. They were gone for a night and a day with no food or water. Something happened there, but Iehuda could never root out exactly what it was.

Shimon, the most solid of the three, said that he had fallen into a deep sleep and dreamed that Yehoshuah was standing with Moses and Elijah, and this dream had the marks of truth to it and he was convinced by it in his own breast. Jona said he had seen the gates of heaven open and the very voice of the Lord had spoken to him by name, but Jona had been known to hear the voice of the Lord in the honking of geese. Jeremiah would say nothing of what he'd seen, only that it had been vouchsafed to him that Rome would burn and the kingdom of heaven would come to earth, which was no more than he had always said.

The longer Iehuda asked, the less this tale became. And yet he heard in the camp that the three men had been taken up in a fiery chariot to the heavens, where the good Lord had spoken to them and told them Yehoshuah was His promised one. He found one man selling white pebbles which he said had been taken from the holy place where they ascended to heaven. Women were sewing them into the hem of their clothes to keep off the evil eye.

Iehuda wanted to discuss the matter with Calidorus, who continued to travel with them, waited on by his body-slave as it pleased him to walk like a pilgrim. But he felt somehow repulsed by the idea. He contented himself with imagining what Calidorus would say. Something Greek, he imagined, something from philosophy. He often quoted from the philosopher whose very name – Epikouros – was a byword for heresy among the rabbis.

He might say, 'The gods, if there are gods, do not concern themselves with us. How can they, when we see the crippled and lame all around us? If it pleases your friends to think that they saw the gods, so be it. It pleases me to go to a play and imagine I have seen Helen of Troy or Agamemnon in his war cry.'

This answer, from an imaginary Calidorus, pleased him. He welcomed the worm into his breast.

An insanity came upon them. They argued over who could sit closest to Yehoshuah, like children fighting over a toy. As if he were already dead and they were arguing over his clothes or the scraps of flesh adhering to his body. Iehuda felt it too. He had always felt it, the desire to be close to the man. The sense that it was impossible to be too close, that he would allow himself to be utterly consumed by Yehoshuah and consider it an honour. This had always been why he struggled so hard to remain separate, to find a place deep in his breast which did not belong to Yehoshuah.

But those weeks, the thing began to tip over into madness. There were more of them every day and at the edges of the group there were more soldiers watching. They all knew that with a rabble this large there would be spies from the Prefect, there would be those who would report his words and deeds and the size of the crowd for a coin or two. But Yehoshuah did not tell them to disperse. It was unwise. They looked now like the kind of rebellious multitude which the Romans dealt with so swiftly and so successfully. They looked like bodies waiting to be nailed up along the road to Jerusalem.

None of the others would say this to Yehoshuah, so it fell to Iehuda again and again to say, when they ate bread together in the evening, 'We should be circumspect. We should disband now and re-form in a few weeks, like we did before.'

Yehoshuah did not reply, except with a smile. The others hated him for saying it. He saw that they were enjoying the sense of danger, for it was also a feeling of power. He could not tell truth from lies any more. He heard someone say that the priests at the Temple were plotting against them and this sounded like absolute insanity. He heard someone else say that the King had paid for information on Yehoshuah and this also seemed madness. But there was such certainty in the group and he was embedded in it so completely that he could not see them from the outside any longer. Perhaps they really were the most important thing in Judea.

It was coming towards a hot, late Passover. The days and months had fallen out so that it was already full spring by the week before the festival. The air was ripe with the green scent of acacia trees and with the hum of hovering insects.

They came to the house of a friend – a merchant by the name of Shimon, whom people had called Shimon the leper because he was so unpopular. Shimon had been impressed with Yehoshuah's teachings on the value of riches. The man had given much of his wealth to the poor and every day now the beggars of Beit Ani came to the back door of his home to receive bread. They were to stay there one night, with Yehoshuah in the bed of honour, and then walk on closer to Jerusalem.

The house was heavy with the smell of a great crowd of the sick and the dirty and the poor. The smells all mingled together: body odour and dirty clothes and women's menstrual blood and a man with foetid sores on his leg and the animals and the tanned animal hides and the half-soured milk in the jars on the floor and the onions on the breath of the camel drivers.

People came for cures, but Yehoshuah performed none that day. His mood was merry and indulgent and he let visitors come with little gifts – a sheepskin, a basket of dried fruits, a silver charm – or to tell him, twisting their bodies, that his face was the face of a holy man, a true prophet of God. Every time they did this, Iehuda felt more uncomfortable.

Towards the end of the afternoon, a wealthy woman wound her way through the crowd. She was dressed in a fine silk robe, her hair elaborately turned in several plaits around her head, and she was mad. Either mad or drunk, as was clear from her unsteady movements, from the way her eyes darted around the room.

She was carrying a small alabaster jar of perfumed oil – the stone was thin, expertly worked, the jar much longer than it was wide, a cool narrow vial. The container alone would be worth a month's wages. She stopped in front of Yehoshuah's chair of honour, bowed low, ceremoniously but with a curious simpering smile on her face. She cracked the stem of the jar so that they could smell what she had brought. It was spikenard, a dense scent of mint and spices and a meaty richness. The smell travelled up and around the room, cutting through the sweat and garlic and sour milk with its scouring sharpness. This was a precious gift – people brought them valuable possessions now, she was not the first, but spikenard was one of the rarest components of Temple incense, brought from Kush in India.

The woman smiled lopsidedly. Her eyes rolled back in her head. Iehuda wondered where she'd got the perfume from, what she'd done to obtain this vial worth more than a year's work for a labouring man. She held the jar in her left hand, and reached out her right to touch a lock of Yehoshuah's hair. Yehoshuah smiled at the woman. She was breathing very quickly, her breasts rising and falling. A sheen of sweat coated her skin. Iehuda wondered if she was about to throw herself bodily on to Yehoshuah – this had happened before.

Instead, she spoke in a slow, slurred voice:

'May I anoint you?'

Iehuda waited for Yehoshuah's easy smile, his way of turning a refusal into an honour. He would say no, but he would show her by his kindness that her offer had been accepted in the spirit if not on earth.

This was not what happened.

Yehoshuah's glance met the woman's eerie, glazed eyes.

He bowed his head before her for the anointing.

She tipped the vial. The oil began to flow out over Yehoshuah's hair. It was enough, more than enough, plenty. Someone rushed to stop her – every drop that fell was a meal for twenty people, every thick glug was a pregnant goat, a pair of good shoes, a field golden with high waving wheat. She laughed and cracked the vial between her hands. The whole fortune of it poured out upon Yehoshuah, coating his head, his shoulders, filling the room with the thick, nauseating, choking scent.

There was no other smell now. The aromas of life – of bodies and animals and dirt and fermentation – all those smells were gone, as if the sounds of the world had been blotted out by the clanging of a terrible gong. This one, too-clean odour, the smell of new-cut pine wood, was all that remained. Beautiful, yes, in a way. But revolting, because it was too strong and because it had destroyed everything else.

The woman was giggling still, crushing the alabaster to smaller and smaller pieces in her oil-covered and now blood-streaked hands. One of the other women pulled out a rag to wipe those poor hands. It was not purely a charitable gesture. Even a rag soaked with spikenard would be worth something. The woman did not resist, even when they led her out to the well.

The house emptied quickly. No one could bear to be near the smell of too much goodness gone to waste. The floor was stained with the oil.

'The worms will enjoy their heaven-scented earth,' said Shimon.

There were only three or four of them left around Yehoshuah. Those who never left.

Something was building in Iehuda now. Like vomit, it would not be denied.

Iehuda said, 'Why did you let her do it? We could have sold that perfume and given the money to the poor people all around us. It's worth a year's wages to any of these men.'

He kept his voice low and spoke quickly. There was nothing to be done now about the spikenard. The oil was dripping still from Yehoshuah's face and hair on to the floor, every drip a meal, a blanket, a handful of good seed. In the streets they would smell the intense foolishness which had been done in this house. Half the village would know it by walking past the door. The earth floor might smell of it for a year or more.

Yehoshuah looked at him, that bright burning look.

'Iehuda,' he said, shaking his sorrowful, dripping head, 'Iehuda, why do you insist on seeing only with your eyes?'

I don't, he wanted to say. I saw you with my heart, and you have led me here, to a place I do not understand.

Iehuda had heard it said: if the rabbis tell you that day is night and night is day, believe them. He thought perhaps he had once been capable of this. He did not know whether he was luckier then, when he could, or now, when he found he could not.

Iehuda tried to swallow it, like a Nile crocodile eating a new lamb. But he could not make it go down. Certain things cannot be right, no matter how you squint at them.

'We could have sold it,' he said again, 'to feed the poor.'

'Do you think I will be with you for much longer?' said Yehoshuah. 'When God himself lays waste to the whole world, do you think anyone will care that some oil was poured on the earth here?'

And Iehuda shook his head.

And Yehoshuah said, 'If you cannot see, I cannot make you understand.'

He trailed behind the group as they walked on from Bethany, pretending to be tired, but he was muttering to himself and the words in his mouth made his pulse quicken.

He said, out loud, to the broken yellow hillside and the scrubby bushes: 'Everything can be justified this way.'

He said it again. In different words:

'If the world is to come to an end, how can we know that one thing is right, another wrong?'

He thought of a dozen problems to ask his master. How if the woman had thrown chests of spices into the ocean for Yehoshuah's sake? How if she had cut herself with lancets, as the Moabites do? How if she had sacrificed her own child? How much waste of wealth, and self, and life, would have slaked him, made him cry, 'Enough, too much!'?

In his mind, he asked him, 'How much do you think is due to you? Have you not yet honour enough?'

He could not find it in himself to speak aloud.

They camped that night and he was quiet.

Yehoshuah said, 'We have come away from Bethany, but the stink of that perfume is still on your head, Iehuda.'

And he thought: how dare you know me so well as this? How dare you use myself against me?

But he said nothing.

In those days, he saw Calidorus again. The man was getting ready to leave the camp, his slaves strapping boxes to the wagon and preparing a soft place for him to sit on the long journey.

'Well,' said Calidorus, 'how goes the quest to overturn heaven and earth?'

Iehuda said, 'There are men casting bones by the side of the road who say Yehoshuah will be king before New Year.'

Calidorus half smiled.

'Would he make a good king, do you think? Would he set appropriate taxes and negotiate successful trade agreements with Rome and array his forces to the north to keep off invaders?'

Iehuda shook his head.

'The man I first followed would never have wanted to be king.'

'You know, I believe that is what Caesar said when he first took power. It seems to be a pattern with them. In this time of special emergency, they say, I must take more power than usual, but this shall be given back in time to the people. Somehow it is always a time of special emergency. It is quite surprising how seductive a crown can be.'

Iehuda looked at him, frowning. Calidorus was a wealthy Roman citizen, in that sense more powerful than almost anyone Iehuda had ever met.

'Why are you here, Calidorus? Here in Judea, I mean. Why here?'

Calidorus shrugged. 'I like the climate. The autumn rains in Rome would make you howl. Much of my trade is here. Interesting people pass through. And Rome is not . . .' He paused, thinned his lips. 'I like to be able to speak my mind, Iehuda. That used to be the foundation stone of Rome, they tell me, but now anyone who opposes Caesar is swiftly found by spies to have been "plotting treason" and apparently,' he said, laughing, 'we leave poets in exile for writing saucy verse. I can speak more freely here than I could in Rome. Here I am no threat to anyone.'

Iehuda blinked.

'Even a Roman citizen? Even you have to calculate like this?'

'Even I, Iehuda, am subject to Tiberius Caesar, a man with all the power in the world and not much idea of what to spend it on.'

'If you could plot against him,' said Iehuda, suddenly bold, 'would you do it?'

Calidorus looked at him very keenly.

'No man should be told he's a god while he still lives,' he said at last. 'It doesn't promote good thinking.'

He knows now he had lost his mind. He thought himself above the others because he did not gather round, begging for a blessing, longing to sit at the right hand of the master. But he noted who sat where. His eyes did not cease from searching out who had received more favouring glances, who seemed momentarily to be the one most praised.

He tried again, in the evening, when the others were asleep. He had always slept lightly and not for long. Yehoshuah did not seem to sleep at all these days. He found him stirring the glowing embers of the fire, blowing on them to bring them back to life, lighting twig from twig and branch from branch.

He said, 'Explain it to me.'

Yehoshuah shrugged. 'The vessel was already broken. What could I have done? Only shamed her.'

'You could have stopped her.'

'Perhaps.'

'You could have spoken out against doing as she did. So that no one else will do it. Others will come with the same idea now.'

'And if they do, what is the harm?'

Iehuda felt that snake rising up in his throat, making him gag and cough. He thought: it is a demon. There is a demon in me and my friend cannot see it or cast it out.

'The harm,' he said. And stopped. And thought.

'We are not here for your glory,' he said at last.

And Yehoshuah smiled.

And Iehuda said, 'We are not here to glorify YOU. Not your name but God's name. Not your words but God's words. Not you, not any one of us. Something bigger than us. The poor, the crippled, the broken. To help them, not to make you into a little god. An idol.'

It was the first time he had let himself think it. He had not known he thought it until he said the words. He was panting, his pulse beating very fast and loud in his ears, his chest aching.

'Are you jealous?' said Yehoshuah.

They had had this conversation before. And Iehuda had admitted his jealousy freely and felt cleansed of it. He wanted to say yes and to fall into his friend's arms, and to be free again of everything.

He shook his head slowly.

'This is not because I want what you have,' he said, 'but because you are using your possessions wrongly.'

And Yehoshuah shrugged and said, 'What I own it is my right to use, as a master orders his servants to perform one task and leave another.'

'Like the love of those who follow you? Are we your possessions too?'

Yehoshuah looked at him, his eyes very brown and clear and fine.

'Only for as long as you wish it, my dear friend.'

Was there a command in this? A wish? A suggestion? Or just a piece of understanding, as two old friends have of one another? The way out is always simple. All it takes is courage.

Losing one's faith is so very like gaining it. There is the same joy, the same terror, the same annihilation of self in the ecstasy of understanding. There is the same fear that it will not hold, the same wild hope that, this time, it will. One has to lose one's faith many times before one begins to lose faith in faith itself.

Iehuda left the camp before dawn. He felt elated. The sky expanded overhead. The moon big and low nearing the horizon, the stars rejoicing in their dark sea. They had turned the stones of the hills of Jerusalem to silver, to opal, to bone. The air was clear and cool as well water and the whole of the house of Israel was sleeping the sweet pre-dawn sleep with soft breaths and gently curled hands. He felt the world move under his shoes as he picked his way across the rocky hillside down towards the city, a gentle tug because the very land was with him, urging him on. It was a blessed night. God, he knew, was watching and smiling upon him.

It was God who had kept the other followers soundly asleep when he left, and God who made the night unclouded and the moon bright so that he could find his way. God had touched his head with a cool calm hand and said softly in his ear, so that no one else could hear, 'It is time, my son, time for this to be at an end.'

He arrived at the Temple when the faintest hint of dawn was beginning to touch the sky. Like God had dipped his thumb in bright yellow pollen and run it around the edge of the vellum world. This would be a day like no other.

Men were sleeping in the courtyard, their heads on their full packs, or the sacrifice sellers under their tables, but the priests were already about their business. They were cleaning out the old ash from the last day's sacrificial fires, and washing the steps and the flagstones. Every morning and every evening, a lamb. They would make the first sacrifice shortly. As they always did. How had he imagined that anything they did would overturn any one of these unchangeable things?

He felt suddenly like a child who had been playing a game all this time. What had they thought they would do? Dismantle the great Temple stone by stone? Defeat the Roman army? Overturn the traditions handed down from Moses? Had they thought that they could take the place of God?

Like a child coming in from a game, like a penitent returning to grace, like a servant yielding to his master, Iehuda spoke softly to one of the priests. He was a man of maybe sixty years, with a good full grey beard like Iehuda's father.

Iehuda said, 'I have come because I know you are looking for Yehoshuah of Natzaret.'

The priest nodded gravely.

'I know where he is,' said Iehuda. 'I can take you to him.'

The priest nodded again, three times, and said, 'Come with me.'

And as they walked towards the house of Caiaphas, the High Priest, Iehuda said to God,

'I have returned to you. I am sorry for my absence.'

And God, who is a loving Father said, 'You are welcome in my house, my beloved son.'

Caiaphas was a bustling man, unexpectedly cheerful. Avuncular. He bobbed his little head and said, 'I think we have enough influence with the Prefect that if your friend admits his crimes and declares that he has no claims to the throne, no more harm will come to him than a few lashes. You've all inconvenienced us a little, you know.'

And Iehuda thought: is this what we were? While we imagined that we could change the world, these men of high office thought of us only as irritating children, throwing stones and firing blunted arrows? And he thought: really? Men had been put to death for far less than this.

Caiaphas busied himself with sending messengers to the soldiers and to the Prefect. There was little enough for Iehuda to do. He sat quietly on a stone bench in Caiaphas's study and felt as if a heavy weight had been lifted from him. It was relief, at last, knowing that things would be put right now. Yehoshuah's claim to the throne was at an end. They could go back to spreading his message, instead of putting everything in the storehouse of one man.

The sun was high in the sky when Caiaphas said to him, 'It is time for you to go back now, do you not think?'

Iehuda blinked. Yes. He had not thought as far as this, not further than doing God's holy work. But yes. Yehoshuah would miss him, would ask after him. No special alarm would be raised for him, but he might be in danger if his friends knew what he had done. He thought of the mad woman with the rolling eyes cracking the alabaster jar and bleeding and laughing. Followers like that would send a knife after him once the thing was done. Safer to go back now and pretend surprise with the others when the guards came to take him.

'We will come tomorrow morning,' said Caiaphas.

This was longer than the matter needed to take.

'What if we move on from our camp before morning? Yehoshuah sometimes . . .' The truth was that he sometimes told them that God had commanded him to move them on. 'He sometimes moves us on unexpectedly.'

'We will be watching you,' said Caiaphas mildly. 'Just stay close by him now. Do not leave his side. And we will come and find you.'

He saw them on his way back across the hillside to the encampment. They did not even seem to be walking in the same direction as him. Sometimes they came directly towards him, sometimes they were far in the distance, watching him walk away. They were cunning and they were swift, and they watched where he went and what he did.

The encampment had not moved. Taddai greeted him with a kiss on both cheeks and a punch to the shoulder.

'Mattisyahu said you'd gone whoring,' he said, and some of the others round about laughed because they could not believe it of Iehuda.

'I took myself off to pray,' Iehuda said at last, and they all nodded.

Yehoshuah was speaking with some of the women under an open-walled canopied tent, and did not see Iehuda return and did not look at him with suspicious eyes or ask where he had been. And on the top of the ridge, behind Taddai's head, he saw the faint smudges of the men waiting for him, and for Yehoshuah.

They ate together that night, as they often did. This was the first night of Passover, though – they went to the Temple to purchase a lamb, sacrificed it, brought it back for the meal – it felt significant. So many people were in Jerusalem for the festival. The atmosphere was febrile, still, every man wanting to be the one who prompted Yehoshuah to say words which they would all remember as long as there was breath in their bodies. They were excited, like children.

Shimon wondered aloud whether the High Priest in his home was wishing he was here in this room among those who truly cleaved to God. Yehoshuah frowned at him and said nothing. Netan'el ate his share of the Paschal lamb and spoke of how the rich priests like Caiaphas and Annas, close bosom friends of Rome, could not understand the meaning of the sacrifice – that some men would only eat the meat of a lamb on this night, that many beggars would fill their bellies to the point of sickness. He hoped thereby to encourage Yehoshuah to speak again about how the poor are close to God, but Yehoshuah merely smiled. One of the hangers-on shouted that when the Messiah came, Rome itself would burn like the charred flesh of the lamb and some others laughed and cheered.

They walked in the fields after the meal, the ones close to Yehoshuah. They talked of the great miracles God would surely make, and of how many in Jerusalem already longed to follow them. They were anticipating the end of days which God would bring soon, so soon the day of judgement. And in the corner of his eye Iehuda saw his tails always, a few men melting into the shadows. Enough to keep watch and to send word.

'They will come at dawn,' he said to himself. 'When the world is quiet but they have light to see what they are doing.'

At some point between dusk and dawn he dreamed. Or thinks he dreamed.

In his dream, Yehoshuah came to learn with him, as they had

learned together two years before, at the very start. They studied in the great hall of scrolls that is heaven, the kingdom of God. They read the words of the Torah from the stone tablets which Moses himself had carved and Iehuda saw that the letters were fire.

And in his dream he said to Yehoshuah, 'Why me? Why did God send you to me, knowing that I could not accept you?'

And Yehoshuah kissed him on his forehead and on his cheeks and said, 'God knew His business. Now we will see what that business was.'

And in the dream Iehuda knew that Yehoshuah had forgiven him. But when he woke, with the dew settling on him in a quiet orchard with his friends, he knew that the matter had not concluded yet and the serpent in him was a great sickness and he wished he could vomit it out. But the clatter of arms and shields was at the crest of the hill and it was too late.

They had not sent enough soldiers for a quiet surrender. There were thirty or forty of them, no more. Yehoshuah's camp was five hundred men – although they were mostly still asleep and a little distant. The soldiers had their swords but the men had wooden staffs as cudgels, slings and stones, cooking and hunting knives.

'You shall not take him!' shouted out Shimon, and stood between Yehoshuah and the guards.

Yehoshuah's closest men were awake and with him in the orchard. There were probably as many of them as of the soldiers. Several of the other men hefted their staffs meaningfully, shifting their stances to legs apart, knees slightly bent. The soldiers drew their swords.

'Give him to us,' said the leading soldier in heavily accented Aramaic. 'He is accused of treason. He must be taken for trial.'

He nodded to two of his deputies, who came forward. One of them took Yehoshuah by the arm. And then it began.

One of Yehoshuah's friends raised his cudgel and struck the soldier a glancing blow on the side of the face. Iehuda, hanging back, remembered Yehoshuah saying, 'If a man strikes you on one cheek, give him the other to hit,' and thought: why, then, are they fighting? But they did fight.

The soldier fell to the ground. Shimon thrust Yehoshuah far behind him as the leader of the soldiers barked three words at his men and they advanced in formation, holding small shields before them, a forest of blades. Two of the soldiers lashed out with their weapons and two of Yehoshuah's men fell – one with a gaping wound to his neck pumping rich red blood, the other clutching his side.

Yehoshuah's men looked less certain now, but their anger was up and some ran forward, flailing and yelling. In a lucky strike Jeremiah pulled one of the shields forward and leapt over it, hacking at the face beneath the helmet with his knife, and suddenly blood was spurting from the soldier's face, and Jeremiah was shrieking because he had cut off the man's ear. It flopped limply in his hand. A piece of gristle cut from an undercooked joint. He brandished it, grinning. Another soldier hit him hard in the stomach with a shield and he fell to the ground.

They were outmatched, Yehoshuah's men. They were dealing the odd blow to the soldiers, but more of them, five, six, had been felled already. There were awkward wrestling matches, soldiers attempting, as far as Iehuda could tell, not to kill if they could avoid it. Several men were knocked out by a heavy shield blow. One of them, a young man Iehuda did not know, was attempting to fight although he was wearing only a wrapped linen sheet. Two soldiers grabbed the garment, trying to throw him to the ground, but he wriggled out of it altogether and ran away naked.

Angry, the soldiers returned to using their swords, and more men would have been cut down if Iehuda had not raised his voice above the din and shouted, 'No! More soldiers will come! They have told me! All of us will die if we do not give Yehoshuah to them.'

It was then that they realized.

'You,' said Mattisyahu, 'it was you who brought the soldiers.'

The shock of it made them stare.

Ah, thought Iehuda, so there is no going back for me now. No returning to the person I was. Now they know.

He had to walk with the soldiers as they took Yehoshuah away. What else was he going to do? He could not stay with the other disciples. They would have torn him to pieces.

They walked as far as the Temple. There was a form to these things. First a hearing in the civil court of Israel, then justice at the hands of Rome.

Yehoshuah was quiet as they walked. They did not have to bind him or carry him or prod him with the points of their swords.

At the gate of the Temple, he clasped Iehuda's shoulder and said, very softly,

'Now we will see.'

And as much as Iehuda has thought of that since, as much as he understands the world of dreams that spoke in those words, he cannot experience it as anything but courage.

They led his friend away through the dark doors. He tried to follow but Caiaphas, standing at the doorpost, shook his head. Thus far and no further. His job was done.

As he left the Temple, the head of the Levite administrators, kinder than the rest, pressed a purse into his hand. He shook his head, but the Levite frowned and said, 'You cannot go back to your friends now. Use this to go home. Buy a piece of land and begin again. Forget everything that happened here. You have done a good service to keep the peace, remember only that.'

He had thought about it, what he would do if he were free. And suddenly he was more free than he had ever been or ever thought to be. What is freedom, in the end, but that no one cares any longer to try to restrain us?

In the marketplace, he bought a sharp blade of the kind the Romans use to shave themselves, a jar of good sheep's fat and a pail. And he walked out of the city to the north, until he came to a place he knew, under the shade of three fig trees, with a fast-flowing brook of icy water.

At first, he pulled great tufts of the hair of his beard out and cut them with the blade – remembering Elkannah wriggling on his lap and feeling that sorrow which would never now leave him. When the bulk of it was gone he filled the pail and let the water go still, so he could look at his own face in the reflecting surface. He looked different already. Not a pious man, not a good Jew. A madman, with sprouting clumps of hair on his face. No longer a person who believed in anything.

He rubbed the sheep's fat on to his face. It smelled half delicious, like a good meal, but with a rancid edge. He massaged the fat into the coarse beard hairs with the heel of his hand, feeling the bristles and tufts scratch his skin. And then he began to scrape the blade slowly, carefully, down his cheek.

He had never done this to himself before, but he had watched with interest as some of the Greek and Roman hangers-on at Yehoshuah's camp had made their toilet in the morning, so he had a rough idea of how the thing was accomplished. When he had scraped half a cheek of hair off and rubbed the bristle-sheep fat mixture on the dry grass, he looked at the smooth patch in the mirror of still water. It was like the skin of a woman's face. Soft and pink, though a little raw in places from the blade. Suddenly, he desperately wanted a woman.

He shaved the rest of his face more quickly. He had the knack of the blade now, keeping close to the skin but not piercing it. He cut himself once or twice, but they were only small nicks. His face felt cold and the skin was stinging. And when he was done he stared at himself again in the water and saw a different man. He had not seen his own face thus since he was fifteen years old and his beard came in. But the face that looked back was not that of a boy. It was a Roman man. An idol-worshipper. The man he had been was as dead as if he had cut his own throat with that razor. Good.

This new face did the work for him when he returned to the market. He had passed through the invisible veil separating Jew and Roman. The Jewish men scurried away from his gaze, the Romans met his eye approvingly. The whores by the market wall called to him as they had never addressed a word to him all those years when he was pious.

He paid one of the whores – a woman about his own age, with dark eyes and grey hairs streaked through the black – he gave her a small coin and had her in a small tented enclosure at the edge of the wall. She did not undress, just bent over the straw bales and flipped up the back of her skirts to show herself to him. The power of it was overwhelmingly arousing, the absolute lack of consequence, her lack of interest in him. As he fucked her, he remembered his wife and knew that what he had grieved for all along, when he thought he grieved for her and his God, what he had grieved for all along was the young man he had been who would never now return. The whore didn't even see his circumcised cock, that young man's last trace. He could be a Roman now, if he wanted.

He waited by the gates for news of Yehoshuah, and when he heard what had happened he went to the crosses. He wore a wrapped scarf like the tent-dwellers, shielding his face, and one of their cloaks bought for two small coins, more than its value. But he need not have bothered. Few of Yehoshuah's friends were there, and those who were could not see him. Their eyes glided over his face as if he were just another Roman, or Jew-turned-Roman.

Even Yehoshuah gave no sign of knowing him. He was near death – the day was hot and several of the men around him had already died. Iehuda wondered whether, if he had come hours before, Yehoshuah would have berated him, or screamed at him. But by this point his eyes were glazed and the flies were settling at the corners of his mouth. He would not have recognized his own mother if she had come then.

Iehuda waited there until he saw the light go out of his eyes. Even till then, though it took until the sun was low in the sky. He squatted on his haunches and watched it out. And even till that moment he had thought that perhaps God would make some miracle. But he saw his friend die. And at the moment that the limbs went limp and the head slumped forward and the chest became still, he thought: well, then, now we know. The Messiah becomes king, he does not die as a traitor. So now we know.

He should have known when the nails went in. Or when he had arrived at the Temple. Or when the snake first began to twist inside him, he should have known that nothing was keeping his friend alive but the faith of those around him. And he went and slept in an apple orchard near the walls of Jerusalem.

He stayed in Jerusalem a few days after that. He went to his friend's grave, hoping to take the body and bury it on that ridge where they had talked, but one of the boys playing with a spinning top at the side of the road told him that the body had been stolen. There was a trade in such things for magical purposes – the dried heart of a man who had died by violence, the fingers or toes, all these things could be used to cast spells. Or, he thought, to fool the gullible and line the pockets of one of Calidorus's fakers.

He wept a little, thinking of his friend's long bones and brown skin going to such a purpose. With the weeping, he touched the corner of his sadness inside his heart. It was like dipping his hand in the ocean, allowing the waves to run through his fingers, thinking for a moment that he had caught the whole sea in his palm, understanding at last that it was a sadness deep enough to drown in. He closed the box in his heart on that sorrow. It is the only way to continue.

He waited for the last possible day to leave Jerusalem safely, when the final pilgrims were returning home after the festival. And he struck west with a band of travellers – Syrians and Egyptians and Jews and Greeks mixed – heading for Caesarea. It was not hard to find Calidorus's house. The man, to do him credit, welcomed him and sent a slave to wash his feet.

Nothing ever happens except that God wills it. This was the teaching of Yehoshuah which Iehuda remembers every day. It is the truth. Everything that happens has been willed by God.

This is not how he ends the story he tells to Calidorus's guests. For them, he is witty and clever enough to make them feel vaguely flattered by the way he tells the story. He brings up Greek myth, tells them that he would have gone down into Hades to find his friend except – he winks – the Hebrew god frowns on such love between two men. The guests roar with laughter. They are in their cups now.

He jokes that perhaps, like the Emperor Augustus, his friend is already transformed into a god by his death. The men grow a little quiet at this – even to suggest that a criminal is on a par with Augustus is faintly seditious.

'But of course,' says Iehuda, 'just as Augustus, who died in majesty, now reigns in majesty on high, I'm afraid my friend Yehoshuah will still be dragging his cross around with him in the heavens!'

This is the best joke of all. One of the men falls on the floor he laughs so hard and pulls himself up still wheezing. Pomponius chokes on his own laughter and has to take more wine, which sets him off in another fit of giggles.

When the men leave, they agree that it has been an excellent party. Calidorus smiles. Iehuda wonders how long it will be until he has told this story to all of Calidorus's friends and business associates, and what his use will be then.

It is not long after this that the thing is broken forever.

Iehuda sees the woman again in the marketplace. Her red hair flames under the modest veil which covers the length of it. She is looking at some glass lamps – very pretty but impractical. He stands beside her, close enough to sense her body through her clothes and his. She does not notice him until he speaks.

'You could never light it,' he says, his voice low, pointing at the lamp. 'The heat would shatter the glass.'

She looks up. Her eyes are green. She shows no surprise that it is him. A wry smile is on her lips and he remembers his wife, suddenly and with a sharp pain.

'Perhaps,' she says, 'I do not intend to light it. Aren't those the most beautiful things of all? The things that cannot be used without breaking them?'

She is poised. She holds her shoulders just so.

'Like a woman's maidenhead,' he says, without thinking. It is a very forward remark to make to a woman in a public place.

She blushes a little, but her expression does not change.

'Like a man's unwarranted faith,' she says. And pauses. And then. 'I know who you are. My husband is a friend of Calidorus. Any man who has a fortune or wants one in Caesarea is a friend of Calidorus, you know.'

'Ah,' he says. 'And who is your husband?'

'Pomponius,' she says. 'He knows you and your funny little story.'

The thought of the arrogant self-satisfied prick of Pomponius thrusting inside this woman makes him hot and angry and, again, aroused. And the little smile playing on the mouth of the woman when she says 'funny little story', this stirs him too.

'Did you know it was me in the temple that day?' he whispers low in her ear. 'Was it my funny little story that made you so wet?'

He grabs her arm, his fingers digging into her soft flesh so that she gasps, and this he finds even more exciting.

Her eyes flick to the stallholder, who is watching them curiously. They are in a busy marketplace. She has only to call out and a dozen men would be on him, for she is a respectable Roman matron and he, if they cared to examine him, would be found to be only a Jew.

She does not call out. She looks at his hand around her upper arm, at the place where the skin is white because his grip is so strong.

She says, 'Yes.'

He fucks her in a disused stable not far from the market, where the musty smell of horseflesh is in the damp straw, and as she reaches her height she bites him on the shoulder so hard that her mouth comes away red with his blood.

She does not leave immediately this time. They sit together, leaning against the wall of the stable, listening to the sounds of the busy street outside: the vendors calling their wares, hooves striking stone, children playing and shouting, the mad-eyed preacher who stands at the corner of the market telling out the end of days.

She sits across his knees and fumbles with the garments at his waist until she has uncovered his exhausted cock. She cups it in her hand, thumbing the rim of the head where he is circumcised. She smiles.

'I heard that some Jews hang weights from it, to try to grow the foreskin back.'

He shrugs. 'Some men plunge their hands into a nest of bees hoping thereby to gain honey.' His hand finds her, under her skirts. His thumb begins to work. She gasps. 'Most men are not so foolish.'

'And what do you think Calidorus's house is?' she whispers in his ear, leaning close to him.

After a little while he fucks her again: frantically, insatiably.

There is an evening when he sits drinking and talking with Calidorus. Everything now reminds him of something else, distorted and confused. Calidorus is a parody of Yehoshuah. Pomponius's wife is a stir-about of his own wife. This evening with Calidorus is a broken tessellation of another evening, long ago. Once a man has lived long enough, every moment is a reflection of some other moment.

Calidorus says, 'My father was a freed slave. He was over fifty when I was born, and his first forty-five years he was owned.'

Iehuda had heard something of this sort about Calidorus. It is not exactly a mark of disgrace, but neither is it a thing to boast about. Calidorus has drunk a little wine. So has Iehuda. The slaves have withdrawn. They are alone in a private chamber with a good fire and Calidorus's little house-gods lined up on a side table.

'The master freed him because he saved his life. From a fire. He ran into the burning building to save his master. He had scars on his face and his body all his life, because his clothes caught fire as he ran and he did not stop to put them out until his master was safe. A long tight patch of red raw skin from here –' Calidorus motions to his waist – 'to here –' he touches his right temple. 'The hair never grew back on the right-hand side. That is how he won his freedom. That is why he was permitted to take a wife and why I was born. But until the day he died, although he was free, he still called that man "Master".'

Iehuda nods.

'And now I am a wealthy man,' says Calidorus. 'If I were so minded, I could become interested in politics, take a seat in the Senate. An able man can rise and rise in Rome, with no one telling him he has not the right father to be a High Priest, or the right lineage to be considered for king. That is what makes us strong. You are still waiting for your "rightful king", the son of David. We take for a king any man who has the will and strength to govern. There is no law to say that a freed slave may not become emperor; it may happen one day.'

Calidorus clears his throat.

'I have heard from friends in Rome,' he says, 'that the Emperor Tiberius has run mad. He spends all his days on the island of Capri, fucking children.' Calidorus raises an eyebrow, stretching the skin across his bony forehead. 'If I uttered this in Rome, you know, someone would inform on me for a few copper coins and I would be taken and killed.'

'It is because every man needs a father,' says Iehuda slowly. Calidorus narrows his eyes. 'Or a master,' Iehuda continues, 'it is all one. Without a father we look for another master: a teacher to follow or a patron to please or an emperor to fear. A man like your Tiberius has his head open to the sky, with no master to obey. That is why he has run mad.'

'And what of you?' says Calidorus. 'You have killed your master.'

Iehuda shrugs. 'God alone is my leader and my master.'

Calidorus barks out a laugh.

'The gods will not keep you from madness. They have not helped the old goat of Capri.'

And Iehuda could not say what was in his heart: that his God was the true God, and those little statues of squabbling deities were just pieces of stone.

'Do you know what I have heard, Iehuda?' Calidorus leans forward, mock-earnest. 'I had it in a letter from a business associate in Egypt. There one of your old friends is preaching that Yehoshuah yet lives.'

'I saw him die,' says Iehuda.

'Oh,' says Calidorus, 'certainly he died. But, as you say, every man needs a master.'

'The governors and prefects will kill them for saying it.'

Calidorus nods. 'Most men would rather die, you know, than give up a master. In some kingdoms, the ruler's slaves and wives die with him, entombed in his grave. Most men have not the flexible heart you have. They cannot turn from one to the next. They must remain steadfast, even unto death.'

'It is a little noble,' Iehuda says slowly.

'It is idiocy. Do you think I still call my father's master's family my betters? I could buy them a hundred times over. We cannot cleave to the same thing forever. In this life, eventually, one is either a traitor or a fool.'

It is easy to leave, once you are used to leaving. Easy to feel the moment of it approaching, to sense the loosening of the ropes that bound you to the earth. One becomes adept in noticing the absolute apex of love or belief from which it will inevitably decline. There comes a point when one can even begin to love leaving, the only constant we carry with us. The man who wanders forever is not cursed, he is blessed.

He leaves before dawn. He takes food for a long journey, and three rings Calidorus gave him freely when he had told a particularly good tale, which will pay his way or be stolen by bandits, only the road will tell him in time. A few other necessary things, including two good knives. A man with two fine knives, good shoes and strong arms is wealthy, or never far from wealth. He will thrive as he has always, somehow, thrived.

He says to God, 'Are you there?'

And God says, as God always says, 'Yes, my son, I am with you.'

The pious would like to believe that God does not speak to the sinners, that one has to earn the right to hear His voice. The pious are wrong. God speaks to Judas of Qeriot just as he spoke to Yehoshuah of Natzaret, just as he would speak to the Emperor Tiberius of Rome if the twisted king had the wit to listen.

'What shall I do?' he says to God.

'Go west,' says the Lord. 'You are in a port. Take passage on a ship and sail away.'

And he thinks he will. Here, this story is the only story of his life, the only thing he has ever done or will ever do. But there is this to be said for Rome: a man can become something new. He is not tied to his birth or his ancestral lands. There are great kingdoms yet to be seen. In the west the debauched Emperor Tiberius sits on his golden throne. In the west the Greeks ply their trade in wisdom. In the west, he has heard, there are demons and witches and uncircumcised barbarians with beards down to their navels and patterns on their skins. He is ready for them. And let them think in Israel that he is dead.

Caiaphas

They tie a rope around his ankle so that, if he dies, they will be able to haul him out.

People say that, a thousand years ago, under the rule of King David or King Solomon, such a precaution was not necessary. The High Priest would enter the Holy of Holies alone on Yom Kippur, perform the sacred rituals, burn the incense, sprinkle the blood, and the Holy Breath would descend and the people would be forgiven.

Even five hundred years ago, after they had had to rebuild the Temple following the exile in Babylon, there was not so much danger. Even then, under the fabled High Priest Shimon the Righteous, the thread on the horns of the goat would turn from red to white and the people would know that they were forgiven.

But not now. Now, when they send a High Priest into the Holy of Holies, they know he may not come out alive. It happens not infrequently.

The Holy of Holies, the chamber at the centre of the Temple, is built on the navel of the world. It was the first piece of land created when God said, 'Let the land be divided from the sea.' It is from the earth of this spot that God scooped up the dust to make Adam and Eve, the first man and woman. It is the place where Abraham went to sacrifice his son Isaac, and where God stopped him and gave him a ram instead, which is how we know that the sacrifice of human life is not pleasing to Him, and that He instead desires the sweet savours of animal flesh. In the end of days, it is from this spot that the word of the Lord will radiate out like the sound of golden trumpets, so that all the nations will bow down before Him. It is the holiest place in all the world.

The whole world is arranged in concentric circles around this spot. There is the world outside the land of Israel, and within that there is the land of Israel. And within that the holy city of Jerusalem. And within that the Temple. And within the Temple the courtyard of non-Jews, and inside that the courtyard of Jewish women, and inside that, closer yet to the holiest place, the courtyard of Jewish men, and inside that the courtyard of the priests. And within that courtyard of the priests, at the heart of the Temple, the reason for the whole edifice of marble colonnades, for the city, for the country, for the world. At the heart of the Temple is this holiest place in all of creation.

The chamber of the Holy of Holies is a small perfect cube, ten cubits, by ten cubits, by ten cubits. Its walls are marble. Its entrance is covered by two curtains. A raised marble platform shows where the Ark of the Covenant used to stand before it was lost – or hidden and its hiding place forgotten – during the Exile. Other than that, the room is empty. Apart from God. This is the place where God is.

And on Yom Kippur, when God brings his face very close to the earth, when he listens and observes His people most intently, on that day the High Priest – the Cohen Gadol – walks into the chamber alone. Alone he burns the incense on the glowing coals, and scatters the blood, and falls upon the stone dumbfounded in the presence of the Lord. Alone he mumbles his prayers into the cold smooth floor and squeezes his eyes tightly shut and finds his whole body shaking. And his head is filled with the smell of the incense and the speech of God, which is so far beyond words that when God Himself describes it in the Torah He can only say that the people hear the sights and see the words, so inadequate is our language to describe the Almighty.

And often, the High Priest does not, these days, survive the experience.

And because the square chamber is so holy, because they themselves would die if they dared to enter it, for it is certainly forbidden to them, they pull on the rope tied to his ankle to remove the body.

This is always a terrible thing. If the man dies, by this token the people know that they have not been forgiven.

It is since the Romans, of course. Since Pompey with his iron boots strode about the holy chamber. Since the wall was breached and the treasures were examined by a Roman note-taker, wiping his nose on the back of his hand as he counted the golden vessels that once were made for the hand of Moses.

And yes, it is because of the men themselves. The High Priests, who once were chosen by their fellow priests for their wisdom and holiness and the force of the spirit in them, are now servants of Caesar, picked by Pilate the Prefect for other, more practical qualities. There are men who have bought their way to becoming High Priest by gifts to Pilate.

They do not always survive.

It is this which Caiaphas carries with him every morning when he rises and scratches, and kisses the head of his sleeping wife and goes to wash and put on the robes of his office and begin the services every day. Today is ordinary, and tomorrow will be ordinary and the next day in all likelihood. But once a year he will stand in the full presence of the Almighty and see if he is worthy to survive.

He has a suspicion regarding his wife.

He has seen her in the courtyard, her hair oiled with perfume but neatly covered like any modest woman, and a jar of water under her bent arm. He has watched as she asks one of the Temple Levites, a man called Darfon, to pull down the branch of the tree so she can pluck some of the sun-warmed dates. No, she smiles, not those ones, they are not quite soft yet. She does not like the crunchy dates. She wants them from that branch, where they are dark and sweet.

The Levite, Darfon, jumps up and grabs the branch with both arms. His sleeves flap down, revealing muscular brown arms, the hair wiry and strong like a young lamb's. She smiles, and he can see her watching the man's arms, and his sturdy legs kicking against the ground, so she can reach her hand up bending only at the elbow and pluck a soft warm date. She plucks two. She presses one to her lips, licking the brown skin with her small pink tongue. She gives the other to Darfon. He takes it coyly, smiling at her under his eyelashes, biting into it with a small, careful, hungry bite.

Caiaphas, watching, finds himself imagining a wolf, down out of the mountains, lean and ravenous from the famine in the land. Imagines the wolf stalking his wife, bringing her to bay in a grove strewn with rocks and broken pottery. Imagines the wolf growling and leaping to rip out her throat.

Or he imagines bruises slowly spreading across her face, turning her eyes bloodshot and her neck scarlet and blue. Imagines, and his hands feel how good it would be, throwing her to the ground, because it is not that he does not love her and desire her, but a thing like this must be paid hurt for hurt.

He is not a violent man; he has sacrificed enough young bulls and yearling lambs to understand the precious delicacy of life. He is startled by the strength of his feelings, how they leap up in him like a wolf he had not known was stalking by his side, or within him, all his life.

It is high summer. Passover is long gone. The sun bakes down on the cool marble plazas of the Temple, and on the north gate, where the drovers bring in their hot and reeking sheep for the slaughter. It heats the marketplace, where the fruit sellers lazily beat palm fans to keep the flies off their wares and the donkeys' tails twitch, raising clouds of gnats. It cooks the houses of the wealthy and the hovels of the poor, it turns the swimming ponds into warm pools of bubbling algae and frogs. In the minds of King, Governor, Prefect, soldiers, priests and farmers it raises the spectre of famine, for what if the rains do not come? They always come if God wills it and why would he not will it – yet there have been years when they did not come. Jerusalem is languorous in the heat, unable to move, slow-witted but fretful. But just because Jerusalem does not move, one cannot believe she is asleep.

The Prefect, Pilate, wears a ring with a wolf's head. The wolf is the animal of Rome, of course: in another room Pilate has his little shrine to the God-Emperor Tiberius, and above it a picture of Romulus and Remus suckling at the teat of their wolf-mother. Like the wolf, Rome hunts with a great pack. Like the wolf, she protects her own but to those outside her circle she is nothing but teeth. Pilate's ring, on the third finger of his long bony right hand, is a great disc of amber with the wolf's head carved into it, snarling, showing fangs. When Pilate slams his hand on to the table, the bright summer light glints off the sharp bevels and lines of the carving, making the teeth sparkle and the eye blink.

'Three months!' he shouts, and then, appearing to calm himself, although this is all for show and Caiaphas has seen it before, he repeats again more softly, 'Three months.'

Caiaphas stares at a point just behind Pilate's head, to the niche where the man has his little statue of Mars, bearing a sword. There would be a riot in the city if they knew he had brought this idol so near to the holy sanctuary. There had been a riot four years earlier when he brought a new garrison of soldiers into the city bearing their banners showing Caesar's head. It is forbidden to bring a graven image or an idol or an image of any kind this close to the Temple.

'Are you so stupid, Caiaphas?' Pilate asks slowly. 'Is it that you are stupid? Is it that you have not understood what I have asked these three months? Do I need to ask you more slowly so you can follow my request? I. Want. The. Money.'

Caiaphas licks his upper lip.

'I have tried to explain . . .' he begins, and he hears his own voice wheedling like a child's and the wolf in his own throat growls at him and before he can stop himself he says, 'It is forbidden. It is utterly forbidden. What you are asking is impossible.'

Pilate stares at him, and his nostrils flare and his mouth works.

He brings his hand down on the table again, so hard that the ink pot jumps and spatters.

'It is not impossible if I command it! The city of Jerusalem,' says Pilate, 'is dying of thirst. There is fresh water in the mountains, there are men ready to begin construction, there is stone in the quarries. Look!' Pilate opens his hands magnanimously. 'Look at your city.' Out of the window, Jerusalem bakes and shimmers. 'Give me the money from the Temple so I can build the aqueduct and bring the water from the hills.'

Caiaphas wonders whether, if he angered the man enough, Pilate would pull down one of those swords from the wall and run him through. Remember, he says to himself, how vulnerable you are. Remember how swiftly the life would run out of you, like the life of a young lamb under your blade. And yet the wolf in him will not hear it.

'The money that is given to the Temple is for its use alone,' he says. 'It is a sacred trust, given to us by God.'

He remembers the widows and the orphans who bring their tiny offerings to the Temple, because they know God will be pleased with their sacrifice, however small it is. They bring it freely. It is money they meant for the Temple. It is not his to give away.

'Fuck on your God!' shouts Pilate. 'That Temple is piled up with gold and decorated with marble, while not a single aqueduct brings water to the south of the city.'

'They have their wells. No one suffers from thirst in Jerusalem.'

Pilate bangs his hand on the table again.

'Five hundred talents of gold! You will hardly miss it from your coffers. We could begin to quarry the stone this week!'

It is a power game, of course. Pilate could request the money from Rome, but his standing is not good enough to have any expectation of receiving it. This Caiaphas has from various spies in the orbit of the Governor of Syria, Pilate's superior. But he wants to leave Jerusalem more like Rome than he found it. No Roman can see a city without wanting to drop an aqueduct on it, for all that the well water is clean and plentiful. And if he persuades the Temple to pay for the project, he will report in one of those dry military dispatches that the people are 'beginning to understand the benefits of Roman rule'.

Caiaphas shrugs. It is a gesture calculated to irritate Pilate and he knows it.

'If you were to send the soldiers in,' he says, 'I could not prevent them. My priests are not warriors.'

'Oh no,' says Pilate, 'I know how this will go. You will force me to send soldiers into the Temple. And we will desecrate some sacred urn or tread in the wrong way on a holy pavement, or distress the spirit of the blessed sheep or breathe improperly in the presence of the consecrated midden heap. And then there will be another riot and I will have to call in troops from Syria to quash it and that would make them say . . .' He blinks and stops himself. 'That would be very inconvenient. These fucking people!' He wipes the sweat beading on his brow with the sleeve of his robe. 'One cannot walk from one end of the square to the other without insulting an ancient tradition of some tribe or other.'

Pilate pokes his finger at Caiaphas. 'You will give me the money and tell them that your God has commanded it. Tell them you had a dream.'

Caiaphas inclines his head as if to say 'an excellent idea', or possibly, 'I will try but I cannot promise', or possibly, 'You are a fool and hold on to this city by a tiny thread.' He has been ending conversations this way for months now. Appearing to concede, never quite consummating his promises.

Every morning and every evening, a lamb is sacrificed. But this is only the beginning. Every morning and every evening, incense is burned on the altar in the Holy of Holies. Every day, there is the seven-branched candelabrum to be filled with pure-pressed oil. On the Sabbath, a meal offering of flour and oil and wine. And at the new moon, two yearling bulls, a ram, seven lambs. To say nothing of the particular sacrifices during the three yearly festivals of pilgrimage, and at New Year in the autumn and Yom Kippur ten days after that. And the sin offerings brought to seek God's forgiveness by penitents around the year. And the peace offerings. And the thanksgiving offerings, for recovery from illness or escape from danger.

'And do you think this is easy?' Annas had said to him when he was a young man. It was when Caiaphas first began to be taken notice of in the Temple and by his fellow priests. Annas was High Priest then; he had these conversations with many young men who had been taken notice of. 'Let us take the incense, for example. Do you think that when the servant from the house of Avtinas comes to bring the incense that it has come from nowhere?'

Caiaphas, attempting to impress the older man, had spouted the lines he had learned.

'There are eleven spices in the incense,' he said, 'frankincense and myrrh and cassia and spikenard and saffron and –'

'Listen to yourself. Stop. Understand how much is necessary for that list you spool out. Where does the saffron come from?'

Caiaphas shifted his weight from one foot to the other. 'From flowers?'

'From only one flower, which grows most plentifully only in Persia. We use a sack of it every month. A good handful of saffron is the product of ten thousand flowers. A hundred handfuls in a sack. A hundred men labouring crouched over their flowers are needed to supply us with saffron alone.'

Caiaphas looked out over the Temple courtyard, where he could count easily a hundred priests hurrying about their duty. He nodded slowly.

'You are not impressed, I see. You think that a hundred men labouring in the hills of Persia are not so very much for the glory of God. Then consider. They dry those tiny threads in the sun. They bundle them into sacks – and where do the sacks come from? Someone must weave them, someone must stamp them with our seal. They put the sacks into the back of a closed wagon – and who made that wagon? Who bred those mules? The wagon is driven by a strong man, with five other men guarding it. They pass through mountains and valleys. A dried-up riverbed. A pasture of waving grass and biting gnats. They fight off bandits who attempt to steal the precious treasure. At night they take turns to sleep. Perhaps in the crossing one of their usual waterholes is empty. Perhaps one of the animals dies. They must change the route regularly or the bandits will ambush them. They must check the sacks for weevil and mould – if it rains too heavily and the saffron becomes wet, their journey is in vain. At last they arrive in Jerusalem, if we are lucky. And of all these things, do you know what is the most needful?'

'The cunning of men,' said Caiaphas wonderingly, 'all the craft and skill given to them by God, to elude the bandits and to keep their cargo safe.'

Annas shook his head.

'A thousand dangers threaten. And to make the incense, we need not only the saffron threads but also those other ten fragrant ingredients: frankincense and myrrh, spikenard and fennel resin, cinnamon and ginger, cassia and balsam, distillation of rock roses and wine from Cyprus. And we need salt from Sodom, amber from Jordan, lye from Carshina. Think of the many wagons bringing them from around the world. And consider that all these go to make just the incense, and not any of the other sacred matters of the Temple. And you are correct that cunning and skill are needed to make them and bring them to us.

'But most important of all, none of this can happen if at any point along the way a war is being waged. If an army is laying siege to a city, the saffron wagon will be requisitioned. If angry defeated soldiers are wasting enemy land, the saffron will be burned. If the men who tap the trees and pluck the stems and brew the wine and mine the salt have been taken for an army, their work will go undone. To bring us all these things, that which is most needful is peace.'

Annas drew himself to his full height. He was an exceptionally tall man, over six feet. 'That is the role of the Cohen Gadol. To maintain the Temple services. To maintain the peace. Nothing is more important.'

Two people come to him with a disputation. Natan the Levite shrugs apologetically as he brings them in and whispers, 'I've tried to sort this one out myself, but the two stubborn goats insist on seeing the High Priest. If you order them both flogged I won't blame you.'

He has a mock-rueful smile on his face as he bows his head low and leaves the room, muttering, 'The Cohen Gadol, if his judgement is sufficient for you and you do not require a voice from heaven.'

They are traders in the outer courtyard of the Temple. They both sell the pure white doves that are used for the thanksgiving sacrifice brought by a woman after she has given birth and recovered safely from those many dangers.

It is holy work to sell the birds. There are three or four families who have done so for generations. They breed the birds in dovecotes just outside the city, catch them by hand – for no bone can be broken before they are sacrificed – keep them docile with a special mixture of seeds which each family guards closely.

And now this. A tall gaunt man of about fifty with a close-cropped beard and a loose skullcap stands before him. Next to him, a short woman in her sixties with sun-cured skin and a heavy gait. Caiaphas would ask each of them what the matter is, but neither of them will let him speak.

'I am but an old woman,' she says. 'I have no strength left in my bones. The place nearest the entrance is fitting for me, for I cannot carry my wares across the great courtyard.'

'Pah,' he says, 'pah. I suppose you have not four strong sons whom I have seen carrying your wares and your stall for you! I suppose those four strong sons did not threaten my Jossya with cudgels unless she moved her stall to the far end of the courtyard.'

'My sons would never threaten,' the woman snaps, 'unless they were provoked. Isn't it true that your daughter Jossya crept behind their stall and released the birds intended –' and here the woman sheds an impressive tear – 'for the Lord's holy table, so bringing shame on the whole house of Israel?'

'If she did it is because she knew that your family have stooped so low as to catch the birds with nets! I have seen birds dragging a broken wing on your stall, sold at a low price to farmers who know no better. I have seen them try to make their sacrifice and be turned away by the priests and come in shame to buy a good bird from me or my daughter. It is you who should be ashamed.'

'You spread these lies about my family so that people will pay your inflated prices! Everyone knows you have grown rich off the piety of the poor!'

'You have grown rich yourself, bringing shame on the holy house of the Lord!' he says.

'You have tried to steal from an old woman in her last years on the earth!' The woman has brought herself to the point of real half-hysterical tears now.

'You are a liar and a thief!' The man is so angry his face has turned pale, his nostrils flaring, the skin of his neck beginning to redden.

'Do you see how he speaks to me? In the chambers of your holy presence!'

Caiaphas continues silent. He watches. He waits. They are in a chamber of his house next to the Temple. Through the small half-shuttered window which looks on to the inner courtyard, he can see the sacrifices being performed. A meal cake and oil are utterly consumed. The Lord forgives the sin which prompted the sacrifice. The man and woman burn themselves out after a few more angry expostulations and before they come to physical blows.

He smiles his diplomatic smile, the guileless face he puts on to deal with common men and with the Prefect. He is all sympathy, all respect. He is sometimes amazed by the way his mouth carries on speaking and his face composes itself into such a usefully sympathetic arrangement while inside his mind he is thinking only of, for example, his wife leaning in to take the ripe date from the sticky fingers of Darfon, son of Yoav.

They reach an agreement after a time: the woman will have her stall near to the front all days of the week but Friday – a day when many people come to buy offerings – and they will both submit to stock checks by one of the Levite treasurers under Natan's command. Outside, the sacrifices continue.

Annas comes to see him at the end of the day, as he is relaxing in his city home. He has two homes: the official residence at the Temple, which he uses during the day for his business, and this, his own house in the city, the place he had built for himself and which would still be his if he were no longer High Priest. Here he is a private man, in so far as he can be.

His daughters have put out fresh goat's milk and bread with soft white cheese mingled with thyme leaves and good black olives from the north. They have poured the cold clear well water into an earthenware jug and flavoured it with citron. The courtyard of his house is cool and still when Annas comes to visit.

Annas arrives unannounced, as he so often does, but he is welcome. He is a powerful man still, both physically and politically. He is wide in the shoulder and his arms are well muscled – when he was High Priest, it is said he could bring a fretful ox to its knees by the force of his grip. And his personality, Caiaphas thinks sometimes. Annas is a clever man with a strong will.

He became High Priest just when the old King Herod died, when his various heirs, mostly also named Herod, were squabbling and pleading with the Emperor for pieces of the kingdom. Many said that Annas bought his way into the office with bribes to the Prefect and the captains of the army, but he stayed there because he was able to broker deals between the Temple and the Prefect, between the King and the people, between heaven, it sometimes seemed, and earth. He had spies – 'Not spies,' he would say, 'friends' – in the courts of the Governors of Syria and Egypt, and even some said as far as Rome itself. He is no longer High Priest now – an earlier governor had taken that position away from him when he tried to execute a man for murder, because Rome does not allow its occupied states the privilege of executing their own criminals – but he still has as much influence as ever. He gives good counsel, and Caiaphas embraces him as a welcome guest when he arrives.

'I hear the sellers of doves have come to blows,' says Annas, chewing on an olive and spitting the pit into the bushes of the courtyard.

Caiaphas shrugs. 'They have been ready to kill over the bird of peace for the past five years.'

'I also hear that you dealt with them extremely well. Both families seem to feel they have come out best from the bargain.'

Caiaphas smiles in spite of himself.

'It was no judgement of Solomon.'

'Even Solomon is remembered for only one case. Your day may yet come. Besides, it is a good training ground for you. I will not live forever and someone will have to do my work when I'm gone.'

Caiaphas is well aware that Annas says this frequently, to various men, including several of his sons. Caiaphas is some way down the list of successors. And yet it is true: it is hard to imagine who will stop the various factions in Judea from shattering apart and breaking themselves on the wheel of Rome after Annas is gone.

'You have many good years left,' says Caiaphas.

'Mmm,' says Annas. Then, staring up through the vine-laden trellis above them to the cool night sky, 'have you heard that there will be war between King Herod Antipas and the Nabateans? There's no way to prevent it. King Aretas of Nabatea is still fuming on his throne in Petra that Herod dared to divorce his daughter. He'll use these border scuffles as an excuse to invade the south.'

'A war? Over a dishonoured daughter?'

'Men love their daughters, Caiaphas.' Annas grins, showing his teeth, and bites off a piece of bread.

*

Caiaphas's wife serves them boiled whole Galilee-fish wrapped in herbs and freshly cooked flatbread, with two sauces, one of yoghurt and one spicy with tomato and hot peppers. There are aubergines stewed in olive oil and doused in hyssop and dried parsley, and roasted onions seared from the fire.

She bends this way and that as she lays out the food and gives them their plates. She is beautiful and he cannot help but watch her still, the way her robe outlines her buttocks when she stoops and the sky-blue square covering her hair slips a little as she moves. She is past forty and has given him two sons and three daughters and still he desires her. And he wishes his suspicion were not true. And he hopes that it is not. But he thinks of her eyes darting to Darfon and a fire burns in his veins.

When she has finished with the food, she comes and wraps her arms around Annas's shoulders, leaning in close, and he kisses her on the cheek.

'Is he treating you well, my darling?' Annas says, laughing.

'Oh, father,' she says, 'he's terribly cruel and beats me every night.' She winks and smiles and they all laugh, because it is so very far from anything that could ever be true.

Caiaphas would not be High Priest if it weren't for his wife. He knows it, the whole city of Jerusalem knows it. There is no shame in it, not really. This is how a man becomes powerful: by becoming precious to men who are already powerful, by impressing an older and wiser man with his skill and his cunning and by marrying his daughter.

Annas was High Priest for ten years before the Prefect demanded he resign the office. But Annas's power has not waned. He has been succeeded as High Priest by his sons, one after another, none of them for quite long enough to secure a power base for themselves. And now it is the turn of Caiaphas, his son-in-law, who has been gently shepherded through the twists and turns of office, spoken of highly to the Prefect and the other priests and to Herod Antipas, the king in the north. And by dint of diplomacy, and through Annas's support, he has somehow clung on longer than all the others. Annas has given him special favour. Men love their daughters.

The next day, after he has finished with the morning sacrifices, there are various pieces of business to attend to. Natan the Levite arrives carrying a jar of wine from Tyre under his arm.

'From that Asher family in the north,' he says, 'the people who had the trouble with bandits. They've offered fifteen casks in place of their tribute.'

'Is wine less likely to be stolen than grain?'

Natan shrugs, scratches his grizzled beard.

'Fewer wagons for the same value. They can protect it with a smaller number of men.'

'And keep more men to work their farm, and send fewer of their sons to make the offering at the Temple?'

Natan pours the wine into Caiaphas's two earthenware cups, rough red pottery on the outside, smooth blue glaze inside the bowl. The wine smells good as it gushes into the cups.

They taste together. The wine is exceptional, scented with orange and spring grass. Caiaphas rolls the good red richness around his mouth. It is the hills of the north and the deep peace of childhood.

He meets Natan's eyes.

'Yes, then,' says Natan.

'Ask them for this in future instead of the grain they owe.'

Natan nods. Pauses.

'And then there is the other matter.'

He looks at Natan, a little confused. Natan shifts uneasily in his chair.

'You'll have to remind me, my friend.'

'Livan's daughter gets married next week.'

'Ah,' says Caiaphas. 'Yes.'

There is a pause. Caiaphas contemplates Livan's daughter in his mind as he last saw her. A dark-skinned girl of fourteen, sweet small breasts under her shift, her hair caught back with a garland of flowers.

147

She kept her eyes modestly lowered when she met him. And he thought: yes, as well this one as another, if God wills it.

'How old is she now?'

'Seventeen.'

'Yes, then she has waited for me long enough. Very well. Good. Do you have a new girl for me to meet?'

'I have her waiting in the outer room.'

'You should have told me she was there. We could have dealt with her first.'

Natan chuckles.

'It is good for her to become accustomed to waiting.'

Caiaphas laughs.

'I believe you kept her outside just for your joke.'

Natan shrugs.

'Whose daughter is she?' asks Caiaphas.

'Hodia.'

Caiaphas nods slowly, impressed. Hodia is a wealthy man, whose generous gifts to the Temple have already secured him a certain amount of political power.

'He has three sons, Hodia, yes?'

Natan smiles. 'And he is a Cohen.' Hodia is a member of the priestly class. His sons would be candidates for high priestly office, perhaps even High Priest. 'I'm sure he would be delighted to be so close to you.'

'Well, bring the girl in.'

This girl is different to the last. Hodia's daughter is round-cheeked, with skin burnished like bronze, black hair and bright black, searching eyes. She does not keep her gaze modestly cast down. Her body is already that of a woman, with broad hips and full breasts. She is sixteen.

Typically these girls remain silent unless he speaks to them, but she speaks before he has a chance to address her.

'Sir,' she says, a small smile at the corners of her mouth, 'is your wife in good health?'

He laughs, without intending to.

'Very good health. Should I apologize?'

'Are you that much of a prize?'

And he and Natan are both laughing.

'I see you've had the thing fully explained to you.'

'Perfectly.'

It is not a complex matter. The High Priest – the Cohen Gadol – must be married. It is not optional. He alone goes into the holy sanctuary on Yom Kippur, the most sacred day of the year. The entire people wait for his sign that they have been forgiven by God. And to atone for the sins of the whole house of Israel, he must be a whole man: he must not be crippled, he must not be unusually ugly, he must not be deaf or blind, he must not be unmarried. To expect an unmarried man to carry that burden of sin would be as foolish as expecting it of a child, or a woman.

This raises a problem, of course. For what if the wife of the Cohen Gadol should chance to die on the eve of Yom Kippur? Then there would be no High Priest able to intercede with God on behalf of the people. So there must be another girl waiting, just in case. She may never be needed. But it is as well to have chosen her in advance. There is, of course, another Cohen waiting to take his place if he himself dies. The needs of the people go on, though men die and other men rise to take their place.

This girl is attractive, with her sauce and her talk. He thinks it would be good to lie with her, to make her gasp and teach her how to please and be pleased. The wife of a Cohen Gadol must, of course, be a virgin. It is not that his own wife is displeasing to him physically or that he longs for another woman, but one must consider the thing properly. If it happened, there would be no time for doubts, and it would seem ill for him to divorce her very quickly.

'You understand that you must be beyond suspicion? For this next year?'

She wriggles her shoulders in a way which reminds him how very young she is – as young as his wife was when he married her.

Her shoulders say that she is uncomfortable with the question, but her smile is bold. Her mother or grandmother must have told her all she needs to know.

'I understand,' she says, and her pink tongue licks her dark upper lip. 'I shall remain precisely as I am now, and consort only with old women, and discuss only housework with them. For this next year.'

And there is something about the way she speaks that makes him wonder. It is interesting. They would not have brought her to him if there were a shred of doubt about her chastity – to do so would risk the whole of the house of Israel. And yet.

Natan leads her out of the room, closing the door behind her and waiting for her steps to recede before he grins and says, 'Well? Don't tell me I haven't found a good one for you.'

'Yes, she'll do very well. Only . . .'

Natan raises an eyebrow. Waits.

'Only are you certain of her innocence? She had a way about her which –'

'No young man has ever even held her hand. Hodia has another priest waiting for her when your year is up. She knows she has to keep herself pure. Don't mistake what your cock knows for what her cunt knows.'

Caiaphas laughs, in spite of himself.

'She'll do very well,' he says.

'And may your wife remain in perfect health until she reaches one hundred and twenty,' says Natan, grinning.

'Amen.'

He tries to reason it out to himself. He is not a stupid man or an uneducated one. His father, a Cohen as well of course, for the thing passes from father to son, had owned a string of vineyards and olive presses in the east, enough to pay for the best possible education for his son. His father had an idea that the boy might be material for a Cohen Gadol, so he had him learn Latin and Greek as fluently as his own Hebrew and Aramaic, and brought a tutor from Antioch. So he's read Greek philosophy and Roman military history, as well as the texts of his own people. He knows the value of reason.

He says to himself: why would she do such a thing? He says to himself: it would be death to her. And yet he cannot reason it himself. One needs a friend for such conversations. He waits until an evening a little later, when he and Natan have finished their business, when the lamb of the evening has been slaughtered, when the day cools and the night blows gently across the hills of Jerusalem.

'Did you ever . . .' He looks at Natan. He had been intending to ask the question in one way but finds now that he cannot. Natan's wife is buxom, loving, several years older than him; the man can never have suspected her. 'Did you ever know a man who had a suspicion about his wife?'

Natan's usual merriness instantly sobers.

'Kef,' he says, 'your wife? Do you think your wife . . .'

Caiaphas finds his practised High Priest smile, the liar's smile, comes quickly and naturally to his lips.

'By the enemies of God, no,' he says. 'No, no. I heard a story from one of the other priests,' and he can tell that Natan is already trying to calculate which of the other priests it could be and whether he is lying and what this might mean for the smooth running of the Temple, but he must talk to someone and if Natan guesses so be it. 'I heard a story that one of them suspected his wife of adultery. Did you ever know a man who thought so?'

Natan leans back in his chair. He scratches at his beard.

'All women look at other men,' he says at last, 'it's natural. Means that there's still juice in them. The day a woman says she never notices another man is the day you know she doesn't want to fuck you any more.'

Caiaphas breathes out through his nose.

'Looking is one thing,' he says, 'I'm talking about something else.'

Natan puts his cup down, leans forward, hands on his knees.

'What are you talking about?' he says. 'Your wife is the most sensible woman alive.' He reaches his hand forward and clasps Caiaphas's knee briefly. 'Even if she did pick you for a husband.'

Caiaphas finds he is laughing. It is the politician's laugh, the one he is surprised to find seems so convincing when it does not touch him at all on the inside.

'Tell me about Darfon, son of Yoav,' he says quickly.

'Oh,' says Natan, 'is that all this is? The man's a flirt, Kef, an unconscionable, foolish flirt and you're not the first one to notice. I've been thinking for a long time I should send him north, to work at one of the record-keeping houses and get him out of our business here. Let him show off his muscles to the girls of the house of Zebulun and find himself a wife.'

'But I –'

'He will be away from here within two weeks.'

He watches her the next day, privately, quietly, while she dresses in a simple night-blue shift and arranges her hair with two gold pins. His mind vacillates between suspicion and finding himself ridiculous. She would not be so foolish. She would not be so cruel. The simple fact that he fears it means it must be impossible.

It is entirely forbidden for any man to lie with a wife who has been unfaithful to him. Not just for the High Priest but for any man. But especially for the High Priest. It is not only undesirable. It is not only that he may divorce her if he wishes. It is forbidden for him to lie with her if she has been unfaithful. If she has been unfaithful, he must know it and he must divorce her.

Every part of him will go into the Holy of Holies on the Day of Atonement. No part of him may have touched an impure vessel.

So he must know. So he arranges things. He waits for a time when he knows that Natan the Levite, the man he trusts, will be busy with the tribute from the tribe of Gad. He calls another Levite, a man who does not know him.

He says, with his liar's smoothness, 'My wife asked me to send one of these casks of wine home.' He motions to two of the barrels from Asher in the corner of his chamber. 'Will you have one of your men do it?' A pause, just long enough so that it will seem as if the idea has only just occurred to him. 'Oh,' he says, 'why not send that man Darfon? He is strong, and my wife wanted someone to cut a low-trailing branch from the cherry tree in our garden.'

Caiaphas is a wolf, cunning and perpetually hungry.

He gives them a little time. He does not follow Darfon closely in the street. He hangs back and tarries at a market stall, examining jars of oil while he counts the moments in his mind. This would be the time when Darfon arrives at Caiaphas's home unexpectedly. This would be how long it would take his wife to send the servants out on errands. This would be the moment they are alone. Now. It is now. His hands shake as he places a small jar of oil back on the stall and his feet begin to walk.

He pauses before his own front door, thinking suddenly whether he would not rather go back to the Temple. It is the memory of the Holy of Holies that urges him on, the memory that soon he will be summoned back to that tiny chamber at the heart of everything and called on to answer for the whole of the people.

The house is very quiet. The small fountain in the courtyard trickles into the pool beneath. His daughters' bedrooms have already been neatly swept by the maidservants. His own bedroom, the large one that looks out on to the courtyard, is still and silent. Some of his wife's hair is caught in the silver-backed hairbrush on her table. In the bronze mirror, his reflection walks past, creeping like a thief.

It is so quiet here, away from the bustling street, that he can hear the birdsong.

He ascends the wooden stairs at the side of the house leading to the upper floor where the servants sleep. Although it is his home, months can go past without his needing to visit these rooms. Some furniture is stored here, a few pieces he inherited from his grandfather. There are four tiny rooms with small windows and sleeping benches for the slaves, and two larger ones with better beds for the housekeeper and the cook.

He fingers the blankets on one of the beds. Remembers how, when his children were young, he would often find them up here, playing in the dust. The slaves and the servants were kind to them. There is an ointment in an earthenware pot by one bed. He smells it and wrinkles his nose. Some foul-smelling cure for rheumatism or spottiness no doubt.

In a box under one of the beds, he finds a letter in Greek – he had no idea that his cook could read Greek – it is a love letter from a man in Crete, promising to come soon and take her away, calling her his duck, his sweet fruit, his fresh pomegranate. As he reads, his emotions are mixed: irritation that some Cretan will take his cook away, anxiety that he might somehow be discovered reading this letter, even though the house is empty, and a kind of wonder at the secret chamber at the centre of every human heart whose contents are unguessable from the outside.

Even the slaves have their tiny arrangements of possessions. A talisman against coughing. A bone comb. A half-completed carving of a tree on a piece of olive wood. When they are released – and a Hebrew slave must be freed after seven years of service – he supposes they will take these things with them, back into whatever life they came from.

He is so involved in the examination of these artefacts that he half forgets why he came to the house in the middle of the afternoon anyway. Until he hears his wife laughing.

It is a short laugh, a breathless one. It is coming from outside. Peering through the tiny window above the housekeeper's bed, he looks without seeing for a while: only the fountain, the vines growing up the trellises, the bushes and the fruit trees already beginning to drop their harvest on the red stone tiles. And then, craning, he sees them.

They are in the gardener's enclosure, screened off behind the main garden so that it can only be seen from above. He never goes in there: it is where the gardener stores his tools in a wooden box, where the plants which are not ready to come out are grown and tended. He does not even know how to get in: he thinks he has seen the latched gate in the fence at the back of the house but is not sure.

There, in that screened-off place, his wife is sitting in Darfon's lap. She is wriggling, pretending to try to escape. Another bubble of laughter rises from her lips. Darfon plucks a ripe plum from the tree whose branches bend low over the garden and puts it to her lips. She bites it. The juice dribbles down her chin. Darfon meets her eyes, questioningly. She becomes very still. He puts his tongue to her neck and laps at the juice on her chin, her throat, lower. Her eyes are closed. She leans back into his arms.

Caiaphas turns away from the window then. His heart is sick and his body is angry and the wolf inside him stalks and prowls and says to him: go down now and strip her clothes from her body and parade her through the street like the harlot she is. And the lamb inside him says: speak to her, be merciful, warn her, for you have seen nothing yet that damns her absolutely. The little room full of the centre of another person's presence says: every person must have their secret place.

And the wolf says: look again. And he says: no. And the wolf says: look again. You know what you will see. It will make your blood hot and then there will be none of this skulking in shadows. Look again, it says, and find all the courage you need.

But when he turns back to the window, his wife is smoothing off her dress and arranging her hair with the two gold pins. And Darfon is in another part of the garden, lopping down the low branch with a saw.

A man may have more than one wife, but a wife may have only one husband. And this means that if a man should chance to desire or know a woman other than his wife, he may simply take her as a new wife and all will be well. But a woman must cleave only to her husband; this is the law of God. Therefore it is right for a man to keep watch over his wife, to ensure that she is not allowed to stray. He has, after all, purchased her from her father by a deed of contract, and he must be free of all doubt concerning the purity of his possession.

There is a thing a man can do, if he has a suspicion regarding his wife. It is scrupulously fair. It is written in the Torah and so we know that it is good and just. A man who suspects that his wife has lain with another man must go to the priests – or to another priest – and declare that the breath of jealousy has entered him. And then they bring the wife and make a little offering to God: some barley flour. This is to begin, to ask God to enter into the thing they will do next.

They take holy water from the sacred well in the Temple and mix into it a tiny pinch of dust from the floor of the holiest enclosure in the Temple. And finally they write the curse against adultery, containing the holy four-letter name of God on a piece of paper. And they put the paper in the water until the ink dissolves. And this holiest of holy water, this water which contains the unspeakable name of God, this they make her drink.

And then two things may happen. If she is guilty, if she has lain with another man, then the waters will be bitter waters. They will cause her belly to swell, and her ripe thighs to wither, and in the fullness of many days she will die.

But if she is innocent she will conceive a child.

It can be observed how merciful and humane a law this is, for when the breath of jealousy enters a man he may be tempted to beat his wife, or even kill her. But in this way it can be ensured that no sin taints him, even though his wife may be mired in her sin.

Caiaphas could call his wife to be scrutinized by this ceremony. But it would not be a simple matter. If she died of it, he would have killed Annas's daughter, and Annas is a powerful man. And if she lived, he would have disgraced Annas's daughter. And Annas is a powerful man. And men love their daughters.

There is another interview with Pilate the following day. The wolf's head amber ring glints and the man foams and expostulates and makes it very clear that if he does not have his money for the aqueduct he will have to look for a new High Priest, one who is more accommodating to his needs.

Annas has another son waiting to take the office. And would not that be in some ways easier? He is willing to give up over this. Temple money cannot be used to build a civic amenity. What next? Send the priests to work the land? Melt down the golden cups and silver trumpets as Roman coins? They could give all the money for the sacred incense to the poor, but before long there would be no Temple at all this way. Not to mention that he would not be able to remain Cohen Gadol anyway if he allowed Pilate the money. He will have to enter the Holy of Holies again this year, as every year. God will see what he has done.

Annas does not agree.

They drink wine in the evening while the house is sleeping and the wild creatures are calling on the hills of Jerusalem. Caiaphas has not spoken to his wife this day, they have not lain together. He is trying to decide what to do. This conversation must be had in any case: it is more serious than matters of the family.

Annas says, 'Give him the money.'

Caiaphas sloshes the wine in his cup. Annas is playing some long and difficult game. Caiaphas cannot see to the end of it. And he is afraid. Playing a game with Rome is like teasing a wolf, tickling its jowls and expecting not to lose a hand.

'Should I lie to the other priests? Have it done in the dead of night? There is that mute slave, Umman, I could send him to do it.'

'No,' says Annas, 'do it in broad daylight. Have ten priests take the money to him through the Temple at noon. Use that . . . what's his name, Egozi, the one who can never keep his mouth shut, to lead them.'

'But,' he says, 'the honour of the Temple. Once it is known, the people will revile me for a traitor.'

'Not as much,' says Annas, 'as they'll revile Pilate.'

Annas looks to the left, out through the pillars of the courtyard, towards the Temple Mount and the star-filled sky above it.

'His standing with the Governor of Syria grows daily worse and worse,' says Annas. 'And we need to be rid of him. He'll find a way to get his money. But if we do it this way . . .'

'The people will be angry,' says Caiaphas.

'He will not be able to stand against them,' says Annas.

He drains his cup to the dregs. From the thin line of trees marking the start of the mountains comes a single howl, then another, and another.

There is a matter of which Caiaphas never thinks. Not that he has decided not to think of it, but it simply does not cross his mind, as a thousand thousand small matters connected to the business of the Temple never occur to him again once they are concluded.

However, his memory is good. If one were to ask him, he would be able to recall how they sourced new bulls that year when the fourteen sacred bulls destined for the altar all died of a cattle plague only hours before the festival. If Annas requested the information, Caiaphas would be able to explain why, six years ago, the tribute from the tribe of Re'uven had been especially high. And if anyone enquired – but why would anyone enquire? – he would remember a madman they handed to the Prefect for Roman justice.

He saw him only three times, and each time the man seemed less impressive than the previous occasion.

The first time he saw the man, he was a genuine inconvenience. Caiaphas had been studying an ancient text on one of the papyri he had bought from an Egyptian trader. It was a Greek text, a fascinating account of the workings of the human body. His eyes became tired with the close work, and he looked up, through the window of his reading chamber, at the bustling outer courtyard, alive with the people who make the holy necessities for the Temple and those who buy them. There was a madman in the courtyard, with a gang of thugs.

The man was whirling his arms wildly, shouting without cease, and there was white spittle in his beard and his mouth was red and sore like the mouth of a man who is lost in the desert and dried up with thirst.

Caiaphas could not make out the matter of his shouts, only certain phrases reached him: 'my father's house!', 'a holy house!', 'evildoers!'

His rants were screams, his voice cracked as he bellowed. He was a pantomime of pain, an ill man surrounded by a phalanx of serious, stone-faced men with broad shoulders and thick walking staffs.

The ranting was not unusual. The temple brought out such people, particularly now, close to a festival. Only the previous week a woman had attempted to strip naked in the courtyard, declaring that she was the daughter of Caesar and that all the men must fuck her in turn to make the new king of Rome and Jerusalem. Caiaphas had had to send for his wife's maidservants to subdue her.

There would be priests already in the courtyard to lead this man out as kindly as they could. If necessary he would send his personal servants to help them. He stood up, leaned against the window, the soft grainy plaster damp under his fingertips.

The man was overturning tables. Raging like a child. He put both his arms under the planks-on-blocks of the man selling holy oil and hurled them wildly. A hundred tiny ceramic jars shattered on the marble flags. Oil pressed from olives in the mountains to the north and brought here by mule cart over five days' perilous journeying dribbled into the cracks between the stones. The owner of the stall, a straggle-haired fellow of fifty, was struggling to reach the man, fighting against the flint-eyed followers who held him back. All around the courtyard they were holding men back while their leader went from stall to stall pulling down carefully pinned curtains and throwing over piles of clay pots and soft flour cakes, like a Roman soldier bent on destruction.

Caiaphas was shouting for his manservant even as he watched the unholy ruin the man was making of all the sacred appurtenances. The slave came swiftly, watched for only a moment before muttering, 'I will tell the priests,' and hurrying away.

A wave of tremendous irritation broke over Caiaphas like a fine sweat as he watched the man. It was this that he struggled against day after day – wanton demolition. As if they had built the holy Temple of the Lord out of mud and straw and every day the rains came and he had to renew its walls. So many hands were trying to pull it down, so few holding it up. It was against this that he made his daily visits and spoke to his spies and counsellors, to hold the place solid against the rain. And this?

The man was overturning the tables full of coins which the poor people had brought to pay for their sacrifices. Hard enough to come by coin outside the cities. Any piece with the head of any king would be taken, that was the pride of the Temple. No one would be turned away for lack of a particular currency. And because the marketplace was here, the priests could oversee the prices to ensure that the peasants were charged fairly, that everyone, rich and poor, men and women, could offer a sacrifice. One might have to wait, but everyone would be seen. It was organized and sensible, and these are the highest and best forms of kindness.

The metal showered like hail and rang like hooves on the flagstones as the stallholders wailed and the children ran eagerly, stuffing their fists with coins. And Caiaphas thought: this? Is it possible that any sane man would prefer this to peace and quiet conversation and each man conducting his business with good humour? Only a man who had never feared for his own life or the lives of his children.

They chased him out of the courtyard in the end, and the young priests set the tables to rights. Caiaphas heard a few complaints that afternoon, and announced at nightfall that the Temple would make good the stallholders' losses out of its own coffers, for it was not right that men should go hungry because of one madman's actions.

And this meant of course that several men who had lost nothing claimed to be ruined, and he set a trusted Levite treasurer to sorting the true claims from the false.

And then many days passed. There was a rising in the east and a spate of murders of soldiers and Roman citizens by bandits in the west. From the north came murmurs of a bad harvest, and from the south they heard there was another plague in Egypt. The eldest son of the house of Avtinas, the incense-makers, came to tell him that the wine they had received from Cyprus was of inferior quality – it had been delayed coming from the coast by the bandits and had spoiled in the casks. This lawlessness must cease. The young man was as wealthy as his whole family; he spoke disdainfully, and the silk robe slung casually over his shoulders, its hem trailing in the dust, could have bought a dozen barrels of good wine, or a dozen men to guard the wagons. But he was right.

He discussed the matter with Annas, who had spoken to the Prefect. Rome was unhappy. It was time, again, to round up the troublemakers and rabble leaders and make an example of them. The Romans had captured a man called only Bar-Avo – a typically insolent pseudonym meaning 'the son of his father' – who, with his band of men, had been torching Roman houses and disrupting their convoys for months.

It would look well if they could also produce a dissenter or two. They would find some of those twitching, raving men who proclaimed themselves the scourge of Rome, flog them in the public square, and be able to tell Pilate that they, too, were defending the honour of the Emperor. As if the Emperor were a fearful woman. The conversation was uncomfortable, as these conversations always were.

Annas placed a hand on his shoulder and said, 'To keep the peace.'

And Caiaphas grunted in assent.

It was a lucky thing that, among the crazed preachers and the careless plotters, a man Iehuda came to them saying that he knew where they could find Yehoshuah, who he said was the one who had tipped over the stalls in the courtyard that day.

When they brought him, Caiaphas assembled an informal court in one of the rooms of his Temple house. It was only days before Passover. He managed to gather eight men: enough to try a simple case like this. There were a few witnesses willing to speak against the man. This was normal. Any trial would bring a group of people eager to gain favour with the Temple. Everyone in Jerusalem knew about the waste of money and goods and the disruption to the sacred services on the day that this Yehoshuah had thrown over the tables.

'He said he would destroy the Temple and rebuild it in three days,' said the man with lumps on his face.

'He said that the end of days is coming,' said another, and none of these things seemed hard to believe to Caiaphas. He had seen the man raving. He was another of those, and whether he fomented rebellion against Rome or not, a man who spoke against the peace, who whipped people up, who destroyed property, was not likely to be let alone.

The witnesses began to shout over one another. Ugly, angry calls. Yehoshuah had spoken against the Temple. They had heard him call himself the Messiah, the rightful king – this was a very serious charge. Under Rome, there is no king but the Emperor and those whom it pleases the Emperor to set on little thrones for a time.

Caiaphas, seated at a long wooden table with four men to his left and four to his right, had the witnesses ushered back, then called one of the Levites to bring Yehoshuah forward. The man had been held at the back of the room while the testimonies were heard. Now he stood before them, seemingly calm, though his face was sunburnt. They sat him in a chair before the judges. Caiaphas stood up. The hubbub from the back subsided a little.

He made his voice loud but low, a trick he had mastered during the endless prayers and services to give his words gravitas without exhausting his throat.

'Yehoshuah of Natzaret,' he said, 'we need an answer from you. You've heard what the witnesses have said. If it's not true, if they're lying, just tell us.'

There was general nodding from the men around the table, an encouragement to behave reasonably. It was surprising how often even a raver, when faced with the calm interrogation of a court, found his wits long enough to deny the most serious charges, which gave them the necessary leeway. For blasphemy, the sentence is generally only a few lashes. There are ways to make an offence less severe in the eyes of the law. That is the purpose of the court – not to condemn but to make the most peaceful accommodation between the person before them and the community which surrounds them.

A Sanhedrin which kills only one man every seventy years has wrought enough harm to be scorned with the name 'a Bloody Court'.

But this madman said nothing. A small smile twitched at the corners of his mouth. And he said nothing in his own defence and he did nothing to show that he understood the charges, and the only movement was his foot twitching under his robe, and Caiaphas thought: this man is entirely mad, but it may still be possible to save him.

He said, 'You know what the most serious charge is. Do you say that you are the Messiah, the expected rightful king of Israel?'

And if he had only remained silent, they could have said: he is a madman struck dumb. They would have assigned him lashes in the marketplace, because one cannot condemn a man to death on hearsay alone if the evidence is contradictory in the least particular, and these witnesses' stories contradicted each other wildly. If he had only remained silent, the case would have fallen.

Instead, with that eerie smile and his eyes affixed on Caiaphas,

Yehoshuah said, 'I am the expected king. And very soon you will see me sitting at the right hand of Yahaveh. We are going to descend to earth on the glowing clouds from heaven.'

He spoke the sacred name of God, the name which is spoken only by the High Priest in the Holy of Holies on the most sacred day of the year. He spoke it as if it were the name of some casual friend.

At this Annas let out a short involuntary breath. And Jonathan, one of the oldest and wisest men on the council, threw up his hands, and Micah, younger and less circumspect, muttered too loudly, 'Now he speaks?' The men on the court exchanged glances. Caiaphas looked at Yehoshuah. He had gone back to that strange unsettling silence. He was rocking back and forth very slightly on his chair.

Caiaphas had the feeling that the man had been waiting for many years for this day, for this hour, when he would say this ridiculous thing to the court and force their hands.

He stood up again. He took a knife from the table, where it stood next to the bread and cheese and wine his wife had laid out for them. He pierced the bottom of his robe and pulled the knife through to the hem. Then he took both sides of the cut cloth and pulled them apart. With a shredding sound and a scatter of fibres in the air, he ripped the garment halfway to the waist. The others around the table nodded, knowing that ripping one's clothes, the sign of deepest mourning, is the only proper response to hearing the true name of God spoken in the wrong place and at the wrong time. The power of the name is strong enough to kill, though it grieves the hearers beyond measure.

He said, and he found his voice hoarse despite himself, 'If this is what you say, then we have no need for witnesses.'

And the verdict was made. And they tried another two men that evening and found them guilty of more minor blasphemy, and sentenced them to the usual punishment – forty lashes, the final lash withheld in case they had miscounted. And he heard that Rome had taken a couple of thieves and intended to execute them too, because

Rome never served up her mercy in portions more generous than a thin dribble.

They might have found a way to save the man even yet. To take a son from his mother and a man from his friends is an evil thing. They could have left him in that locked stable by the Temple for a week or two, until their own memories had faded a little, until if they had asked each other, 'What exactly did he say?' they might have contradicted one another and so proved false witnesses. There are ways to save a man from judgement. But it was the festival of Passover and the streets were thronged with people and the Romans feared that another rebellion might be rising in the city.

And so Pilate summoned him in the morning. He stood by a table covered in scrolls of messages and vellum maps, and a soldier standing quietly to one side, with his sword hanging at his belt. Pilate always greeted him in some similar way, so that he should never forget the power he represented.

'I hear,' he said, 'that you have a man found guilty of blasphemy.'

Who had told him? Some spy among the witnesses, no doubt. One must never lie to Rome.

'Yes,' he said.

'This is a sin against Rome, you know. Against the sacred cult of Tiberius the Emperor. And it is a crime punishable by death according to your laws, is it not?'

And again Rome, whose currency is death, can never hear equivocation. Others are weak for not dealing death, weak for seeking to avoid it. Rome's daily business is death, her nightly amusement is the death match. Death is cheap and easy among them.

'Usually, yes.'

'But of course you cannot enact this sentence.'

Death is the gift Rome reserves for itself. The people it occupies cannot pass their own sentences of execution.

'No, we cannot,' said Caiaphas.

'Give him to me,' said Pilate.

And this was not a request, and to refuse it would have meant death as surely as God smote the Egyptians at the Red Sea. If Rome wants something, Rome will have it.

And he surrendered, as if the waters of the sea were closing over his head.

'Yes,' he said.

He had the man brought up to him first of all, to tell him that they were handing him over to Rome. Yehoshuah did not respond, though he must have known what it meant. His head wobbled a little on his neck. His eyes almost closed and then jerked open. There was a bruise on his face: very probably someone had kicked him or hit him while he was imprisoned in the stable. It is impossible to root out this kind of mindless cruelty; with so many people coming and going in the Temple, it could have been anyone. He swayed. The man was ill, it was obvious. Caiaphas felt ashamed. Before they came into the iron embrace of Rome, they would have found a way to save his life. When the soldiers escorted Yehoshuah away, Caiaphas found himself staring at a door that had closed on him for a long time.

Annas told him later that they had crucified the man along with a few others, and in some piece of public theatre, had released the rebel Bar-Avo – a mistake on Pilate's part probably, but Bar-Avo was the more popular man. Perhaps Pilate knew he could recapture Bar-Avo, or thought that he could trust the man to keep the peace out of gratitude. Perhaps he was genuinely offended by this Yehoshuah's claim to be a god: Pilate has always thought that Rome would be pleased if he pressed the cult of Tiberius upon the people. In this as in so much else, he is mistaken: Annas has it on good authority that Tiberius is a little embarrassed by the whole business of worship, and refuses to allow many temples to be built to him.

Caiaphas, thinking guiltily of the man's cracked lips and wild rolling eyes – and fearing, after Annas had set him thinking on it, that his tomb might become a meeting place for rebels – sent two slaves to bury the body honestly in an unmarked Jewish grave. But by the time they arrived, the corpse had already been stolen, they said, probably by his friends or family, for who else would have taken the trouble? A pity. The whole thing had been a foolish waste of life.

And if anyone were to suggest to Caiaphas that this little episode, this regrettable but unavoidable matter, were the Holy of Holies of his life, the tiny chamber at the centre of his heart which is somehow larger than the whole edifice which surrounds it, he would frown, and half smile, and attempt to be polite, and think afterwards that he had not understood the joke. If this is a secret chamber, it is entirely empty.

It does not come from nowhere. A city does not catch fire in an instant. It has been months and years. It has been the taxes and the tribute. It has been the way the Romans look at the Jews, the little taunts, the kicked-over fruit stalls and shoulder bumps as they pass. It has been the sons and daughters who look at Rome and say to their family and to themselves, 'Why can't we live like that?' And the girls paint their faces and show too much of their thighs. And the boys shave off their bristles and go to the gymnasium to exercise naked. It has been the friends of these boys and girls, seeing them become strangers and collaborators.

It was Pilate bringing the legions with their idolatrous banners into the city when his predecessor knew well enough not to do that. It was Pilate's way of administering justice: swift, merciless, unpredictable. It was the fear that grew in the city so that no mother could see her son leave in the evening without fearing where he was going and whether he would return.

And these things rise and rise and no one stops them. And the city is full of angry men.

And the city bakes in the sun. And the city is dried up by the sun. And the city is as dry as a tinder box.

Pilate sends word again that he will have the Temple money. Caiaphas has ten priests go down into the storerooms to bring up the gold. He picks them at random, but this is all it needs. They walk through the burning-hot marble plaza at noon with their boxes of gold, saying, 'Make way, make way, these chests are bound for Prefect Pilate.'

And the curled cedar shavings are smoking in the sun. And the flint is struck. And the spark flies off.

They wait until dark. Through the roasting day, people go about their business with stiff bodies and dark waiting eyes. By the fifth hour of the afternoon the shops close up their shutters and the mothers bring their children in, and somewhere the young men are waiting but no one can see them, not yet.

In the evening, the second daily sacrifice. Every morning and every evening, a new lamb. To remind us that we must die. Caiaphas can see it in the men who come to the offering.

One of them mutters as they leave, 'Stay home tonight, Cohen.'

The others look and nod, to see that he has understood.

They wait until dark, and past dark. Into the night, they wait, standing on street corners, their cloaks pulled up around their faces. And the soldiers know something is wrong, but the garrison at Jerusalem is small and they are just standing, and they cannot arrest people for standing, and besides where would they put so many men?

One of them begins to shout. It is the old call.

'David!' he shouts. 'For David, King of the Jews!'

They take it up and throw it between them. 'For David!' 'For David!'

Like a wolf pack taking up a howl.

Their pockets are full of stones. One of them throws a stone at the shield of the small tangle of Roman men standing at the gates of their storehouse. It bounces off the shield with a dull thwack of stone on wood and tumbles clattering to the ground.

And then the sky begins to rain stones.

And the tiny smouldering spark on the cedar shaving bursts all at once into huge and beautiful and all-engulfing flames.

*

The riot goes on through the night. They set the grain store on fire, the one the Romans keep as supplies for their garrison. A thousand days' worth of wheat for a hundred men burns with the sweet smell of roasting and then the black scent of wasted wood and the death of summers past. The flames leap to the stable and the horses begin to scream in terror, kicking at the doors of their stalls, but the doors are built to withstand precisely this. Someone gets one of the stable doors open and the animals stampede through the streets, rolling their eyes and rearing and foaming, but not all of them are saved and their screams grow louder and soon there is the smell of blackened flesh, and death is always the same, whatever set the events in motion that led to it. Death and destruction are always just the same.

There is a glory in it, for the young men whose blood is up and whose limbs ache for battle and for the sweet exhaustion of the hunt. Most of them are young indeed, twelve or thirteen, or fourteen or fifteen, and they yearn for a fight. There is a delight in it, because those Romans have taken their land and laid their people low and desecrated their holy places and it is good to see them suffer.

But in the morning the streets are full of broken pots and the smell of burning in the air and the market traders are afraid to set up their little stalls and the people look at each other with downcast eyes. And Caiaphas thinks: this?

They begin to gather in the afternoon, at the Prefect's palace. They are spent now, tired now, but there are so many of them and they keep coming. All the people of Jerusalem are here, shouting out that the Temple money is holy, that the Prefect must not use it for this watercourse, that he must abandon his plans. It is not that they object to having an aqueduct, but this way of trampling down the things that are most sacred to them is abhorrent. He has not tried to understand them. They must make him understand.

The crowd grows a little ugly, in their chanting and their jeers.

'Pila-ate. Your mother was an ass and your father was a donkey.'

'No one wants you in Syria, and they hate you back in Rome, just leave us alone and crawl back home.'

The crowd is thick, full of men and women who have brought bread and water and intend to spend the day protesting. Men seem to have come from outside the city, for many of those standing quietly in the crowd, faces shaded from the sun by the hoods of their light robes, are newcomers. There are no soldiers.

A wise man, perhaps, would have let them shout themselves out, encircled them with quiet armed men and, at dusk, had them escorted from the plaza. But Pilate has too much pride for peace, that is his disaster. He leaves it until the late afternoon to address the crowd, when they are hot and thirsty after many hours, at their most irritable. He shouts down from the balcony words that are, perhaps, meant to recall Cicero, addressing an angry mob with enough vivid clarity to calm and soothe them.

But of course Pilate is no Cicero; his words are not those of the great orator, and his delivery is weedy and thin. And the language is a problem: he begins to speak in Greek and is immediately shouted down. He has Aramaic enough to try it again, but this is perhaps a mistake.

'People of Jerusalem!' he shouts, and his accent is wrong, and he puts the stress on the second syllable – ru – and not at the end, where it belongs. 'I have heard your voices!' And this is wrong too, because it sounds like a mockery of God's words telling the Children of Israel in Egypt that he has heard their cries. But nothing that Pilate says in this tongue can work. His accent proves he is not one of them and can never understand.

'Let me be clear. I seek only –' he hesitates, searching for words – 'to make your lives better, to bring you comfort and relief.'

'Fuck off home, then!' shouts one wag in the crowd, and a laugh ripples through the square.

Pilate flushes, the pink coursing up his face across his bald skull. His hand grips the marble balustrade in front of him. If the crowd were not buoyed up by their sense of invincible oneness, they would understand that they should be afraid.

'People of Jerusalem, Rome bears great love for you!'

'Shame, cos we fucking hate her!'

Another ripple of laughter. Can any man bear to be laughed at? Pilate's knuckles are white against the marble. If it were possible, his fingers would have crushed it to powder.

'It is time for you to disperse. Rome simply wants –' he coughs, as if he is being strangled – 'Rome simply wants to improve the streets of your beautiful city.'

'The streets belong to us!' someone shouts, and the crowd take it up as a chant. 'The streets belong to us! The streets belong to us!'

And Pilate's face has gone from red to white, and his nostrils flare and his eyes widen and his whole posture stiffens.

'You are common criminals,' he says, though he does not speak loudly enough for his words to reach across the crowd, 'and you deserve all that is coming to you. If you are old enough to riot, you are old enough to face the consequences.' And Pontius Pilate, who has never suffered, who has never lived under occupation, who has never been trapped by soldiers or known what it is to see those things in which you believe trampled by an overwhelming force, raises his right arm high and brings it down on the balustrade three times.

The signal is understood.

All over the square, quiet men mingling with the crowd throw back the hoods of their simple travelling cloaks and uncover their faces. And pull out their daggers.

The crowd is unarmed. It is angry and it has hurled insults, but it is not violent. They do not even have stones to throw.

The first people die before anyone has even understood what is happening. While Pilate watches grim-faced from the balustrade, five hundred plain-clothes soldiers among the crowd of ten thousand unsheathe their knives. Pull the nearest man to them by the shoulder. Lean in close. Cut through his neck so that he dies without a sound. All around the square men fall to their knees gasping, clutching at mortal wounds. Or crumple to the floor. Or try to cry out and are silenced by a swift swipe to the throat.

And then there begins to be screaming. There are men in this crowd who burned the grain store, who killed the horses, who threw the stones, this is true. But the soldiers do not differentiate between the innocent and the guilty. There are women who fall to the ground with bleeding wounds to the stomach. A young man who had stood quietly at the front of the crowd, calling for peace and dignity, is set upon by two of the soldiers, who plunge their daggers into his chest in unison and withdraw them bloody as the young man's heart struggles and ceases.

The people try to run, but those quiet men with their blades . . . well, they are human too and have suffered daily abuse from the people whose land they occupy and they are angry. Many of them are not even Roman: they are auxiliary troops brought in from the local population in Caesarea, or Samaritans brought in from north of Jerusalem. They bear Rome no more special loyalty than do the Jews. If Pilate thought he could control this once it began he was wrong. He does not have the common touch and has never sought to understand the people he governs, either the Jews or his own soldiers. He makes some other signal, a hand waving in the air, but no one is looking.

The soldiers block the exits to the square and begin to advance, forming a net around the unarmed protesters. Some people escape through the buildings and up on to the roofs. Some manage to barge through the guards at the exits, using the bodies of the dead as shields. Some soldiers have died now – only a handful compared to the three hundred, four hundred Jews dead or bleeding out under the Prefect's balcony, but enough that some of the Jews have managed to arm themselves with daggers from the corpses. They make a desperate run at the soldiers at the southern end of the square, where the line is weakest. At first the charge seems to succeed. Five soldiers fall, blood fountaining off them like water pouring from a broken aqueduct.

And the people run screaming still in all directions, but when they see the gap in the line they begin to stream through it, making for home or for safety, carrying their injured and their children away from the place of carnage. But the line closes up again and it takes two more attempts and another fifty people dead on the blood-slick stinking floor before the soldiers give in and let them run weeping from the place.

And when it is done, there are four hundred or so soldiers in the long brown robes that made them indistinguishable from the Jews panting in the sun. And six hundred bodies on the floor around them, so that the place is heaped with corpses. And the sun beats down, drying out the blood to a sticky film. And the flies settle on the bodies. And the soldiers go to wash and congratulate each other, because what else can they do now? The deed has been done and so it must have been mighty. And Pilate stands alone on his balcony and looks at the field of conquest and perhaps he wonders if this is how great Caesar feels after a battle and why it does not feel more glorious. He had read *The Gallic Wars* at school and had expected something different.

In the evening the women come weeping to take back their dead, and wash the bodies and bury them according to their custom. Great Pilate sits alone before his little statue of the God-Emperor Tiberius and utters a prayer of thanksgiving, for he is a pious man in this way and believes what he has been taught, that the mightiest man in Rome becomes its god. And in the courtyard outside Caiaphas's house, Annas and Caiaphas sit together in silence, drinking wine and listening to the wailing ululations from every part of the city.

'No one said he could possibly plan this,' says Annas after a long time.

'Did you expect he would lie down like a yearling lamb? He is a wolf, son of wolves.'

'I thought . . .' and Annas is broken. He has rarely miscalculated. 'I thought there would be a riot. And he would burn down some houses and crucify some of the rebels, but the riot would show that he had not the love of the city and Rome would take him back.'

There is a woman screaming and screaming in the night, she will not cease. The screams never waver from complete shock, as if she were discovering an insupportable tragedy over and over again.

'And what now? Will Rome summon him back for this?'

Annas shakes his head and his eyes are great and wide and staring. Caiaphas sees the tears begin, but says nothing.

'I do not know,' says Annas. 'I have sent swift messengers to Syria and to Egypt and surely they cannot leave him here now, but I do not know. No one in his own house told him not to do this. Perhaps he even took advice from Rome. I don't know what it will take to get rid of him. I do not know . . .' He pauses. 'I do not know whether God meant me to do what I have done.'

And the screams go up again, through the night that smells of blood.

Days pass and no word comes from Rome or from the Syrian Governor, and Pilate sits in the Prefect's seat yet. The people bury their dead and Pilate decides that, all said and done, perhaps he will not have that aqueduct after all. Most of the money is returned to the Temple: most, but not all. And even though this is done with the greatest ceremony and loud announcements, no one seems to take particular notice of it.

Six of the priests died in the riots and Caiaphas speaks with their families. He doesn't have to do it. Natan the Levite tells him that he can arrange it, but still Caiaphas has those conversations. When they realize, after two days, that Elikan, a young priest of eighteen, is the one whose hacked-up body they dragged from the plaza because it was dressed in priestly robes, Caiaphas himself walks down the hill to visit Elikan's older brother and tell him.

It is a sorry job. When they see him coming across the orchard, the brother's wife starts to wail in a thin, reedy tone. Nonetheless, the brother, a stern man in his forties, does not believe it until Caiaphas has said the words.

The brother holds his breath, when Caiaphas says, 'I have come with bad news for you,' and pauses, and says, 'There was fighting in the square in front of the Prefect's house. Some priests were caught up in it, we do not know how,' and the brother is still holding his breath when Caiaphas says, 'Elikan is dead. We knew him by the scar on his leg from the dog bite when he was a boy.'

And the brother lets his breath out in a single violent puff, as if someone has punched him, and says, 'I told him not to go near that dog, but he swore he could tame it.'

Caiaphas stays with them from the ninth hour of the morning until the third hour of the afternoon, and when he goes they beg him to take a little food with him for the walk and a skin of water, but he refuses.

'It was not your fault,' says the brother's wife, who seems, when she has finished weeping, quite reasonable and kind. 'No one could keep Elikan from excitement, not even the discipline of the priests.'

But as he walks back up the hill towards the gleaming white marble Temple he thinks: it was my fault, who else's fault could it be?

He does not lie with his wife at all for several weeks. And this, suddenly, is not abnormal or to be remarked on. Some people are drawn together at such times, driven to press their bodies against one another to remind themselves that their blood still courses and their loins still flame. But many find they do not have enough of themselves to spare, for a while. That the piling up of corpses has turned them inward, and no one can say that one response is natural and right and the other is not.

But nonetheless, the other matter does not leave his mind. They cannot send Darfon away for a time now, there is too much turmoil in the streets and in the land of Israel. He has Natan the Levite give the man constant duties, forbid him ever to leave the Temple enclosure.

And one afternoon Hodia's daughter comes to see him. She who, if some terrible illness or accident were to kill his wife, would become his wife. She who is therefore, in some sense, already his.

She looks shaken, as all the people in Jerusalem look shaken now. He finds these days that when he passes a man in the marketplace he has only to hear a snippet of conversation – 'Liata has not seen her son since . . .', 'They say he brought them in from Egypt so that . . .', 'I heard that Bar-Avo's men plan to . . .' – to know exactly what subject they are talking about. There is only one topic on the lips of Jerusalem. Only one thought, refracted through thousands of minds and hearts. There is a look on the faces of the people, a look of quiet uncomprehending shock, like the face of a man who has lost his father. Such a look is on the face of Hodia's daughter.

She says, and her voice is very calm and measured and low, 'Tell me how this happened.'

He shrugs and he says, 'All Jerusalem knows as much as I know.'

She shakes her head, her gentle curls stirring, the scent of her perfumes rising.

'There are a thousand different rumours. I've heard that the priests let Pilate do it because he bribed them with the Temple gold. And I've heard that Rome sanctioned it. And I've heard that it wasn't really about the money at all but revenge for an assassination plot. Which of those things are true?'

It is unusual for a woman to ask a question like this. Of a man who is not her husband, of someone she scarcely knows. But they stand in an unusual relationship to one another. He supposes she has as much right to know what kind of husband he might be as he has to ask himself and others what kind of wife she would make. And times like this change things. People meet each other's eyes differently in the streets. Strangers swap remarks or theories about the terrible events. Something has broken down in Jerusalem. And she is right in thinking that he might know more than the gossips on the street.

'No,' he says, 'it was nothing so complex. Pilate demanded his money and we gave it to him. And word got out –' he leaves a hole here, a lacuna unfilled, hoping she will not notice it – 'and we thought it would pass with a little disturbance.' She is looking at him with such shining eyes of trust. 'But Pilate is not a good man,' he says.

'He is a Roman.'

'There are better Romans and worse,' he says, 'don't listen to anyone who tries to tell you otherwise. There have been prefects we've been able to come to an accommodation with, who've tried to learn how things are here, to bend with us as we bend to them. Pilate is not like that.'

She nods. 'He put Caesar's head on the coins. My brothers said that was an offence against God.'

He runs a hand across his hair. She moves fractionally closer to him. He notices it. They are sitting in chairs next to each other. The door is slightly open, though. She moves her chair closer to his.

'People are too swift to find offence against God,' he says, 'and too slow to recognize the truth of our situation. Look.'

He stands up and walks to the window. She follows and stands close to him. A little closer than he had expected.

He points out of the window, past the Temple courtyards. She leans in close to see where his finger is pointing. It is the red-roofed Roman building facing towards the Temple, its eyes always open, its lookout always manned.

'The garrison,' she says. 'I know. I see it every day.'

'But do you know what it means?' he says.

'It means that soldiers walk among us. That strangers tread our sacred streets.'

'It means,' he says, and his hand is touching her arm, because he suddenly wants to make her really understand what he is saying, 'it means that none of us is free. Each of us is shackled, I as much as you. If we destroyed the garrison they would send a legion, and if we destroyed them they would send four, and if we fight it can only end with the sacking of Jerusalem. Rome couldn't ever lose that fight, you know, never.' He finds his wheedling politician's smile creeping across his mouth and he stops it, pursing his lips, making his face stop lying for him. 'We are trapped. All of us. No matter how high or how low, we must make accommodation with what they demand of us. I am as trapped as you.'

Her fingers find the back of his hand. She is very warm, and he realizes how cold he is.

'Is there nothing but duty?' she says. 'Nothing at all but that?'

He glances behind him. The door of the room is closed now. When did that happen? He does not take his hand away.

He shakes his head. 'Not for me. Not if we are to keep Rome from our door.'

'Nothing at all?' she asks again, and her voice is very low, and her face very sad and serious as she looks up at him from behind her lashes.

Is it possible she is a virgin? With the way she looks at him and the way she is dressed? It is possible, he knows it is. Some girls bloom like this at even twelve or thirteen: knowing, without understanding what it is they know. Watching for an effect.

Making himself examine it, he realizes she is dressed so modestly, it is impossible to fault her. A pair of loose white trousers, showing nothing of her legs. Apart from that slice of bare foot slipped into her leather shoes, visible when the trousers move just so. The brown, bare, warm skin. The tunic is loose also, seemly, white with a pale blue woven belt at the waist.

And yet when she stands, the daughter of Hodia, her black hair around her shoulders and her dark skin next to her white clothes, he can detect, somehow, the shape of her breasts under this modest garment. When she stretches her shoulders, pulling her arms back, he can see the nipples outlined for a moment against the fabric, as hard as dried beans and ringed by the raised zone of bumps he could read with his fingertips like words carved into stone.

And then he cannot help himself any longer. He pulls her towards him by her arm and she utters a little squeak but does not struggle, acquiesces softly and warmly, and he places his hand between her legs, cupping her where she is so hot, she is a furnace and he had forgotten what young girls are like, giving off so much heat.

She begins to move against his hand. This is overwhelming.

He pulls at her tunic, releasing a breast, and the excitement of feeling that warm softness and seeing the dark bruise-coloured nipple makes him hold his breath before he descends on her with his mouth.

She is soft and she is warm and she is wet and she is hard. She smells of cloves and rain.

If he fucked her and did not marry her, she would be forbidden to any other priest of the Temple. This would be a terrible disgrace. She is the daughter of a wealthy man of the priestly class. She is expected to marry a priest. And he cannot marry her while he and his wife are yet married, for the Cohen Gadol, the High Priest above all, may truly have only one wife.

He stops short of entering her, and is astonished at himself, at his own maturity and composure, at the way that he almost, almost, straining towards her, almost does so but then remembers and pulls back. He finds that what he wanted after all was to consume that body, not to be consumed by it. That his desire had been to feel out every part of her, to see the gentle undulations of her soft belly and the way her breasts fall back when she lies down, and to hear her pant and cry out, and it would not have been right to go further, he knew that before he began. They may still have a wedding night. It is not entirely impossible.

He lies with her in the stillness of the hot afternoon on the floor of his chamber.

He says, 'You were really never with any man before?'

She shakes her head gently, the sweat glistening on her cheek.

'Never a man,' she says.

Hmm, he thinks. Then: oh.

'Oh,' he says. It is the secret dream of the priests when they see the women's enclosure and the curtained-off places where the women go. He allows this thought to grow in his mind, relishing the way it almost overwhelms his control. Almost, but not quite. If he wanted, if he were willing to relinquish certain other things, he could have this woman, she could be his wife. It is not impossible for a High Priest to divorce, just, in his case, unwise.

A thought occurs to him.

'Tell me,' he says, 'I do not know your name.'

Her smile is mocking.

'You have never thought to ask one of your many servants and advisers?'

He shakes his head.

'What would you have called me on our wedding night? "Hodia's daughter"?'

He reaches a hand to her soft breast again.

'Beloved,' he says, 'I would have called you beloved, as in the Song of Solomon. And kissed you with kisses of the mouth, for you are sweeter than wine.'

She does not seem displeased by this, but there is a thinking mind behind those dark eyes.

'Did you ever love a woman without noticing whose daughter she was?'

He looks at her, while his hand kneads at her breast and the desire rises in him again, pleasingly.

'No,' he says. 'Did you ever love a man without noticing his power?'

'Never a man,' she says. And try as he might, he never gets more of the story than that from her.

She leaves before it is time for the evening service. Though he is sad to see her put away her dark and comely body, he knows that it must be so.

At the door, she pauses and says, 'Batsheni.'

He frowns.

'My name,' she says.

'Ah.' It is not a respectful name for a woman like this. 'I think I would rather call you "beloved".'

'Nonetheless,' she says, 'Batsheni is my name. "Second daughter". In case my father ever forgot which order we came in, I suppose. The boys are called "God will make me strong", "God will enrich me", "God approves my right hand" and so on.'

She closes the door softly as she leaves and the scent of her oils still hangs sweet in the room.

And that evening, when he visits the sanctuary, the chamber next to the Holy of Holies, for solitary prayer, he bends down and picks up a pinch of dust from the floor. He folds it into a scrap of linen and tucks it into his waistband. He keeps it safe.

★

Every morning and every evening, a yearling lamb makes sweet savours for the Lord – the perpetual daily sacrifice. And after that, between the many sacrifices brought by the people for sins and to make peace, to give thanks to the Lord for saving their life, in between all that at some point, every day, Caiaphas makes the offering on behalf of Rome. Every day, he sacrifices a pure white-fleeced lamb for the glory of the Emperor far beyond the Great Sea.

It is a compromise. For Rome has found it cannot operate in Judea in the same way that it franchises out its business to all its many other conquered states. There is an accepted routine which has worked well in these many other nations.

'Congratulations,' says Rome, after its armies have torn down the defending walls and set alight the pointed fences and killed the fathers and husbands and sons and brothers who had gone out that morning painted with war paint and screaming battle cries, 'hearty congratulations to you, for you are now part of the Roman Empire. We will defend you against barbarians and bring you roads and aqueducts and various other civic amenities. In exchange you will give us tribute and we will take some of your people as slaves and exhibit your king and your precious objects in a triumph in Rome.'

'Yes,' say the conquered people, barely able to draw their eyes away from the smouldering heaps of men and animals and timber and stone, 'that seems . . . yes.'

'Very good. And one other thing,' says Rome, 'tell me, what is your local god here?'

'Why,' mumble the people, 'we worship the Great Bull of the Mountain,' or it might be the Heron King, or Almighty Ba'al along with the Sea God Yam, or Mother Isis and her son, who dies and is born again each year.

'How charming,' says Rome, 'we worship our current Emperor, Tiberius, and various members of his family, both those living and those forever alive, for they have conquered death. Here are their statues. Place them in your Temple and worship them as you do your Great Bull. That will be all.'

'Yes,' say the conquered people, as the stench of burning enters their nostrils and their eyes begin to water.

This approach, so helpful in tying conquered peoples into Rome in all other places, was surprisingly ineffective in Judea. It was because of the particular laws of the people: not to make an image of their one God, not to accept that His powers could be divided into separate entities, not to create any statue even of their most revered prophets or to allow any such emblem to be placed within their Temple. No man, say the Jews, can become a god and that is an end of it.

They attempted it, early on. Just a little statue of, let us say, the Blessed Augustus. Just one, here in an outer courtyard. The battles were so long and so bloody that even the Romans became sickened by the slaughter necessary to keep that little figure in its place. These people would rather die, each one of them, even the children, than give up the sanctity of their holy places. It is an unusual and puzzling level of dedication to a god who cannot be seen or touched or felt.

But Rome is nothing if not flexible. Within limits. Annas, who was High Priest at the time, suggested a way around so many difficulties.

'We cannot worship your God-Emperor,' he explained sadly to the Prefect, 'the people will not tolerate it. But we can dedicate some of our worship to him.'

And Rome sighed and said, 'Very well.'

So, instead of the forbidden statue in a courtyard, there is this. Caiaphas slaughters a lamb every day, just one sacrifice among many, but this one dedicated to the health and well-being of the Emperor Tiberius, whose reach stretches even to this distant province.

And there are those who call him a traitor for this. In general, the young priests are so eager to perform Temple services that they race to compete for them, or draw lotteries to see who will get the honour. But not for this sacrifice. They go to it grudgingly, having to be summoned repeatedly. Even the lambs do not behave, bucking and bleating and kicking out.

But what can one do? One lamb among so many, to keep Rome

happy. But, say the mutterers, nothing can keep her happy. But we must try to keep her happy. This is my task, he says to himself as he brings the knife towards the lamb, this is my duty, this is how we keep the Temple standing and the services being offered. This, this, only this.

In the private pre-dawn light when the household is sleeping, Caiaphas takes a horn of ink and a quill and a strip of vellum cut from the end of a letter he had written to save it for another occasion. He dips the sharpened feather into the rich black ink. Holds it so that the bead of excess liquid drips back into the horn. Tamps it against the silver-rimmed edge so that his first stroke on the vellum will be clean and clear.

He holds the parchment still with his left hand and begins to write with his right. It is the words of the curse against adultery. 'If you are defiled by a man who is not your husband, the Lord shall make you a curse and a watchword among your people. And the bitter waters of the curse shall go into your bowel and make your belly swell and your thighs wither.'

He takes particular care over one of the words. The short horizontal line of the *yud* with its tiny tail at the right, like a tadpole. Then the house-like structure of the letter *hei*: a solid horizontal line held up by a long vertical coming down on the right, and a small vertical line inside, as if it were sheltering from the rain. Then a *vav*, proud and tall, like a *yud* grown to manhood. Then the final *hei*. The pen scratches on the parchment. The black ink runs minutely into imperfections in the vellum. It is done. There is the name of God.

He waits and watches for the ink to dry. It seems wrong to leave the paper. He has turned it into one of the holiest things on earth. So he just waits, as the ink soaks in and changes colour slightly. He blows on it a little. It does not take very long. The sun is just peeping over the horizon when it is done. The ink is dry. He holds the vellum in his hand. This thing is so holy now that, if it were to become worn or tattered, it must be buried in a grave, like the body of one whose soul is departed.

He places the ink horn and the quill back on their appointed shelf. He goes to the well in the courtyard of his house. He fills a small slender-necked jug with water. He sits beneath the vines and fruit trees as the birds begin to call out with joy for the start of a new day.

He looks at the parchment for a long time, taking in the letters. The curse which cannot harm unless harm has already been done. The name of God. An impossible tense of the verb 'to be', which suggests somehow at the same time something which both is and was, something which has been and will be. It is entirely forbidden to destroy this name once it is written. Except for one sacred purpose.

Without thinking too hard, at last, he plunges the paper into the water. Waves it to and fro. Watches as the letters dissolve until there is nothing on the paper at all. The name of God is now in the water. The curse is in the water. They are bitter waters. He takes from his belt the folded-over piece of linen he keeps with him always. He retrieves from it the pinch of dust he took from the outer sanctuary. Drops it into the water. Shakes the jug to dissolve it.

He brings an empty wineskin from the kitchen – the servants are just beginning to rise, he can hear them moving slowly upstairs. He pours the holy water into the skin. Holds it close to his beating heart, as if he can feel the name of God inside it. It is done.

A week goes past with no disturbance. Then two, then three. Shops and market stalls begin to reopen. The barber in the road next to Caiaphas's city house sings one morning in the late summer as he used to do. The maker of pots produces a new design of interlocking wheat sheaves, very pretty. No one fulminates in the market square or passes seditious notes from one hand to another. It is like the silence after a thunderclap.

It has been a little while since Annas came to visit. He comes now cheerfully, as if that moment of self-doubt is entirely expunged from his mind. He bears scrolls of parchment with some good news. The harvest in the north is successful. And Pilate has received a sharp note from Syria about the massacre in the square.

'They have warned him that if this continues he will be recalled,' says Annas, as his daughter pours for them the wine of the evening.

And the daughter, Caiaphas's wife, looks up suddenly and says, 'If this continues? So you are saying we will have to have another massacre before he can be sent home?'

If she were another man's daughter, or merely Caiaphas's wife, Annas would have raged at her. Caiaphas has seen his rages: terrifying and cold when they arrive, and sudden. Caiaphas prepares himself for the onslaught, feels the muscles of his shoulders tensing and his thighs bunching and his heart beginning to race.

But there is no rage. She has taken the fire out of him with a few words. As a man's daughter can, sometimes, if she knows him well.

Annas stares off into the distance. His face crumples. He looks older suddenly than he did. He is becoming elderly, he is nearing sixty.

'Yes,' he says, his voice deep and rumbling. 'Yes, I think we will have to have another massacre before they recall him. I think that is what will happen.' He looks at her. 'Is that what you wanted to hear?'

She raises her eyebrows. 'I wanted to know that you knew it.'

She brings another wooden chair from the covered part of the garden and sits with them. She sits closer to Caiaphas than to her father. She covers Caiaphas's hand with hers and squeezes it. There is a reason that he married her. Not just because of who her father is, but also because of who she is for being his daughter. He did see her, when he agreed to marry her. He could not see through her skin, but he did see something.

'You've put Caiaphas in a hideous position,' she says, 'I suppose you know that.'

'Is it my fault?' starts Annas, and then, 'No, you are right. In the southern kingdom they've already sent word that they want you removed, Caiaphas. They have their own man for the job.' He shrugs and chuckles. 'He wouldn't be any improvement, let me tell you.'

'Removing you solves nothing,' she says to Caiaphas, 'I think Pilate will trust you a little more after all this. Because it ended so badly, because he lost control of his own men. He thinks you're in it together now. Despised by your own side. Neither of you wanting to admit how it happened.'

Annas nods slowly. 'He thinks you miscalculated. Good.'

Caipahas wants to point out the obvious thing, but cannot. For fear.

His wife says it instead. 'He doesn't know it was you, father, who miscalculated.'

Annas shrugs his shoulders. 'Let him think he has a friend. You can play that part, can't you, Caiaphas?'

Caiaphas, whose special gift is to lie so well he does not even notice himself doing it, says, 'Everyone thinks I am their friend.'

The next day, he takes his wife on a long walk in the hills.

'Come,' he says, 'while the countryside is safe and the bandits are quiet. Let us walk in the quiet of the hills and today another priest will perform the daily sacrifices.'

She looks at him oddly. For he is speaking oddly. And it is an odd request. But they used to do so when they were newly married. He brings wine with them, and a little dry bread and hard cheese. And skins of water, including one which he is very particular to keep separate from the rest.

The hills are stepped and dotted with cypress and twisted olive trees. The earth is red and yellow, and the path is dry. Lizards sit basking on rocks, blinking as they approach, too lazy to move. Their feet become dirty from the dust, but it is good to walk and walk, as if their bodies could outpace their minds. They talk of the children and the family.

He finds a shady place for them to sit. His wife is smiling now, puzzled, as if she did not know him. He does not know himself.

He passes her some of the bread and the cheese. They eat. They drink the wine. They are softened by the sun.

He says, and he had not known he would begin like this, 'I have seen you with Darfon the Levite.'

Her whole body stiffens. Like the turning of the crowd when

Pilate raised his hand and gave his signal and the soldiers showed themselves. He has revealed the traitor in her midst.

'I do not know who that is,' she says slowly and at last.

'I could take you to the Temple,' he says, 'and bare your breasts in front of the high altar and accuse you of adultery. I could put that shame on you.'

She says, 'You would not dare to do it.'

He shrugs. 'I have never known you at all, I think,' he says. 'You were only ever Annas's daughter to me, and perhaps I was only ever a man suitable to be High Priest to you.'

She looks at him, her eyes dark and angry.

'If I were a man,' she says, 'I would be High Priest and make a better job of it than my brothers.'

He gives a little nod to show that he agrees. This is not the matter at hand, though.

'I could divorce you,' he says, 'but it would bring shame to the children and we want Ayelet to be married next year.'

'I did not lie with him,' she says.

And he shows her the wineskin of bitter waters. And tells her what it is. She starts to laugh.

'At your foresight,' she says when he asks. 'At the plans you have made when Jerusalem was burning around you and men were slain in the streets.'

'It is the same thing,' he says. 'It is all part of the same thing. All the different lies, and the plans, and the men we give them.' He has learned, under Rome, to be careful and cunning and never to act too quickly and never without a smile or a pleasant face.

'Yes, I know,' she says, shaking her head. 'Do you think I have not heard all this before from my father? I know how it is. To keep the Temple standing, we do this and this and this, and –' She breaks off. Stretches her arms behind her so that he is reminded for a moment of Hodia's daughter.

She snatches the wineskin from his hands. Looks into his eyes.

She says, 'My father told me about applying this curse to women

187

suspected of adultery. He said that often they never had to drink the water at all. That women who were guilty would start to weep and shake when they saw the bitter waters and confess. And those who were innocent would drink it down without fear.'

She says, 'I swear I am no adulteress and may all the curses of heaven fall on me if I am.'

She meets his gaze as she drinks and drinks, gulping it down, some water spilling over her chin, drinking it all until the wineskin is empty and she takes it from her mouth and her mouth is full of water. She does not look away from him as she takes the last gulp. She wipes her mouth and chin with her forearm. She throws the wineskin at his feet.

They walk back to Jerusalem together, not talking. She does not help him when he stumbles. He does not give her an arm over the high stone wall of a farm. The silence between them is as thick as woollen fleece. But still they walk together. For there is a presence howling and prowling on these hills and, if they separated, they would become prey for the wolves.

Nothing is settled forever. Every peace is temporary.

The dove sellers come before him again, this time one with a blackened eye and another with a tooth missing.

It is a man in his forties who brandishes the tooth like a nugget of gold.

'Do you see what they've done to me? Do you see? Those mongrels, those monsters, that pack of dogs!'

This time he bans several of the men from the Temple court-yards altogether, and tells them to make reparations for the disturbances amounting to more than a talent of gold in total. It cannot go on like this, and yet there is no other way for it to go on.

The brother of Elikan – the eighteen-year-old priest who died in the riot in the plaza – comes to visit him. His name is Shlomo, the brother, he had not thought to ask that before, or perhaps he had forgotten the name. His wife has given him four living sons, thank

God, and the eldest is now approaching thirteen, when it will be time to begin his Temple service. The son belongs to the Temple, as do all male children in the family of the priests.

'Perhaps,' says Shlomo, 'you would be prepared to meet the boy? To offer him some guidance? He remembers his uncle Elikan with great fondness.'

And Caiaphas knows what Shlomo is asking.

'Is he with you?'

Shlomo brings the boy in. He is gangly and nervous, with a voice on the edge of breaking which wavers from high to low pitch within a single sentence. He does not speak much.

'What is your name?' says Caiaphas, trying to be kind.

'Ovadya-Elikan,' says the boy.

'He took on the name himself, after his uncle died,' says Shlomo proudly.

'Come to see me Ovadya-Elikan,' says Caiaphas, 'when you begin your service. And we'll make sure you get to know everyone in the Temple.'

Shlomo is grateful. He himself serves his turns at the Temple offices but has never had a friend in such a high position before. Much good may it do him, thinks Caiaphas.

Natan the Levite tells him that Darfon, son of Yoav, will set out this very afternoon for the north, where his strong arms will be of the greatest use in loading barrels of wine and oil on to carts and his cunning brain will be most welcome in figuring the accounts. Caiaphas feels a certain relief at that, but then at once his mind starts to seek out whom his wife might turn to now, in Darfon's absence. He cannot send every man in Jerusalem to the north.

'And Pilate wants to see you,' says Natan. 'No,' he continues, before Caiaphas can ask the question, 'he didn't say why and I didn't ask.'

They look at each other. Every peace is temporary.

Pilate is full of himself. The rebellion has been quashed; Rome surely sent disapproving words merely to placate their own guilty consciences. But he has acted strongly and rightly. This is how a Roman man behaves.

He greets Caiaphas warmly. There is no soldier standing guard today.

'Can you sense the mood in the city, Caiaphas?' he asks. 'They have felt the touch of my power. They know who is their master now, and they have given up all resistance like obedient slaves.'

Or like clever slaves, who will heal their wounds and gather their resources before beginning to plan the next rebellion.

'Yes,' says Caiaphas, 'you have shown them what you are willing to do.'

'They cannot help but respect it, Caiaphas! Like a woman, they long to be governed.'

Like a woman. Yes, exactly like a woman. Who has laboured and survived, who has raised a child. Similarly fearless of pain, careless of self in protection of something greater than herself.

'I think I will bring the golden images of Tiberius back from Caesarea. He is their lord and high master, he is their god and rightful king. They should kneel before his statue and kiss his feet.'

'Exactly as you say, Prefect.'

'This is not a bad country, you know. A few rotten apples in the barrel, but mostly decent hard-working families. They will be grateful to me for rooting out those bad elements. I will turn around the lives of those families. With this rioting on the streets, your society has become morally degenerate, but I will repair it!'

A memory skitters across Caiaphas's mind, as if he has heard a speech before delivered with the same shining eyes, the same absolute self-assurance. But the memory is gone before he can recall the dingy robes and the glowing clouds of heaven.

'Certainly you are right, Prefect,' he says, 'but I do not know if the people of Jerusalem deserve your love. Look at how they rebelled: not only against you but against me! Lavish your praise rather on Caesarea, on the Decapolis, on the loyal regions.'

'Come, come,' says Pilate, 'you're letting your injured pride get the better of you. And yet you are right . . . perhaps this city is not yet worthy of the statues of Tiberius, their God-Emperor.'

The conversation continues. This, here, is the work of Caiaphas's life. This.

There are only two outcomes to the ritual for a man who has a suspicion about his wife. She must drink the bitter waters. And if she is guilty the curse will fall upon her and she will die. And if she is innocent she will conceive a child. And if neither of these things happens?

Caiaphas's wife does not die. She does not talk to him any longer except about matters connected to the family and the running of the house. She sits and comments on his conversations with Annas and gives her opinion. Her belly does not swell and her thighs do not wither.

But nor does she conceive a child. How could she, indeed, since he does not lie with her for several months? He waits, and no sickness falls upon her and no child grows in her womb. In the end, without conversation, he begins to lie with her again in the nights. If she conceives a child, then at least he will know, he thinks, as he ploughs her again and again. She does not resist him. It is fierce between them now, as it never was when they lied and pretended to love one another.

There is another option. The rabbis tell us that if a woman has studied Torah in great detail, the merit of her learning may delay the enactment of the curse on her body. Her knowledge is a shield, keeping her husband's will from blighting her. If a woman is learned enough, the curse against adultery may never kill her. This is why it is vitally important never to teach a woman Torah.

Caiaphas doubts whether Annas bore these strictures in mind when deciding upon his daughter's education. She does not conceive a child. She does not die. He reminds himself that he did not perform the ritual entirely properly: that she should have made a meal offering at the Temple first, that it should have been done in front of several priests. Nonetheless. She drank the bitter waters willingly, having accepted the curse on herself. Perhaps Annas taught her a great deal of Torah. But perhaps there is another reason.

Something has gone now. The presence of God that howled like a whirlwind, that spat blood and fire upon the Egyptians, that stalked by the side of the Children of Israel through the desert, protecting and terrifying in equal measure, that is gone. There was a time when every man saw God face to face at Mount Sinai, there was a time when His wonders were as clear as the edicts of Rome and when His might toppled mountains and destroyed nations. There was a time when He raged for us and nothing could stand before Him.

But not now. Not since that first stone tumbled from the wall and Jerusalem was breached. We must have done something wrong, for that almighty righteous power to have withdrawn itself, to have become so small that it sits, alone, in the Holy of Holies inside the Temple, and does not bestir itself to protect us even from faceless men following their leader's orders. The only explanation is that we did something terribly wrong.

Natan the Levite comes to inform him that, all being well, Hodia's daughter will be betrothed after Yom Kippur is over. She is older than the previous girl, it is not right to make her wait much longer. They have found a good man for her – he names a man over twenty years her senior who is thought much of in the Temple. Caiaphas holds the man in his mind, trying to recall him exactly.

'Itamar? That dried-up husk?'

The man is nearing forty and has never married, nor ever shown much interest in women. Caiaphas cannot imagine that Hodia's daughter will take much delight in the marriage, though it will cement a solid bond of loyalty for her father, for Itamar is the brother and cousin of important men.

Natan nods his head slowly with a rueful smile. 'I know. A girl like that. So . . .' Natan moves his hands unconsciously, as if imagining squeezing her breasts.

'Ah, well. It will happen only if my wife should chance not to die,' he says, with that practised smile.

Natan the Levite laughs. 'Yes, only if the faint possibility comes to pass that your young and healthy wife does not die.'

She will not die. Someone has done something terribly wrong, but he does not know who.

Later, in the autumn, it is Yom Kippur again. He is sequestered for seven days. He fasts and prays. On the day of Yom Kippur itself he, like all the Jews, does not eat or drink even water from sunset to sunset, so that they may pray for forgiveness of their sins. He dons his golden robes for part of the ceremony. He sacrifices the bull. And then he wears the pure white linen garments, for it is time for him to go into the Holy of Holies, to risk death in order to secure the Lord's forgiveness for His people.

He balances the shovel with the glowing coals on its blade in his armpit and on the crook of his elbow. He plunges both his hands into the basin of incense, bringing out two thick, sticky handfuls. He walks slowly – the body moves more slowly when it has taken no food or water – towards the Holy of Holies, the place where he will meet God. Two of his priests, with eyes averted, draw back the curtain.

He enters the room. The curtains close behind him. The only light is the dull red glow of the coals. He relaxes the grip of his shoulder muscles, placing the shovel on the raised platform where the Ark of the Covenant once stood.

Perhaps it was different when those holy items were here: not only the Ark, but also the stone tablets on which the Lord had written the laws in letters of fire, the jewelled breastplate whose stones illuminated to give messages from the Lord, a jar of the manna which fell in the wilderness, still miraculously fresh and delicious after so many centuries. We know that these things were here because our tradition is clear on the matter. It was so, but somehow the things were lost when the Babylonians invaded the country and burned the Temple and took our people into slavery more than five hundred years ago.

This generation – obsessed with wealth and status – does not, perhaps, merit the miracles vouchsafed to our ancestors. So perhaps it was different then. It must be that it was different.

He drops the incense on to the shovel. The room becomes full of the scent of the burning resins and gums and spices at once, a thick choking heady multilayered aroma. He breathes through his nose. He kneels. He prays, using the words he has learned by heart, words of the psalms of David, who found favour in the eyes of the Lord. He begs the Lord for His forgiveness for His people, he gives his service faithfully and holds the love of the Lord in his heart. This is the moment for which the whole edifice was constructed: not just the holiest place but the priests and their courtyard, the men and their sacrifices, the women and their prayers, the Temple herself. And not just the Temple, but the whole holy city of Jerusalem. And not just Jerusalem but the whole of the land of Israel. For this moment here, when he will speak to God face to face.

And it is true that other men have died in this place, that their fellow priests have had to pull them out by the rope that is even now tied around his own ankle. But he does not know what has killed them. He prays here until the incense smoke has filled the whole chamber. And his heart yearns to the Lord, as it does when he prays to Him every day, and his mind is full of the love of the Lord. But there is no crackling light, no sounds that are also shapes and colours, no miracle and no mystery. No force pushes him to the floor, no voice rebounds in his head. He prays, and that is all.

And when the room has filled with the thickly scented smoke, he pulls back the curtain and leaves the empty chamber. And the people rejoice, for he has returned from death to life and so they know that God has forgiven their sins. And his own experience of the moments is entirely irrelevant.

Bar-Avo

There is a Roman sport. It is called 'one of two will die, and the crowd will decide which'.

They love this sport. It is their most glorious entertainment. They play it with slaves and captured enemies, they roar and cheer at the spectacle of it. They set up two men – perhaps one with a sword and shield, the other with a net and trident – in a round patch of burnt sand with the smell of other men's sweat and blood still in the air. And they say: fight. And if the men say: we will not fight, they say: then we will kill you both. If you want to have a chance to live, you must fight.

And when one man is beaten and bloodied and breathing in ragged gasps on the floor, the first man raises his sword and looks to the Governor or the Prefect or the Emperor, who listens to the shouts of the crowd. Mostly, the people like to see a death, but if the crowd shout loudly enough for some beloved gladiator, the man may be spared to fight another day.

In this way, the Governor or the Prefect or the Emperor seems to have the gift of life in his hands. In this way, he appears to be rescuing one man from death. Rather than the truth. Which is that he has condemned both men to die some day, in some place if not in this, for no better reason than that the sport and the sight of it please him and the crowd. It is a good trick, to kill a man while still appearing to be the one who saves a life.

When the time comes for Bar-Avo to look into the face of the Prefect, he knows that he sees a man who, like him, has killed so many men that he can no longer remember their names or count the number or think of how each death felt as it escaped between his fingertips. Men like these recognize each other, and he sees the same sense at the end of it all of looking back across one's life and

197

thinking: so many and still not done yet? So many dead and still the business is not finished?

But Bar-Avo rarely looks back, if truth be told. For a man like Bar-Avo, everything is a constant present. Like a fight, where each blow must be landed or dodged now, and now, and now. The life that he lives is like that. He is always looking into the face of the Prefect, and he is always listening to the crowd calling out, 'Barabbas! Barabbas!' and he is always, always feeling the knife in his hand and advancing on the old man and attempting – he knows not exactly why – to comfort his shuddering as he brings the blade towards his throat and bleeds him in less time than it takes to draw one in-breath.

There is Giora to his left, and Ya'ir to his right, and they are roaring at the soldiers. Ya'ir is shorter, stocky, already sprouting hair across his chest although they are only fourteen. Giora is tall, athletic, nimble. He, in the centre, is neither particularly strong nor particularly fast, but he is brave and clever.

'Come on!' he shouts to the soldiers, and it's easy because he knows Giora and Ya'ir will back him up. 'Come and get us if you're not too fucking scared!'

It was like those dare games they'd played as children. Dare you to climb that tree. Dare you to walk into the dark cave alone. Dare you to dive from that rock.

'Did you leave your balls back home, Samaritan scum?'

That one's his too. It makes Ya'ir and Giora crease up laughing.

He starts a chant: 'No balls! No balls! No balls!'

'I dare you to throw a pebble at those soldiers' shields. Just a pebble. I dare you,' he says to Ya'ir.

A boy, dared to do something, can he refuse? Would he even want to refuse? When the pebble is so shiny and smooth in his hand, and the sea of shields is so gleamingly tempting. Ya'ir stares at the pebble, feeling it with his fingertips. For a moment they think he won't do it. Then he throws it. It bounces off the metal and pings on the ground. And nothing happens. Behind their helmets the soldiers are impassive.

A few other boys are watching them now. Standing behind them on the street. Maybe backing them up, maybe ready to run if something kicks off.

'Come on,' says one of them, 'something bigger. Come on.'

Come on. That pottery jar, the small one. Giora, greatly daring, spins around, noticing the dark-eyed girls watching them from a rooftop. He hurls the jar, it shatters and still the soldiers do nothing. The boys are getting bigger by the moment now, strutting and squaring their shoulders. They smell of boy-sweat and bottled-up anger. They're remembering how the soldiers treat them in the streets, how they get pushed to the back of the line in the market, how the soldiers laugh at them, how they accuse them of thieving when they were just looking, how they search them for weapons in the street like criminals. All of them are suspect just because of who they are. They're remembering how one of these soldiers took out that girl they like. Because isn't this always how it is, over and over again?

Come on. It's his turn now, Bar-Avo's. He hefts half a brick, feeling the weight of it, then hurls it in a wide arc. It bangs against a shield. It leaves a dent, and the boys laugh and shout, 'Look what you've done!' just like their mums would. They surge forward towards the soldiers but then lose their nerve before they reach the line of bronze men. They jeer at each other, fall back.

Someone throws a cobblestone. It gets a man on his head, he falls down. He's all right, he's moving, but the boys are shocked for a moment. Bar-Avo can see him holding his head, moaning. It's a nasty sight but at the same time exciting. Something's going to happen, his whole body knows it. The soldiers start shouting: angry barked commands. The boys don't understand, the soldiers' accents are thick, the words they're using aren't Aramaic or Hebrew.

Bar-Avo feels himself becoming strong, the blood coming to all the right places as if his heart knew that this is what a man is made for. Now he'll be a man, right here, father or no. The soldiers start to advance, orderly in their phalanx, and now it's on. Giora runs towards the soldiers, roaring and throwing cobblestones with both hands, and he gets another one, knocks him down, and then the line breaks, because one of the other men decides to chase, even though his commander shouts at him to come back, to hold the line, not to be an idiot.

Bar-Avo shouts and laughs and grabs his friend's arm and now they're off, leaping and running, and the blood surging and their limbs singing, and shouting with fear and delight like a toddler chased by a parent pretending to be a monster. They whoop as they scramble over stalls and climb lumber piles, and grab on to roof struts to run along thatch or tile, grabbing handfuls of mud or broken pots to hurl at the soldiers. It is like the feeling when they first held a girl, because even though they had never done the thing before they knew exactly what to do somehow.

Ya'ir is the first one to set a torch of straw and oil aflame and throw it among the soldiers with a jar of oil, which splashes fire on to the men's legs and feet, causing a great howl. He laughs when he hears the sound, baring his teeth, and the others let out a rallying cry and begin to find flaming things to hurl.

And now it is a running battle on the streets. The soldiers advance, and the boys retreat, but each time they retreat they've done a little more damage, and the soldiers are a little more ragged, and the boys are a little deeper into the streets of houses where they've known everyone all their lives and anyone would take them in. Bar-Avo and Giora slip through the tiny gap between the house of Shulamit the seamstress and Zakai the spice seller, the gap that doesn't look like it's there at all, just wide enough to take their skinny frames, and collapse in the courtyard for a moment, their bodies aching from laughter and fear and exertion all at once.

They climb up on to the roof. Bar-Avo shows his bum to the soldiers. All around the streets, there's laughter and shouting. From another rooftop, three girls are watching the battle, whispering behind their hands and giggling. The boys fighting down below spot them and play up to it. Giora does a backflip along the street as other boys throw pots and bottles. The girls applaud and shout – commentary to the boys on where the soldiers are coming from, admiration for the acrobatics, anger to the advancing troops.

The thing turns from comedy to violence and back again as swift as a knife. One of those flaming jars of oil hits a soldier – his leg and arm begin to burn and his screams are hideous before his fellows smother the flames with a blanket and even still he whimpers as they carry him off. A red-headed boy is caught by the soldiers and, as he struggles to escape, one of them pulls out a sword and cuts off – somehow, in an awkward close-fought struggle – three fingers of his left hand so he is suddenly howling and bloody.

And yet over here Bar-Avo is clambering between buildings when a goat rushes out from a backyard enclosure, panicking at some small fire, and knocks him to the ground so that his friends laugh and point and howl with mirth. He picks himself up. His pride is a little injured and he makes up for it with a brilliant scheme, luring the soldiers down an alleyway with taunts, then scrambling up the wall with his friends' help while, from the rooftops, the others pelt them with rotten fruit in a box they'd found left over from the market.

There is no conclusion to the battle. It goes on like this until nightfall, with the soldiers making sudden rushes, capturing a few boys, and the boys throwing stones and sometimes fiery things and sheltering in houses and shouting rude slogans. A storage barn burns and they watch the flames together, fascinated by the slow crumbling tumble of the building folding in on itself. The fighting peters out before dawn, and Bar-Avo has still not been caught.

He has had a good riot. He was one of those young men throwing fire-bottles but they did not take him, although a soldier had his leg at one moment and at another he scaled a wall to find a soldier waiting for him with a red shouting face on the other side. He and Giora helped one another escape through a soft place in the roof of a cowshed and then patched it up so that the soldiers who followed them in could not find them. Giora laughed so much that he fell to his knees and almost sank through the roof again.

There were girls watching them, and there was much pretence of protecting them even though the girls could easily have got away, but they nonetheless stayed on that roof, playing at being protected. And after sunset, as the day began to grow dim and the sky was the colour of bright blossom shrivelling to black and the night sounds of the mountains began to rise up, the soldiers slunk away back to barracks. They were dragging a captive or two but went so sullenly and having taken so little that the boys shouted catcalls behind them and the girls whispered, 'You won, you really won.' There were two sets of hands around Bar-Avo's waist in the dark and two sweet pliant bodies pressed against him and the girls did not seem to mind sharing as the night closed in and their hot mouths found him ready.

That is his first riot, and it seems as far away from death as it is possible for any experience to be. When he wakes the morning after, his head so clear and alive that he feels that God has made the sun rise inside his own skull, he wants to do it again, and again, and again, and wishes with his whole heart that every day would be a day of climbing and shouting and throwing and goats and manure and backflips and oil jars, and that every night could be like the night that has just passed sweet and warm and that every morning for the whole of his life would be like this blue radiant dawn.

He's been taken notice of already. His cleverness and his daring and his eagerness for the fight – that last one most of all. Men older than him, men who never gave up the battle even when that stone in the wall fell in and the Romans breached the citadel, those men look at the rioters and pick out which ones seem to have something more than the rest.

There is a man, Av-Raham, who sits in the marketplace most mornings, sipping occasionally from a bowlful of smoke. He has a little pot belly and his hair is thin at the crown, but he has a shrewd eye, and men come to him all morning long with questions and requests. He is the one who knows where those cartloads of wheat looted from the Romans ended up. His friends are the people who receive the extra measures of oil which somehow appear when there are bandits in the north. It is he who owns the sharpest swords in Jerusalem, and he to whom one goes if one needs medicine, or aid, or revenge.

They bring Bar-Avo to him the morning after the riot. Bar-Avo is cocky, at least at first. He's only fifteen and he doesn't know what he's doing here. A small corner of him suspects that he's in trouble. A larger part of him doesn't care, because last night he had two girls and nothing that happens this morning can ever erase that. He's still buzzing from the fight.

They'd found him naked under a pile of old sacks, fucking one of those two girls again, his hair a cloud around his face, both of them moving slowly, tired but unable to stop. They'd waited until he was finished and then said, 'Av-Raham would like to see you.' And Bar-Avo had taken a swig of water from a jug by his side, swirled it around in his mouth, spat it out into the straw and said, 'What if I don't want to see him?' They had explained most politely that Av-Raham was a good friend to his friends. And, swaggering, Bar-Avo had gone.

There was something he liked about the deferential air surrounding Av-Raham. He couldn't help imagining how it would feel to be the man whom others talked to in low voices, asked favours of and consulted. He was old – over fifty probably – and not handsome, not like Bar-Avo, but there was something charismatic about him. Over the years Bar-Avo would watch him closely to see how he did it. The formation of the inner circle within his group of followers. The constant denial that he was a man of any importance whatever. The impression that he was holding secrets and that, perhaps, he spoke to God. These are the skills by which a man leads, inspiring both love and fear.

That morning, the conversation was brief.

'They tell me you acquitted yourself well in the battle yesterday.'

Bar-Avo has all the humility of a teenager.

'Yes,' he says. 'No one can climb as well as me, no one else hit as many soldiers with the oil pots, I think those are the most important things.'

Av-Raham smiled an amused smile.

'The most important things. Tell me, do you hate Rome?'

And there's no question, none at all. Rome is all the things that are wrong in all the world.

'Yes.'

'Then we may find a use for you. You are the son of Mered, aren't you?'

The mention of his father stings him. He was not a good father. Bar-Avo has not seen him for a long time.

'I'm a man now. It doesn't matter whose son I am.'

And Av-Raham's eyes meet those of one of the men standing beside him and they both laugh. Bar-Avo cannot read the laugh, cannot see that it says: yes, we understand that, we have said those words ourselves when we were boys.

Bar-Avo shouts at this ring of slow, thoughtful men, 'Do not ask me about my father! My father is dead! I have no father!'

And Av-Raham says, slowly, 'None of us has a father.'

Bar-Avo looks around at them, trying to see if they are mocking him.

'Or at least, God is our father,' says Av-Raham, 'no other father matters. You can be simply His son with us. Or mine, for I am father to many.'

Bar-Avo squints and thinks and curls his lip.

'I will be the son of some father,' he says at last, and that is how he gets his name, which means 'the son of his father', and no other name he has had before has ever suited him so well as this. He is this now, a man who carries his own father with him, a nameless, invisible, intangible father.

Av-Raham, whose name means 'the father to many', laughs.

'Either way,' he says, 'now you belong with us.'

And that is that.

They give him little tasks at first, and he deals with them handily. A set of daggers to be smuggled past the guards – he conceals them under a cartful of vegetables a farmer asks him to take to market and gets paid twice for the journey, once by the farmer and once by Av-Raham's men. Messages to be carried. Lookout to be kept as they cut open the leather thongs holding a prized horse belonging to the Prefect in its stable, slap its thigh and send it skittering across the plaza, where, terrified by the smells and the noise, it falls and lames itself. Conversations to be overheard in the marketplace – there is always a use for information carelessly dropped.

He is bored sometimes, but also paid fairly well for his trouble – so much so that he can be the man now of his home, bringing his mother meat and bread. And when there is going to be a riot he knows it, and he is the one who can tell his friends where to be and at what time. And he knows where the fires will be lit and where the roofs will be torn off and what can be stolen early on because everyone will think that this saddle or that blanket or that wheel of cheese must have burned in the flames. A long campaign of resistance and anger is nothing if it is not pragmatic. Young men must be found to fight, and must be rewarded and encouraged, and people must eat.

Many days are dull – days of waiting for the fighting or for anything to happen. He does not mind the dullness. He finds himself more patient than he'd realized. The more he thinks on it, the more he wants what Av-Raham has. That quiet command, honour in the hearts of men. One has to wait, and work hard, and become trustworthy, before these things start to happen.

There is a day when Av-Raham shows him a map of Israel. He has never seen more than a little plan before – drawn on a table in wine, perhaps – to show where the grain store is in relation to where they are now, or which of three roads leads to the house of the girl he likes. This is a brushed-vellum masterpiece, kept rolled in a cloth bag and brought out ceremoniously when the men sit discussing their affairs.

Bar-Avo has come to bring wineskins he stole from a Roman officer when he was distracted by a commotion in the marketplace, and to receive his orders. But when he enters the small back room where these discussions are held, he cannot help staring at the map.

'They have moved their troops here,' one of the men is saying to

Av-Raham, putting a finger on the map, 'so their supply lines will have to go through the mountain pass.'

Bar-Avo sees at once what the map is. There is the sea, inked with fine blue waves. Here is the coast, here are the roads leading in from Yaffo to Jerusalem, up to Caesarea, down to the desert. He has imagined the countryside with this eagle's view when he walks from place to place. And all over the map are dried black beans – from one of the sacks kept in the storeroom which conceals the entrance to this chamber. Av-Raham sees him looking.

'They are the Romans,' he says, pointing out the beans, 'here is the garrison –' a cluster of beans near Jerusalem – 'and here are the outposts –' all around the countryside. 'We keep watch on where they go and what they do, so we know when new supplies will be dispatched to them and when they will be isolated.'

'So you can decide when to strike,' says Bar-Avo wonderingly.

'These are guesses really. Merely that. Our information is often out of date. But we try to steal from them when we can. There is nothing sweeter,' Av-Raham says, smiling, his little pot belly shifting against the table as he leans forward, 'than killing a Roman soldier with his own sword.'

Bar-Avo smiles too. He has imagined himself a killer before, like all boys. Has swished a sword and imagined running someone through with it. He has taken lambs to offer at the Temple and seen the life go out of them and understood how simple and how important the thing is.

'How many of them will we kill before they leave?'

Av-Raham looks into Bar-Avo's eyes, then takes his left hand by the wrist, palm up. He plucks a bean delicately from the table and places it in Bar-Avo's palm.

'This is how we proceed now. One by one. But with God's help . . .'

Av-Raham sweeps the beans off the parchment with the back of his hand. It takes two sweeps, three, to clear them all.

'That is what we must do. Every one of them out. No peace until every single one of them is swept away.'

'We'll drive them into the sea,' says Bar-Avo, looking at the beans on the floor.

Av-Raham pulls Bar-Avo towards him, so Bar-Avo can smell the older man's scent of onions and spice and the cloves he chews. Av-Raham holds him at the back of the neck and kisses the top of his head.

'With a thousand boys like you,' he says, 'we will do it.'

He is trusted, as time goes on, with bigger things. He is taught where the caches of swords are, and how to grease and wrap them so that they will not rust in their long months underground. He learns the different ways to set a fire in a building so that it will take with little kindling and without time to waste. He learns the names of the important men up and down the land. Av-Raham even has one of the old men teach him to read, though he always does so slowly and hesitatingly, for this is a skill necessary to a revolution.

And it is entirely true that some of these skills are dull and he has to be convinced that learning them is necessary. But then there is the day when he first kills a man. That is not a boring day.

There was no reason for this to be the day, though he knew the day would come and that it would be a moment like this. He is nearing twenty now and commands a handful of men of a similar age or a bit younger. They make mischief, steal things where they can, riot and destroy property, telling themselves every time that, piece by piece, they are pulling Rome off their land.

Today it will be the baths. Rome has not built a grand bathhouse in Jerusalem as she does in many of her conquered cities, but there is a small pool, one storey only, near to the dormitories for the soldiers stationed in Jerusalem. The soldiers bathe there and that is enough to make it worthy of attack. And it's used by some of the people in the town, those for whom the traditional ritual baths are insufficiently Roman, those who want to show their loyalty to the occupying power. Traitors, therefore, in their treacherous waters.

They have decided on a plan. There are open windows in the roof of the baths, and the building is next to several houses, one owned by a man who owes a great deal to Av-Raham and has been persuaded to let them use the window which leads out on to the curved bathhouse roof. Four of them go: Ya'ir, Giora, Matan and Bar-Avo himself. They shin down the wall from the window, each of them carrying a leather bag over his shoulder, each of them suppressing laughter.

Through the windows in the roof, they look down on the Romans at their bath.

They are hilarious, strutting about, each man naked as a child, caring nothing for their modesty, their decency, their honour.

'Look at that!' whispers Giora, the youngest.

He's pointing out the men being oiled by slaves. One in particular, a man in his fifties with a soldier's physique, has two male slaves working on his back, rubbing thick drops of yellow olive oil into his skin.

'I've never had a woman work so hard on me as that,' mutters Ya'ir.

The man whose back is being oiled lets out a little moan of pleasure and the boys on the roof collapse in laughter.

'Neither has he!' says Ya'ir. 'He's never touched a woman in his life, look at him!'

There are six or seven men being rubbed with oil in a similar way.

Bar-Avo says, 'My mum does that with the lamb before she roasts it.'

'Let's see if they bring out the herbs!' says Ya'ir, and they start laughing again.

'We brought our own herbs, remember?' says Bar-Avo, indicating the leather bag on Ya'ir's back, and Ya'ir's face cracks into a grin.

They position themselves at four different downward-facing windows. It will be important, for maximum impact, to start at the back and work forwards. Giora is over the window the furthest away from the exit from the baths. Beneath him are the hot steamy rooms where men are exercising to cause the sweat to run from their pores before they go to be oiled. They are all naked, jogging on the spot or punch-

208

ing at imaginary enemies. Giora pulls the bag from his back and hefts its sloppy weight in his hands. The contents are runny. He undoes the leather draw-cord holding it closed just a little and gets a whiff of the contents. He screws up his face. They have each come with a bagful of liquid animal faeces. They have mixed it with water and let it rot in a barrel for a couple of days just to enhance the effect.

Giora leans his body half over the window, lowers the hand holding the bag down and then, holding on to its handle, begins to whirl it round and round and round.

The rotten, liquid, soupy faeces splatter in wide arcs across the roomful of naked men. The stench is appalling. The stuff is sticky and smells of vomit and disease.

It splashes on to the bodies of all those naked men, across their pink scraped torsos and in their hair, and one man, a young soldier, looking in an unlucky direction, gets it across his face and in his mouth and eyes. He starts and then begins to retch as he realizes what it is.

They run, of course they do. They make for the room with the plunge bath, which is next in line and where Bar-Avo is waiting with another thick full bag. He had found some dog's vomit to put into his, mixed with the shit. As the men start running through the building away from the whirling stench, Bar-Avo begins to empty his bag too, swinging it to make a splatter of filth, and then on, as they run in disgusted confusion, two of the men already vomiting, Matan empties his bag, and one of them, looking up to see where the pollution is coming from, takes some full in the face. They barely need Ya'ir's bag, so much destruction has already been wrought in the place, but he empties it anyway, into the plunge pool, where some of them had leapt, attempting to wash themselves.

The boys are laughing as they drop the bags through the windows and can't help staying to watch for perhaps a little longer than they should, as the men desperately try to clean themselves, and one of them knocks over a huge tub of oil, which spills slick and green across the tiled floor. Another man comically slips and falls in the oil – it's too good, like players performing just for them – and manages to tip more of it over himself and, struggling to get up, pulls another man covered in brown slime down on top of himself. There's a sharp snap as another one falls, and his arm is twisted awkwardly where he tried to break his fall – he's evidently broken a bone and this is the funniest thing of all. Ya'ir rolls on his back laughing and Giora shouts through the window, 'Go back to Rome!'

They are of course watching too intently. They do not notice that a man has scaled the back wall with a ladder until it is too late and he is almost on them. He is not covered in oil or shit. He is a soldier in his full uniform, one of the men stationed outside in case of an attack on the bathhouses. They do not notice anything until Giora starts to shout and Bar-Avo turns his head from observing the men covered in oil trying to stand up and sees this soldier, his eyes like gleaming stones, his teeth bared, raising Giora above his head only to hurl him through the window down on to the floor below. There is a loud crack as Giora lands and Bar-Avo cannot see if he's moving, has no time to see.

The soldier draws his sword and the three of them, Bar-Avo, Ya'ir, Matan, scramble to their feet and back away across the roof. They are unarmed. The soldier roars and lunges. Ya'ir almost loses his footing on the edge of one of the windows and Bar-Avo pulls him back by the waist of his tunic. Taking his advantage, the soldier slashes at Ya'ir, brings his sword back red. Ya'ir screams, frightened, intense, like a child. The soldier's taken a great slice of flesh out of Ya'ir's raised arm and seeing this brings such rage to Bar-Avo that he surges forward, not thinking of himself, only of his anger and finding a place to sheathe it.

He is lucky. If he had tripped or missed his step the soldier's downward slash with his sword would have caught him on the back of the neck and his head would have rolled down through the window to the tiled floor beneath. Instead he manages to lunge low, while Matan dances backward and the soldier is confused for a moment.

Bar-Avo kicks out wildly at the soldier's knee and hits the perfect spot, at the side. There's a gristly crunch and the soldier trips, falls to his knees, shouts and grabs out, reaching for the back of Bar-Avo's tunic. He has him, he's caught him by the tunic collar, he raises the sword in his right hand and Bar-Avo catches at the soldier's wrist.

Bar-Avo is the weaker of the two. The soldier is behind him, pushing his arm down. Bar-Avo is trying to hold it back with his own right arm, but he's not strong enough and the sword is descending towards his ear, his face. And then the soldier gives a sudden start. Matan has kicked his spine and this moment of released pressure gives Bar-Avo enough leeway. He grabs the soldier's wrist, pulls the sword down and back and there, into the soft part of the throat, just above the armoured breastplate.

The soldier falls backward. He chokes and groans and grabs at the sword sticking out of his throat. The blood bubbles down his front like the blood of the lamb when it is slaughtered for the sacrifice. And he dies just as easily, there on the roof tiles, his sticky blood dripping down through the open window. They stare for a minute, startled and silent, before the shouts from the bathhouse remind them to run, to scale the wall, to get away.

Bar-Avo had not quite meant it but had not tried to avoid it either. He feels nothing afterwards, not grief or shock or pity, only perhaps a kind of surprise that it was so simple. And a kind of shock at himself, at his own cool capacity. He knows something about himself now that he didn't know before, that it will not trouble him to kill a man. He thinks: this will be useful.

Av-Raham, when he hears, congratulates Bar-Avo in front of his men and says, 'The first of many!' And Bar-Avo agrees. Yes. The first of many.

There are reprisals. Rome does not know precisely who attacked the bathhouse and killed the soldier, and Giora somehow managed to limp away on a broken ankle before he could be caught and questioned, so the Prefect's men round up a few dozen young men and give them lashes in the marketplace. They execute five or six for 'stirring up unrest'. Av-Raham sends gifts of money and promises of loyalty to the families of those young men. Rome wins nothing by this.

Bar-Avo marries soon after this, because the death has sharpened him somehow and the girls are not enough night after night. He has not got a child on any girl yet but at some point he will, he knows, and this thought, the thought that he might have to take a girl because he has given her a child, makes him think that it is time to marry.

He does not need to look too hard for a wife. There are a dozen girls of the right age – fifteen or sixteen – among the daughters of Av-Raham's friends, and they are sweet and kind and think him handsome. There is one he likes, Judith, not just for the spread of her hips and her neat bottom, but because she seems to understand when he talks.

He has not slept with her; it is not right to do so with the daughters of these men. But once they sat together in a barn during a rainstorm and he told her how he longed to make his mother proud, and take care of her in her old years, and at this Judith leaned her head on his shoulder and said, 'She doesn't know how lucky she is to have a son like you.'

He had kissed her on the mouth and her kiss tasted faintly of cherries, and he tried to do more but she pushed his hands away and moved to put a little distance between them.

'You think everything will always come easily to you,' says Judith, 'but one day there'll be something you can't get and then what will you do?'

'I'll have to ask your father for you instead,' he says, and she laughs.

Judith's father, one of the zealous men, is delighted by the offer of a new son-in-law and agrees rather swiftly.

She is a good girl, and gives him six children in six years, all of whom live to be bright toddlers and then on and on. They are four boys and two girls and Bar-Avo is surprised suddenly to be a father to many small delightful people whom Judith presents to him each evening washed for bed, who ask him if he has apples for them, who are delighted by the gift of a shiny stone or a piece of misshapen clay.

Judith, sensible as she is, does not ask questions about where he goes during the day or who he sees or what they tell him. She knows where they keep the daggers, wrapped in leather in the roof, and knows to keep the children from them. She knows what food to give him to take if he suddenly says that he will be away for a few days, and who to ask if he's away for longer than he said. She is very calm if he happens to give her a message to tuck into the baby's wrappings and pass to a man selling saltfish at the market.

His job, in these days, is to gather followers. A movement of revolution needs an army and each man must be recruited individually.

He travels to Acre, and then to Galilee, and talks to the strong men who are gathering their fishing nets in from the great lake. Their arms are knotted with muscles. Their thighs are bunched like tree trunks. Their bodies are meaty like bulls'. These are men who can thrust with a sword or a spear and pierce straight through another man's body so that the point sees daylight on the other side. It is men like these that he wants. This is how to secure power, he sees. Work hard, be loyal to those who have much help to give you, but secure your own followers too. A day will come when Rome is gone. But before that, he will slowly become stronger and more powerful.

'Come and follow me,' he says to the fishermen, 'follow me and free the country from tyranny.'

'We cannot follow you,' they say, 'we have hauls of fish to pull in and families to feed.'

And he says, 'Is not God the Master of all?'

And they say, 'Yes.'

And he says, 'Then will not God provide for His children, if they will only follow Him?'

And one of them, more curious than the others perhaps, says, 'How shall we follow?'

And at that Bar-Avo gives them instruction. How they will become trusted friends of those who are zealous for the Lord. How they will watch for the words: 'God alone as leader and master.' God alone. He says it again, and he knows how it feels to hear. No disgusting Emperor steeped in seamy sin upon his golden throne. No Roman army. No Prefect laying waste to good men's lives upon his whims. God alone, he says to them, as leader and master.

'What of the priests?' says one, and Bar-Avo knows by this question that he has them.

'The priests connive with the Prefect and Rome and wheedle for their own fortunes. Haven't you heard how rich the High Priest's family is? Where do you think that money is from? It's stolen from the Temple. And it's blood money paid by Rome for our lives.'

And they believe, because they have heard the stories.

'God alone,' he says, 'leader and master of all. None but God. God alone.'

They repeat it after him.

And when he walks on to the next village and the next most of the men stay, but giving him their word that he can call on them. And one or two – young men, men without families or men who long for the fight – walk with him. Strong fighting bodies, and he has them practising their dagger thrusts in the evening and fashioning arrowheads. When he comes back to Jerusalem after three months' walking, he has a score of men built like muscled oxen with him and another twenty times that number who have promised their right arms to the cause. He will not need them yet. But they will all come to Jerusalem to sacrifice for the festivals of pilgrimage, and then suddenly he will have an army.

'There is a logic to battles,' says Av-Raham, welcoming him back with a great feast and a calf spit-roasted over a fire of old olive wood. 'There is a way to feel in the city when it is ready for war.'

All his friends are there: Giora and Ya'ir, and Matan, who broke his leg in the fall from the roof and walks with a limp now but is still useful to the cause. Bar-Avo's own mother has pride of place by the fire and his brothers and sisters with her, because now he is a man of some influence. It pleases him to see his family's hands shiny with grease from the calf slaughtered in honour of his own safe return with many men and good news. His wife is here too, her body newly strange and enticing to him after so many months away, and their children filled to the brim with meat and dozing like a half-dozen little puppies draped across her lap. And Av-Raham and the elder men, who look at him with new respect now. They sent several men out to recruit but none has come back with such good news as he.

'I can feel it is coming now,' says Av-Raham. 'It will not be long. A year or half a year. Have you heard about the holy men each claiming to be the Messiah? This is a sure sign that the time is near. And the people who follow them? They will come to us.'

They drink wine and eat meat. Their moment is at hand.

There are terrible rumours across the land of Israel, stories so shocking that they must be passed from person to person as quickly as possible.

Some say that the Prefect is demanding that the Temple give up its holy money, donated for the glory of God, to build some kind of latrine. Some say that the priests have agreed to it and that the gold will be transferred under cover of darkness. This news alone is enough to provoke angry shouts in the street, insults flung at soldiers, stones and wine jugs thrown from upper windows at them as they pass in the street.

Bar-Avo leads a raid on a caravan bringing wine to a wealthy Roman merchant. It is for actions like this that the Romans call them bandits and murderers, but that is to misunderstand: they are freedom fighters. They kill the guards who resist them and let those who run go free. Inside the wagons they find not only wine but chests of gold and letters for half the most powerful men in Jerusalem and Caesarea. The letters confirm that the Prefect, Pilate, is weak and has been demanding additional resources from Syria. The money goes to shore up their support in the west and the south. Bar-Avo's esteem increases tenfold with this find.

Now he is the one to whom men come for advice, suddenly. Av-Raham is still a leader, a man of much influence, but Bar-Avo is the rising star. They come to tell him about a preacher who slaughtered a cat outside the Temple to represent the sacrilege done there every day by sacrificing for the Romans, and one who has been making cures and upset the tables in the Temple. They tell him about small risings and pockets of resistance. He is the one who decides what punishment should be meted out to men found to have been too generous to the Romans.

What does it take to make a man follow you? Not love. For love a man will mourn you and bury you when you are dead, but not follow you into battle. For a man to follow you, it must seem that you are the one who knows the way out. Every person is in a dark place. Every person wants to feel that some other man can guide them back into the light.

A few days before Passover the city is ready.

All of Bar-Avo's four hundred men are coming to Jerusalem to sacrifice for the festival. His provocateurs do not even have to make up stories, just remind people of what has already happened. They say, 'Remember the Hippodrome?' and even men who were not born when it happened have heard the stories and see in their imaginations the great structure set aflame and thousands of men crucified up and down all the roads to the capital.

He holds a great feast just before Passover. They roast lambs upon great fires and sing songs and call down curses on the head of every Roman. He lays out his plans to the men – how it will be when we take control of the city, who will take which of the gates, who will storm the high places and David's Tower. He is foolhardy, perhaps, because he cannot see every figure lurking at the edge of the crowd or ask where they have come from and what their name is. He holds up the bread and the wine at the meal and says, 'Just as we eat this bread and drink this wine, so we will devour the armies of Rome and drink sweet victory!' And there are great cheers.

Shortly after dawn, when the birds are still calling out and the sky is streaked with pink-tinged clouds, he wakes with his wife next to him, soft and sweet-smelling, and thinks for a moment, why did I wake so suddenly, and then he hears the cry again. Loud and low and afraid: 'Soldiers!'

They are coming from three sides. There is little time to do anything. He and Judith knew this day might come, that is why only the baby is with them, strapped to her body. The other children are safe with his mother. Judith kisses him hard, white with determination and anxiety, and runs to the horse. She is away and clear of the reach of arrows before he joins his men for the battle.

Someone must have given away their position, it is the only explanation. Someone sold them out for a handful of silver. As the soldiers close in, Bar-Avo looks at the faces of his men. One of them, with his guilty expression, will show himself a traitor. Not his dear friends, surely not, not Ya'ir, not Matan, not Giora? He watches them, while his men fight with the soldiers and he fights alongside the rest, even though he knows they will lose. He watches for men who seem to be hanging back in the fight – one of them knows they will not get their money if he is freed – and at last he thinks he spots who it is, though his heart breaks open. Ya'ir. Open-faced, strong and handsome, and the one he loved the best of all. Ya'ir is the one hanging back. Ya'ir is the one who, he remembers, took care to embrace him last night at the banquet and address him by name even though they all knew not to do so.

His men kill four soldiers, but the soldiers kill three of his before they reach him. There are young men – about the age he was when he started to riot – throwing themselves on to the backs of the soldiers and beating their heads to keep them from him. They know to make for him, it seems, presumably to cut off the head of the beast and leave it wriggling on the floor. He fights off two with his short sword, taking one with a slice to the throat, another with a jab to the groin, but more come and more, and someone wrests the blade from his hand and pushes him back.

As the soldiers reach him, he cries to his men, 'Do not deal too harshly with Ya'ir!' and he sees the fear grow on the man's face as he turns to run. They will kill him if they catch him. Good. And if they do not, and if he escapes, he will kill Ya'ir himself, for if the man wanted money he could always have come to Bar-Avo.

And now they are here, three men from Samaria, bought by Rome to fetch him to their dungeons and their Prefect. They will not take him easily. There is a dagger in his boot and he stoops, seeming to let his head go down, beaten, but draws out the blade in one easy motion and slices through the back of the ankle of the man nearest to him. He falls to the ground at once, and in the gap he leaves there's a break in the wall of men. Bar-Avo calculates and thinks: I could run now and regroup the men in the forest. But as he takes one step forward, there is a starburst at the back of his head and black spots before his eyes and then he knows nothing at all.

The next thing is the closest he ever comes to death, although death has always walked beside him like an old friend.

Before this he imagined he would meet death in battle, or that death would catch him when he tried to leap from one building to another and misjudged it and so fell into the waiting palm of death instead. Or that death would be a wolf on the road when he was alone and had left his knife in the camp. Or that death would be a Roman sword where he did not see one coming, the one he failed to dodge. He had never imagined capture.

When he wakes in the cell and realizes what has happened, he tests out how it feels. His head thumps, his arms and legs ache, there is a twisting in his belly. Very well, this is what it feels like to be injured in battle and not to take any food or water. He needs a woman with warm water to bathe him and a boy with a pitcher of cold water to quench his thirst, but neither of those things is here.

It does not feel like a disgrace, though. He had thought it might. It makes him angry and it makes him cunning. While he lives, there is a way out. He has learned that from the countless skirmishes with the Roman soldiers. The only man who can never escape is a dead man – while he lives, even surrounded by a ring of swords, he can look about him, identify what there is to use here and make good his escape.

He sits up and sees for the first time that there is another man, weaker than him, in here. He can tell from the way the man moves that he is not a trained fighter, or trained to endure many blows. The other man coughs and shivers but otherwise is so still that Bar-Avo would not have known there was anyone else in this small stone room with dirty straw on the floor.

'You,' says Bar-Avo, 'what's your name?'

The man remains silent. Bar-Avo can see his dark eyes staring at him, hungrily he thinks. With great intensity. Bar-Avo is not daunted.

'I am Bar-Avo,' he says. 'I command some of the zealous forces around Jerusalem. Tell me, friend, have you fought alongside us against Rome? Or have you battled for freedom in some other way?'

This is an obvious gambit, but in the context it is more likely to succeed than not. Men in Roman gaols have often been rebels, or might like to style themselves so after the fact. At the very least, men in Roman gaols have no love for Rome.

'I am going to die,' says the man slowly.

Ah. Yes. It takes some men this way.

'That is certainly their intention,' says Bar-Avo, 'and they surely aim to carry it out. But if you have made your peace with God there is nothing to fear from death. Do not be afraid.'

'When I die,' says the man, 'the whole of creation burns, and God Himself descends from heaven to judge the righteous and the guilty.'

Hmm.

'I can see you are a great teacher,' says Bar-Avo after some thought, 'and that the spirit of God is in you. Tell me, do you have many followers?'

'All of the earth are my disciples, but it must not be spoken. Do not speak of it.'

It is very possible that this man will be of no use whatsoever. Nonetheless, he must sound him out. He has heard strange men like this before and knows their usual preoccupations.

'The time has not yet come for you to be revealed, I understand.'

The man nods slowly and shifts his hands. The shackles clink.

'The world will burn,' he says a propos of nothing, 'when the abom-ination that causes desolation is in a forbidden place, then there will be great earthquakes and famines. It is then that I will come in clouds with great power and glory. Only then will my name be known.'

There is something about him, it is curious. Although the things that he says are nonsense and Bar-Avo has met ten times ten of his kind, nonetheless there is a conviction to his voice. Perhaps a hun-dred times a hundred such madmen have merely ordinary skill of rhetoric and so they are not believed and people see in them only a sad wreckage of a confused mind, but one in ten thousand are gifted with this combination: the calm manner of self-assurance, the pen-etrating gaze, the low commanding voice, the particular way of holding his limbs even now, even shackled. God throws such a one together from time to time: an arresting man. If he had not been thus mad, he could have been a great man.

'I know who you are,' says Bar-Avo. 'I have heard about you. You are Yehoshuah of Natzaret. You have near six hundred men with you, they say.'

He had not heard that the man was captured. But he had heard that there was such a man: a healer, a caster-out of demons. Some of his own men had gone to seek healing for a wound that would not knit or a deaf ear.

'There will be more,' says Yehoshuah, 'there will be many more. Listen –' and Yehoshuah leans forward and Bar-Avo, despite his mind, despite his sore limbs and his aching head, cannot help leaning forward too – 'listen Bar-Avo, son of no one, don't you think that God Himself will take his revenge for what has been done in this city? You make your plans and gather your forces to you, and you hope to overturn His will, but don't you know that He has sent the Romans to scourge us so that we'll repent and return to Him before the end of the world comes? Bar-Avo, king of bandits, God is angry with His creation and the time has come to fold it up and put it away. You are as much a tool of His will in this as any Roman soldier.'

Bar-Avo shivers. He has thought this himself, alone, late at night. Where is the Lord in all this? When he is fighting to rid the country of Rome, when he wants to see the holy Temple purified of their unclean bodies, isn't their presence a sign that God has turned His face away? And if He has turned His face from Jerusalem, it can mean only one thing.

'Are you a prophet?'

Yehoshuah smiles.

'I may not tell who I am.' He pauses. 'It is no accident that you and I are in this cell together.'

Bar-Avo struggles. There are a thousand false prophets in Jerusalem and he cannot say why this one is striking him so forcefully. Perhaps it is just that his head is sore and he knows this may be his last night on earth.

'If you are God's prophet, why not tell your men to join with ours? To fight with us and drive the Romans from Jerusalem and set up God's house again?'

Yehoshuah smiles and wipes his dirty face with his dirty, shackled hand.

'Bar-Avo, murderer and leader of murderers, do you think God needs help to do His work?'

Bar-Avo is stung and impatient. This is the same rhetoric he has heard a thousand times from the people who support the Temple, who preach moderation, who don't trust in God but in their own full bellies and warm beds.

'God has told us what He wants already. He says that no idol shall be tolerated, that we shall destroy all those who make graven images. He has given us work to do already and we are too cowardly to do it. Join with us, do the work God has commanded, turn the heathens out.'

'We are far beyond that time now,' says Yehoshuah. 'God has cast His judgement on the land.'

Bar-Avo looks at him. His head throbs, his vision pulses with beads of light at the corners of his eyes. He knows he may die tomorrow on a cross set up by Rome.

'Shall we not try?' he says, and his voice is cracked and he longs for water although he knows they will not bring it, for he is already dead in a sense. 'Shall we not strive with all our might to do what is needed, and if God in His wisdom decides to slay us all, shall we not then die knowing that we fought as hard as we could, that we tried for freedom?'

Yehoshuah says nothing.

'Shall we not strive to live? That is all that we know, that life is good. Shall we not fight to gain our own lives?'

Yehoshuah says, and he smiles as he says it, 'God's will, not my will be done.'

And Bar-Avo, who has always been a fighter and a survivor, who has crawled out of holes not quite as dark but almost as dark as this one, finds himself thinking: very well, then. If this is your choice, you make my choice easier. Because he has a notion of what might happen next, since it is getting close to Passover and Jerusalem will be full of angry men and Pilate is a damned coward.

They come for them early in the morning. One guard places an earthenware vessel filled with dank, warm water in front of Bar-Avo. He drinks it greedily to the bottom before he even checks whether a similar jar has been given to Yehoshuah. It has, but the man drinks sparingly, and washes his face. Bar-Avo rubs at his face with the corner of his garment. He knows what is coming.

The guards kick at them to make them stand and, despite their shackled feet and tied arms, hustle them along the passage towards the light. The breath of wind is a cool kiss to the forehead. The sky is bright and clear with early-morning streaks of feathered cloud. Yehoshuah does not look up at the sky, but Bar-Avo cannot keep his eyes from it until they are dragged into the house where Pilate has his office.

They bring both the men in to see the Prefect, one after the other. Bar-Avo waits in the outer vestibule – he stands with his legs shackled and his hands tied behind him and his back aching and his knees aching and his shoulders aching, and he listens to the conversation taking place inside the room as best as he can hear it.

Pilate says, 'They tell me you've been going around calling yourself the King of the Jews.'

Silence. The sound of birds singing in the courtyard outside and of a maid clanging pots downstairs.

'Well, out with it. Are you the King of the Jews?'

'Those are your words.'

This is not a good answer, though it will make Bar-Avo's task considerably easier. It would have been better at this stage to blame the priests, to imply that they had encouraged him to declare himself to foment rebellion against Rome. It would have been better to say that he would lay his men's loyalty, however much that is worth, at the feet of Pilate. It would have been better even simply to deny it. 'No, I am not,' would have been a better answer for a man who wanted to live.

There is a sigh and a sound of rustling paper.

'You understand that this is gross sedition and if you do not deny it and swear loyalty to your Emperor I will be forced to execute you?'

Pilate sounds tired and irritated. This is useful information which he might be able to turn to his benefit.

The man still says nothing when there is so much he could say that might save his life. Pilate doesn't trust the priests any more than he trusts the people. There is always a crack to work a knife into, to twist the blade, to break open.

'Very well. Take him away.' This to the guards. They half drag, half bully Yehoshuah out of the door directly past where Bar-Avo is sitting, but the two men's eyes do not meet. Some men give up their lives for nothing, but Bar-Avo is not likely to do so.

They bring him in. He is standing, with his hands bound behind his back. Pilate is sitting at his ease, sipping on a cup of hot soup, for a little chill is in the air this morning. The whole thing will have to be played as carefully as a game of knives.

'Do you think he has run mad, that man Yehoshuah?' says Bar-Avo, before Pilate has a chance to ask his first question.

It is a bold manoeuvre, to speak first, but it is a calculated risk. This way he sets the tone: reasonable, thinking. But he asks a question also, deferring to Pilate. It is a risk. Pilate could have him killed here, for insolence.

Pilate looks surprised. Looks at him full in the face. Says at last, 'You were with him in the cells, weren't you? Was he mad then, or as sane as day?'

'He has moments of clarity and moments where he falls into insanity. I am not sure he knows what he's done, or why. Everyone is looking for a Messiah. Every leader has followers who tell them that they are the Messiah. I think he's started to believe them.'

Pilate shrugs and raises one eyebrow.

'Well,' he says, 'Jerusalem won't suffer for having one fewer of those. Now. You have brought a great deal of harm to this city and this nation. The sooner the people learn that no rebellion will stand against us, the better it will be for them. I propose to put you to death. However, if you are willing to give up your co-conspirators, I will give you an easy death by the sword. If you refuse, we will torture you and then crucify you.

'We will, for example, slice your tongue to pieces and pierce your eyes with nails. And we will, of course, arrest some others of your followers whose faces we know anyway, so that whatever you do it will be put about that you betrayed them. Do you understand? There is no chance for glory. Either torture and ignominy, or ignominy but a quick and merciful death. I only need a handful of names and locations. Let's start, for example, with Giora. Tell me where he is now.'

'I do not know,' says Bar-Avo.

Pilate sighs. 'You may be surprised,' he says, 'by how much you will start to tell us when the branding irons are applied to your flesh. The ears, they tell me, are surprisingly sensitive. And the bottoms of the feet. Quite brave men find themselves babbling like women after having hot coals and iron scourges applied to the bottoms of their feet.'

It is time to take back this conversation. Pilate's lines are too practised now; he is in a rhythm which will be hard to break.

'Do you think any one of us tells the others where they are to be found?' says Bar-Avo. 'Prefect, you know better than that.'

He lets it hang in the air for a second too long. The insolence of it catches Pilate short.

Bar-Avo pushes on: 'You might as well ask that Yehoshuah where all his followers are now, all that rabble he brought with him from Galilee who fled as soon as he was captured. Every meeting place will have been changed the moment they knew I was taken alive. Every man I ever knew will have moved to another home. Every family will have been told to deny their sons. Prefect, you can beat me and scourge me for as long as pleases you, but don't think for a moment that my bruised body will do more than excite greater hatred of you. Even if they think I am a traitor, they will still hate you more.'

Pilate looks at him. He knows that what he says has the ring of truth to it.

'A true leader,' says Pilate, 'does not care whether he is hated, as long as he is feared.'

'And has it stopped them rising up? You'll never hold Jerusalem like this,' says Bar-Avo. 'Every man and every woman and every child will fight you. You can't take us by fear, only by love.'

And he knows that this is the right thing to say, because his men have intercepted some of the letters from Syria and Rome, and he knows that this is what Pilate's masters have been saying to him for months now. These exact words. Not by fear, but by love. Bar-Avo is not stupid. He is not ill-informed. He is the leader of many men.

'Do you want them to remember you like this, Pilate? As a bloody tyrant? A man who made the streets run red, not one who brought the civilization and order of Rome?'

This is a gamble too.

'They will remember me for discipline. Rome does not bring

marble and gold only, Rome brings order and obedience.' Pilate is talking to himself now, for the most part. Bar-Avo has him. The right words at the right moment and Pilate is his now.

'If I were you,' says Bar-Avo, 'I would release that man Yehoshuah and put me to the sword.'

Pilate stares at him and nods, as if he has said something tremendously wise and interesting.

'Why release him?'

'To show mercy. To bring the love of Rome as well as the scourge. You've done it before at the festivals. You know it works. It is clever.'

Too much to compliment him in this fashion? No. Pilate is as vain as any man.

'They have already come to ask, it is true.'

'Then release him. He has a body of followers, many of them women.' He drops this in as if it is in Yehoshuah's favour. It is not. Rome takes only a little more account of women than Greece ever did. 'That is my advice to you –' he lowers his head – 'in return for a swift and merciful death. I've killed your men. Your soldiers will love you for doing away with me. It will be easier for you to keep them in line.'

Pilate's lip curls.

'The soldiers will obey me because it is their duty so to do. They owe it to me, to Rome, to their Emperor.'

He motions with his head to the little golden statue of the God-Emperor in the alcove shrine opposite the window.

'You should still execute me. If you want to be wise.'

It is so easy to bait Pilate. He is entirely unable to conceal his reactions. He is angry that Bar-Avo has suggested a wise course of action, implied that he is not wise already.

'I know what men like you are. You consider it an honour to die at our hands, fighting. What if I don't want to give you that honour? What if I keep you here as my slave? There'd be no martyr's death for you then, no crowd of wailing women to keep your name alive and use it to spur on further rebellion.'

Bar-Avo shrugs.

'I am in your hands, Prefect. Do with me as you see fit.'

Pilate narrows his eyes, certain now that some game is being played with him.

'And what if I let you go?'

'My men would, of course, be delighted.'

'Yes,' says Pilate, 'yes, your men. Ten thousand of them, they say, across Judea, loyal to you.'

This is not true, but Bar-Avo does not contradict him. There are nearer five thousand and they are loyal not to him but to the cause. To live free is more important than merely to live. Loyalty to him would hurt that cause. They must be willing to give him up if necessary; he would do the same to them.

'Yes,' Pilate muses, 'let them taste the mercy of Rome as well as the kiss of her strap.'

The man is not an idiot, and yet he behaves like an idiot. It is pride. If another man were considering this course of action, Pilate would bring him up easily on five or six points which make it unthinkably foolish. But he cannot bring his mind to bear on his own plans.

'They would be grateful to me, would they not, if I released their master?'

'They would suspect I had turned traitor,' says Bar-Avo, because he can see the growing, gathering shimmer of the way to save his own skin.

'Hah!' Pilate smiles broadly. 'Even better! Gratitude and mistrust. Magnificent. You could not have promised me anything better if you had designed it yourself.'

Bar-Avo tries to make his face as impassive as a stone. As if the thought of what he has done has hardened his heart.

'I'll tell you what,' says Pilate, 'I'll make a game of it.'

His men are in the crowd. Bar-Avo sees them as soon as he and Yehoshuah are brought out blinking into the light of the square below Pilate's home, the place where later on the Prefect has his soldiers massacre all those men.

They are here to see him die, perhaps. Or to start a riot, or join in with one if one starts. They mingle quietly with the crowd. The hoods of their cloaks are drawn up around their faces. There are perhaps a hundred people here and probably forty of them are his own men. Because of the respect and love they hold him. Not to try to save him, but to witness his death and bear witness of it to his friends, and to his mother, and to his wife and sons.

He sees two or three of the friends of Yehoshuah in the crowd. He had a smaller band, of course, and they were not strong men, not used to fighting or to witnessing death at the hands of Rome. He wishes more of Yehoshuah's men were here. Such a united force should see how Rome kills. If they saw, they could not help but rise up.

Pilate addresses the crowd.

'People of Jerusalem!' he shouts. 'I come here today to offer you a choice!'

The crowd stirs and mutters. He has played this little game before. He does not always do it, only sometimes. So they should not become complacent, of course.

'Your will is important to me! Rome does not wish to hurt you, only to bring you order and good governance. Therefore, I have two criminals here: the preacher Yehoshuah, who called himself the King of the Jews, and Barabbas, a rebel who murdered men during the rebellion.'

There is more muttering. Not men, the crowd are thinking to themselves, soldiers. Who do the Jews kill in a rebellion? Not other Jews. Soldiers. Even those who didn't know that Bar-Avo had killed soldiers know it now. Pilate has as good as said: here is a freedom fighter, a hero. Does he know he's said it? It's so hard to tell with that man whether he's being cunning or stupid. Or whether his cunning is the same as his stupidity, because only a stupid man would try to be cunning like that.

'I am going to allow you to decide which of these men shall live and which shall be executed. They are both criminals, both found guilty by your courts!'

But we know who influences the courts, murmur the crowd, we know who tells them whom they may find guilty and whom innocent.

'This man Yehoshuah has blasphemed against your God! And this man Barabbas has murdered men!'

But there are women in that crowd to whom Bar-Avo's men have given bread when the Romans burned the wheatfield. There are men in that crowd whom Bar-Avo's men have fought with, defending their homes from bandits. There are children in that crowd whom Bar-Avo's men have found medicine for. No group of guerrilla fighters can last for long without the love of the people they live among. What could Yehoshuah possibly have to compare with that? No preacher has anything to offer to an oppressed people that compares with bread and water and tinctures and swords.

'So which do you choose?' he shouts. 'You can save one and only one! Which of these men will you save?'

And there's no choice, none at all. Yehoshuah's friends try to call for him, but there aren't enough of them, and they're drowned out by the voices rising up one on another on another saying, 'Barabbas! Give us Barabbas! Blessed Barabbas!'

It is a pitilessly cruel game. If they refuse to call out names – and it has happened before, like gladiators refusing to fight – Pilate will simply kill both men. It is entirely unfair. It makes a mockery of life itself. And yet what can anyone do but participate?

Bar-Avo stares at Yehoshuah. Yehoshuah is looking out at the crowd, where his scattered friends are shouting themselves hoarse on his behalf. There is a man with tears streaming down his face as he shouts, 'Yehoshuah! Yehoshuah!' Bar-Avo can see his lips moving, but the sound does not reach, so great is the clamour of 'Barabbas! Barabbas!'

Pilate is disconcerted by the vehemence of the cries. Whatever calculation he thought he'd made, it seems to have fallen out differently from his expectation. His shoulders slope. He quietens the crowd. They settle down watchfully. He could do anything.

'But this man,' he says, 'don't you want this King of the Jews?'

And it's clear to the crowd that he's mocking them now. As if they've been left with any such thing as a rightful king, as if they'd be able to tell their rightful king when they saw him.

It is nearly one hundred years this year since Rome took hold of Jerusalem and breached her and penetrated her by force. He is asking this question as if every king for one hundred years hasn't been placed on the throne by Rome. He despises them, and it is obvious in every word he utters.

'What shall I do with this King of the Jews?' he says.

'Execute him!' shouts someone in the crowd, and the rest take up the cry of 'Barabbas!' again. The few pitiful voices calling out the other name are entirely inaudible.

How is it possible that a whole life can come down to this moment: seeing how many friends you have and how loudly they are prepared to shout your name?

Bar-Avo wants to live, he thinks, but not like this. But that is a lie. He realizes it as he stands there, with the humility of a man who has been for these past few days half dead, half alive. He wants to live and he does not much care how, as long as it does not destroy the cause he's fought for. He and Yehoshuah are both weeping, and the preacher's friends are still shouting his name, still desperately trying to save him, and it is obvious they love the man. If it were possible to save them both, Bar-Avo's men would be shouting for that. If it were possible to expel the occupiers from the land by shouting, they would shout for that until their throats bled. But there is never the choice to save both. There is never more mercy than absolutely required.

And a look crosses Pilate's face, and he glances to his left and right as if he wishes he had more soldiers around him. If he were to refuse to give them Bar-Avo now, his life would be in danger. There are enough men in the crowd to rush them. Crowds have a single voice and mind and heart. This crowd wants Bar-Avo.

'Very well!' shouts Pilate. 'I have heard your wishes! I hope that seeing the magnanimity of Rome will encourage you to be loyal! To love your Emperor! To stop your petty uprisings! I know that Barabbas, having felt this mercy, will join with me in longing for peace between the two great nations of Rome and the Jews!'

Yehoshuah's friends are still calling out, they are trying to get close to the raised platform on which the men are displayed. Yehoshuah himself stands absolutely silent, his head bowed, his hands tied, like Bar-Avo's, behind his back. Bar-Avo looks at Yehoshuah, while one of Pilate's soldiers saws at the ropes that bind him.

And eventually Yehoshuah looks back. He seems shocked and frightened and alone. He understands that he has failed to win a popularity contest, that he has not somehow made enough friends, or loyal enough friends, to fight for him on this nonsensical battlefield.

Bar-Avo too has heard the sayings of the rabbis: that one good friend is worth an army of hangers-on, that fools consort with a multitude while the wise man keeps his counsel among a few whom he can trust. They are wrong, the rabbis, in this matter. In times of peace a man has the luxury of picking a few good friends. In times of war one must hoard the love of men as one lays down stocks of grain and oil and jars of water against an ill-fortuned time. Bar-Avo's friends are his treasure house. They have saved his life.

Pilate does not have to release him, even still. There is no law that says he must obey the will of the people, just as no statute or edict from Rome has told him to ask them. But Pilate is too fearful a man to be willing to chance a crowd like this. He has rolled the dice hoping for Venus and it has come up Vultures.

They cut through Bar-Avo's ropes at last. His wrists are sore, his hands numb. There is a gash on his right hand where the knife slipped – though they were none too careful with it and perhaps the wound was intended. The soldiers hustle him by his shoulders to the edge of the platform and half lower, half push him off. He looks back. Yehoshuah's head is still hanging down. Their eyes meet as Bar-Avo reaches the ground and his friends begin to encircle him, hugging and patting and punching his shoulder.

Bar-Avo says, 'I am sorry,' and though the sound of his words is obscured by the noise of the crowd he thinks that perhaps Yehoshuah sees the words form on his lips and understands, because the man's head moves. It is something like a shake of the head, something like a thin smile, something like a sob in the movement of his shoulders.

He is touched by the man's ambiguous gesture. As his friends sweep him away, he thinks that perhaps they should attempt to mount a rescue, as they might try to do for one of their own captains. But such manoeuvres are risky at best – they would not have tried one even for him. They are more likely to end in losing twenty men than saving one. It is odd, really, that the idea has even crossed his mind, since this man is nothing to him. Except, of course, that this is the man who will die in his place, whose death has bought his life.

He has lived his life in the exact opposite fashion to the way this Yehoshuah has lived and that is why he, Bar-Avo, lives and Yehoshuah will die.

In the marble-floored plaza, as he is taken out in triumph, a few men and women are weeping. He turns his head again to see Yehoshuah led through the iron gates towards the dungeon from which he will travel to the place of execution. The gate closes fast behind him and Barabbas can no longer see his face.

He goes to sit beneath the men who are being crucified, later. He is the most free bandit and murderer in the whole of Judea now, for the Prefect has liberated him in front of a great multitude and so he can go where he pleases and do what he likes.

Besides, two of the men crucified that day have fought alongside his men, stealing grain and arms from the Romans. He pays the guards to cut their wrists as the nails go in, so that death will come to them more quickly and he waits until he sees them slump. He has their bodies taken down for burial before the evening, as is right. He has already told his loyal lieutenants to bring pouches of silver to the men's families. This is how a man makes friends and keeps them.

He would have told the guards to do the same trick with Yehoshuah, to ease his passing, but some of the man's family and friends are standing by. One of them, the man he'd seen weeping in the plaza, spits and shouts as he walks past, 'Murderer! You should be up on that cross, not my master!'

And he finds he no longer has a mind to help that death go swiftly.

It is not, in any case, the worst method of execution Rome has ever devised. There is a particular thing they do which begins with hanging a man upside-down by his ankles between two trees and slowly, across many hours or even days, sawing him vertically in half from scrotum to neck. It is astonishing how long a man will live like this, upside-down, when he would die right side up. By contrast, crucifixion is merciful. There is another thing he has heard is done in Persia, where maggots of a particular beetle are introduced under the flesh and the man is fed milk and honey to keep him alive while the maggots burrow through his sinews and make their nest in his belly and sometimes crawl out alive through his eyes and ears and nose while he is still himself just living. Sufficiently living to scream, anyway. Death, the only inevitable item on the list of life, is nonetheless such a constant matter of human creativity. He finds he has an odd admiration for it. He would never have had the ingenuity to devise such methods.

He wonders, as he lingers by the crosses, whether it is his destiny to end his days here too, pinioned and waiting to be food for ravens. It is most likely, he thinks. That is how it will probably fall out. He will join all the thousands upon thousands of men whom Rome has nailed up, but the important thing is to make sure he has scratched her face before that day.

He finds the man afterwards who betrayed him. His dear friend Ya'ir, the one who was his most loyal and trusted follower, the one who fought alongside him, his most precious Ya'ir.

Bar-Avo is crying when he talks to Ya'ir.

'I trusted you,' he says, 'I gave you everything, I looked after you and your family, you are my brother.'

Ya'ir, tied with rope at wrists and ankles, gagged across his mouth, says nothing.

'If you had a reason for me, any reason at all,' says Bar-Avo, 'maybe it would be different.'

Ya'ir does not even attempt to speak. His eyes are dead already. What can the reason possibly have been? Only that he had capitulated, taken the Roman money, agreed to betray them because he had accepted that Rome was the only power and had the only favour worth gaining.

Bar-Avo leaps up from his chair and strikes him across the face, but still he says nothing.

They keep him for three days. They have to perform a certain number of unpleasant tasks to be sure they've found out everything he knows. Bar-Avo watches, for the most part, but does not participate, and it becomes clear over time that Ya'ir does not know much.

They hang him in the end, from a tree near the village where they've been hiding, and put it about that it was a suicide. If anyone questions this story or even wonders if it was true, they do not dare to say it out loud.

He sends later to root out what happened to that Yehoshuah's followers and family. It is not only sentiment that makes him do it; a rabble army looking for a new leader could be useful to him. He gets back a garbled tale that the dead man's body was stolen, probably by his family, but perhaps by some of the hangers-on who wanted to set up a shrine to the holy man. He asks his own people to report back if they find out the truth of the story, but no one ever tells him a convincing tale about it.

In those days, Av-Raham dies. It is not sudden or violent; he is an old man now, nearing eighty, and his spirit burns brightly but his body is frail. He has time to gather his men to him, to tell them to keep fighting – they know that – and to name his successors. Bar-Avo is named, of course, as the captain of the north.

They bury Av-Raham just before sunset and stand weeping over his grave for a long time. Bar-Avo lingers after the other men have departed, wanting to wring some final wisdom out of the dry earth. It is for him now to decide how to prosecute the ongoing war.

He says, 'They captured me. They have spies among our ranks. If we push on we may perish and be defeated.'

And from the grave he hears Av-Raham's voice and smells the man's scent, the smoke and the mild smell of frying onions: 'Better perish than live under occupation. Better every man dead than that.'

Bar-Avo is pragmatic. He knows that the dead often appear in dreams and visions, that just because you think you have smelled the scent of a man's clothes after he has died does not mean that you should do what that voice tells you.

Pilate is mobilizing his forces, striking back at the 'bandits' who have harried his supply lines for months. It might be a time to retreat, to scatter the men to their homes and wait for the crackdown to end. It is not Bar-Avo's decision alone, but he is part of the decision. He says no, tell the men to come to the city even still. If there is no fight there will at least be a mighty demonstration of anger. We are ready now, or we will soon be ready. The people want to overthrow the Romans.

And he is right that the city is ready to burn. That is the riot over the money for the aqueduct. Six hundred people die in the public square.

Bar-Avo is not one of them, though he sees his friends cut down, and women, and children. His own son, still just a boy, might have been one of them if he, Bar-Avo, had not gathered him into the folds of his cloak and broken through the Roman line using his teeth to tear at the soldier holding him back, bringing up his mouth red and with a chunk of the man's face warm and bleeding in his mouth.

Men and women and children. It is the smell Bar-Avo remembers most as the years cloud up his memory of precisely how he escaped and who he left behind to die when he ran.

Bar-Avo pricks himself with this memory when he grows weak, when his heart says for any moment 'enough'. It will never be enough until they have rid the land of every Roman on it. It will never be enough.

And perhaps on the same day that Bar-Avo decides this, Pilate begins to think to himself: so many dead, and still the thing is not concluded? Perhaps he does think so, there is no way to be certain.

And then it is the last days of summer and the wheat is high, and then it is autumn when the fruit trees bring forth their goodness, and then it is winter when the winds howl, and then it is spring again and the earth which has died is reborn. And ten years can go past like this quickly and they continue the fight.

Pilate is finally ordered home to Rome after one massacre too many, and there is some brief rejoicing. It is true that he has killed many thousands of Jews, that his men have left the city worse and more afraid and more angry than it has ever been, but at last he is gone, and perhaps this is hopeful.

In Rome the old goat Emperor Tiberius dies and a new emperor ascends to rule. His name is Little Boots and he is full of promise of a new era of tolerant understanding, but it falls out that he is madder than his predecessor and the name Caligula is soon a byword for cruelty and sickness. Caligula believes he is a god – though the people of Judea already know that no man can ever be a god – and sees no reason, as a god, to keep to the old compacts between Rome and Jerusalem. He orders his statue to be placed in the holy Temple. His generals attempt to explain to him that the Jews will rebel, that this has been tried before, that they would have to kill every man in the city to make this happen.

'Then kill every man in the city,' Caligula says. Or something similar to that. Or something as unconcerned as that, at least.

Caligula's madness has encircled him so that although he rules an empire as wide as any ever known, he is entrapped within the labyrinth of his own mind. He cannot see beyond the horizons of his own loves and hatreds, his own family, his own cock. He fucks his sister, they say, and makes his horse a consul, and when his sister falls pregnant he cuts the unborn child out of her belly.

In Jerusalem the new prefect, Marullus, attempts to place the statue. And the anticipated consequences come to pass.

Bar-Avo has three thousand men under his orders now in Jerusalem alone, and more importantly the people are with them, the households give them shelter, the young men come to fight with them. This statue of the Emperor Caligula, his nose upturned to the heaven, a laurel wreath on his mad brow, is too much for the people of Judea to tolerate and the High Priest cannot convince them, does not even try to do so. Caiaphas is gone now, and it is another of Annas's sons who meets with Prefect Marullus to say, 'Not this, not this, there will be no way to stop the killing.' But the Prefect, even if he were the best man in the Empire, would have to obey the commands of his God-Emperor.

Caligula has set himself against the God of Israel. Upon Him particularly and necessarily, for both are jealous gods. All the people who will have to die to wage that war of god on God are insignificant.

Massacres and riots and rebellions and battles are nothing new now. Mothers sharpen weapons for their sons. Grandparents shelter fleeing rebels, saying, 'He was never here, we have seen no one.' Men are slaughtered in the noonday square and their bellies sliced open so that their entrails slide out glistening as they yet scream. There is death upon death, and though it never starts to feel easy, it begins to feel expected. The land is becoming accustomed to living this way.

For every Roman excess there is a rebellion. Every rebellion is put down with increasing brutality. Every act of brutality hardens the people a little further, making the next uprising more violent. Every act of violence justifies a more extreme show of force in suppressing it. There are fewer and fewer people among the Jews who trust Rome at all. Even to speak of trusting Rome now, of wanting peace with Rome, is to forget the murdered sons, the repulsive statues in the Temple, the men with daggers concealed in their cloaks. The thing has no end. Or no end but one.

Bar-Avo sidles up to a man in the marketplace. Who is he? A baker, by the scent of him and the flour dusting his drawstring trousers and his leather shoes. Bar-Avo has never seen him before. He probably does not deserve to die. There is a crumb of dandruff above his ear. The back of his neck is red from too much sun. He has a hot boil starting just above the place where his tunic rubs his neck. Some woman probably loves this breathing body, or is used to it at least. Some woman would have a hot compress with fragrant herbs to draw the poison out of that boil this evening after his work is done. He should not have come here to stand in the marketplace.

To do good, sometimes, one must do evil. He reminds himself that this honest baker has paid his taxes like a good citizen of Rome. That perhaps he sends loaves to the Roman garrison or to the Prefect. That he collaborates, over and over again, just by living in the city and not rising up against them.

Bar-Avo's cloak flows around him in loose, deep folds. Within the cloak is the dagger. The crowd surges and bounces. There are sizzling scents of freshly cooked meat from the stalls. People are loud, shouting for attention from stallholders, watching out for the thieving hands of small children, demanding from one another where they need to go next and have they tried yet the bread with dill, the cheese, the wine, the garlic, the oil? He waits until a surge pushes him forward into the baker.

They learned the lesson Pilate taught them extremely well. Pilate understood the methods of terror. Pilate is no longer the prefect, but his methods are still effective.

Bar-Avo's dagger slides out so smoothly. No one sees it within the folds of the cloak. He finds the baker's ribs with a steadying hand and sends the dagger through just here, behind the heart, with that horizontal slicing motion that cuts the heart in two. The baker says 'ump'. That is all. It was an easy death, in so far as men are ever afforded an easy death. His body slides against the wall but the crowd does not let him fall completely to the ground quite yet, they are pressed so tightly. No one has even noticed. Bar-Avo moves a little away. It does not have to be far. It is not wise to try to run. He has learned that before.

He has already sidled up to the meat stall, is haggling with the vendor over the price of a pound of chicken hearts, when someone else finds the baker is dead. It is a woman. She is screaming over the body slumped sideways against the wall, the red flower blooming across his back.

People still remember the massacre in the public square. They know whose trick it is to conceal men with daggers in the crowd. Bar-Avo says to himself: it is not I who have done this, but Rome, who taught me that this is the way to bring fear to the city. The crowd begins to turn towards the baker's body to find out what the commotion is. Now. It is time now.

'Romans!' shouts Bar-Avo. 'Roman spies! They're among us with their long daggers!'

'Yes!' shouts someone else, because people are always eager to spread bad news and to lie to augment it. 'I've seen them in the crowd! I saw a soldier's knife under a cloak! They're here! They want to kill us all!'

There is a stampede then. Stalls are overturned, hot fat spitting as it fizzles on the moist stone and makes the ground slick, piles of good fresh bread trodden into the dirt, dogs barking and grabbing for unattended meat, apples rolling here and there, women scream-ing and men taking the opportunity to grab where they can. People fall and other people tread on them, and children are crushed up against the walls and little fingers are squashed underfoot. Bar-Avo sees a child screaming, under a teetering pan of hot oil for frying cakes, and he snatches him up, lifting him above his head, so that he is out of reach of the crowd, which now thinks with one mind.

That is what he has learned in his life. What a crowd thinks. How to change what a crowd thinks. How not to think like them.

He holds the child above the crowd, smiles at it as he would at any of his own children, gives it a roll he has snatched from one of the stalls, dipped in rendered goose fat. The child munches content-edly and when the commotion has settled down the mother finds them and takes her baby gratefully, with a smile.

By this time the market is quieter and almost empty, with just a few sobbing stallholders to count the cost. Let the people remember, he thinks. Let them remember that they are not free. That this happened today. Just because the Romans did not do it, the Romans could still do exactly this. They must never forget that these people are in their homeland. Whatever is necessary to do to be rid of them must be done.

This was the special thing Pilate taught them. The cloak and dagger. Bar-Avo and his men do not often do it. But sometimes, when things begin to seem too peaceful, when it seems that perhaps they have forgotten. People need to be reminded all the time. Most men will simply fall asleep if you let them.

They gather more and more men to them. Not just fighters but preachers, fishermen, healers, sailors, spies in distant lands. His men go combing the streets for people who will be sympathetic to their cause. There is a point when they are particularly interested in healers and holy men – people listen to these men when perhaps they will not listen to a man with a sword. If a man can heal, it is a sign that God is with him. They want God with them.

So they bring him, once, a man who worships that dead preacher, Yehoshuah, as they bring many men whom they have found preaching in the marketplace or teaching in a quiet spot at the edge of town. The worship of Yehoshuah is a rather esoteric cult, though not the strangest that exists, and the man seems grateful for the attention.

His name is Gidon of Yaffo and he is almost as old as Bar-Avo, rangy and quietly fervent, speaking as Yehoshuah did of the end of days, which will surely come within our lifetimes. He tells how Yehoshuah died and rose again from the grave and was seen by several people.

'Did you see it?' says Bar-Avo.

'I have seen it in my heart,' says Gidon of Yaffo.

'That is not the same thing. Did any man you would trust with your life see it?'

'I would trust them all with my life for they have seen the risen Lord.'

'But you did not know before to trust them. And if the Messiah is come,' says Bar-Avo, 'why does not the lion lie down with the lamb?

Where is the great crack of doom that presages the end of the world and the final judgement of all mankind? Where is the true king of Israel now, if he has performed this strange trick and returned from the grave? Why does he not take his throne?'

'These things will happen,' says Gidon of Yaffo, 'soon and in our days. I have heard stories from the very mouths of those who saw miracles. Before this generation has passed away, there will be the signs and portents, the lord Messiah will return and the Temple will run red with blood.'

'That last,' mutters Bar-Avo to Isaac, the man who brought Gidon of Yaffo to him, 'will surely happen, for we will make it happen. Fellow,' he asks, raising his voice, 'will you take arms with us to fight the Roman scum?'

Gidon shakes his head. 'We do not fight for this broken land and this corrupt people. When our Lord returns he will cleanse the earth himself.'

'Then you are of no use to me,' says Bar-Avo, and sends him on his way.

Isaac says to him, 'Romans as well as Jews are taking on this teaching.'

Bar-Avo shrugs.

'I have heard it preached in synagogues in Egypt and in Syria. Slaves and women like it, for they say that they encourage all to join in, with no exceptions.'

'Tell me again,' says Bar-Avo, 'when there are as many temples to Yehoshuah as there are to Mithras or to Isis.'

'It might happen,' says Isaac stubbornly. 'My grandfather said he remembered his grandfather telling him of when only a few men worshipped Mithras. There were not always such temples. Gods rise and fall –'

'As the angels on Jacob's ladder, yes, I know. And only our God rises above them all and lives forever. And what good will it do if you are right and the dead man Yehoshuah becomes a god?'

Isaac blinks.

'He was a Jew, Yehoshuah. If he were . . . not like Mithras or Ba'al, but if his worship were even as widespread as the cult of Juno –'

'Juno!'

'All right, Robigus then. Even Robigus, the god of crop blight, if he were even as loved as that . . . a Jew . . . might not the Empire soften towards us?'

Bar-Avo looks at him. What a kind-hearted boy he is. How did he get to be so simple, in a world this hard?

Bar-Avo speaks very quietly and low and very slowly.

'Rome hates us,' he says. 'We are their conquered people and we are dust under their feet.'

'But if –'

'Listen. If they want something from us, they will take it. They will not stop hating us. They will find a way to say that the thing they want was never ours to begin with.'

Isaac looks at him with those trusting cow-eyes.

'Do you think that when they send our good oil to Rome they say, "This is oil pressed by Jews"? They say, "This is oil brought from the far reaches of the Empire by the might of Rome." If Yehoshuah ends by being loved in Rome they will find a way to use him against us.'

Bar-Avo puts his hand on the boy's shoulder.

'You fight bravely,' he says, 'and you love peace. I know it is hard to understand. We want to find a way towards peace. But the only way is the sword. If we do not drive them out, one way or another they will crush us.'

And Isaac is still looking uncertainly towards the man who preached long after Bar-Avo has gone.

And then it comes time for him to do what perhaps he had always been destined to do. If we believe that God has seen all things before they come to pass, that every woman is destined to bear the children she does, and every betrayer is bound to betray and every peacekeeper intended by God to attempt to keep the peace, perhaps too a warmonger is destined for that purpose by the good Lord who made him.

On the hillsides the mothers weep for their fallen sons. In the marketplace men preach curious doctrines and strange new ideas to fit with these uncertain times. In the Temple, Annas the former High Priest and father and father-in-law of High Priests, dies quietly without having secured the lasting peace he longed for. He dies knowing that war may come again at any minute, and that the streets of Jerusalem are no less bloody than when the Empire first breached the Temple wall. His sons gather to mourn him and one of the youngest among them, Ananus, becomes High Priest in his stead.

And it is morning and it is evening. And it is one hundred and thirty years since Rome first breached Jerusalem and still she squats over the city, enforcing her will, enslaving the people. And something must be done. Something more extreme.

It is clear to all that they are on the verge of open war with Rome. There have been scuffles, Romans have been thrown out of the city and are pressing their way back in. Some urge war and some urge peace. Ananus, the new High Priest, makes a speech in the centre of Jerusalem. It is a good speech and a merciful one, calling upon the people not even yet to despair, for they may still come to some good accommodation with Rome and there need not be war. He calls on them to think of the values of their forefathers, and the love which they feel for peace. Annas, his father, would have been proud of his son for giving this speech and the people are moved by it.

Bar-Avo does not hear the speech but he hears word of it from a dozen different men. Well. So much blood spilled and yet still the thing is not done. How quickly people forget the taste of freedom, swapping it for this easy comfortable thing they call peace. Sleep is peaceful. Death is peaceful. Freedom is life and wakefulness.

He feels a kind of contempt for the people of the land these days. He is fighting for them, but apparently they do not understand why or feel gratitude. He has to lead them by the hand through every part of the journey and still they can be swayed off course by any mildly effective rhetorician in the public square.

Well, sacrifices must be made. For the good of the people, sacrifices must be made.

There is a storm the night they invade the Temple. It's not a coincidence. The Temple is guarded by thick walls, by strong men. There are barred gates which are lowered at night to keep the treasures inside safe while the men sleep. The whole city of Jerusalem is a great guard to the Temple also. If they had tried to take the Temple on a dark quiet night, the moment one man saw them he would have shouted the halloo to the city and Jerusalem would have defended her greatest treasure and dearest joy.

So when the storm blows up, they know God Himself is signalling to them that it is time. When it comes louder and louder, when the thunder begins to roll across the sky in almost ceaseless peals and the rain lashes down and the wind screams, then they know that God has given them the cover they need. No one will hear them now, and no shouts of alarm from the Temple will reach the city. They gather their tools and their weapons and they run through the rain up the hill to the place where God lives.

Up on the hill, although they do not know it, Ananus has looked out at the approaching storm and taken a message from it too. God is saying, in words as clear as fire, that no one will stir from their houses this night. The rain has given them a night of peace, while the thunder is His voice shouting His presence over the land. They are safe, they are well.

'Tell your men to sleep,' he says to the Levite head of the guards. 'Leave a few men to stand watch, but let the rest of them sleep tonight.'

And Ananus takes to his own warm bed in the Temple enclosure, sends word to his wife in the city that all will be well this night, gives his prayers to God for a good night and that his soul will be returned to him in the morning when he awakes. He plugs his ears up with soft wool to drown out the noise of the storm, pulls his pillow under his head and sleeps.

At the gates of the outer courtyard of the Temple, Bar-Avo's men gather. They are sodden already. The driving rain which the wind sweeps in all directions has poured on them like buckets emptied over their heads and flung at their bodies. This is not the gentle rain of blessing. It is the rain of anger, of the God who knows that His terrible will is to be done this night and who is already full of rage at those who dare to carry out His plan.

There are ten of them at this gate. There will be others elsewhere. Even with the protection of the storm, the work must be done as quickly as possible. Bar-Avo is not here yet – this is work for young men. The team at the gate is headed by Isaac, who will one day distinguish himself gloriously in battle but today is simply extremely competent, directing the men to cut through the five iron bars of the main gate.

They bring out their saws. There is no other way. The saws shriek, metal biting metal. It could not have been done on any other night – a single howling cut would have wakened a dozen men from the deepest slumber.

The rain drives and they are soaked through and dripping and their fingers slip. One man makes a deep cut in his own hand with the serrated saw blade, filled with flakes of rust and iron from the gate. They wrap it up and continue to work. A lone guard makes his solitary round of the ramparts at the top of the Temple wall. They press themselves into the shadows as he passes. Soon enough, one bar is free, then another, then another.

The skinniest of them presses himself through the gap and they can work the saw two-handed, so it goes faster. The fourth bar is out when a guard dozing in the outer courtyard thinks he sees something hazily, through the rain, moving at the gate. He is a large man, fat and tall, carrying a stout belly proudly before him and a stout club by his side. As he sees the men at the gate he shouts back behind him and breaks into a heavy run.

There is not enough space for the others to get through yet. The skinniest of the men at the gate – his name is Yochim – freezes, his shirt and cloak plastered to his skin by the rain. He is shuddering.

The guard grabs him by his clothes, hurls him against the gate, shouting and calling through the storm, but the thunder crushes his words. He bellows again for the other guards, as he picks up Yochim and then roars into the boy's ear, 'Where are the others? Where are your fucking friends?'

Yochim, dazed, blinded by the rain, deafened by the blow, lashes out with his hand, which he finds is still holding the saw, and the guard goes down, his face raked and his eye sliced in two. He is screaming and writhing as one of the other men passes Yochim a sword through the gate and, after a nod of confirmation, Yochim brings the point down through the guard's throat.

The body jerks and trembles and is still. Yochim sinks to his knees for a few quiet moments while the wind whips up again around them and the thunder roars and there are three quick flashes of lightning one after the other. Then he scrambles to his feet again, wipes his face, leaving a long smear of bright red blood on his wet cheek, and they begin to saw again.

The bars pop free one after another. Isaac squeezes through the gap, scraping his arm on a protruding tongue of metal. Ariel and Joseph follow him, then the others, carrying their swords now openly in their hands. They walk towards the guards' gatehouse. No one could see them if they looked out of that window, the rain is driving too hard and the night is too dark. They might see a shadow moving, but it could as well be a barred cloud moving across the face of the moon.

They stand by the door of the gatehouse. Inside it is warm and dry. Isaac boldly places his ear to the door. If someone inside opened it now, they would have his head off before any of the others could stop it. But no one opens the door. Isaac listens for a moment and holds up three fingers. Three guards.

They burst in, swords drawn, shouting with the raging voice of the storm that batters on the Temple. They slay one man before he has even been able to look around, a sword digging down into his neck from the top of his shoulder and dragged out again, leaving his head toppled at an awkward angle. The other two throw down their mugs and draw weapons to fight, but the numbers are too great.

One of them is a boy not much older than Yochim. He fights like a demon, whirling his arms and screaming and yelling. It is Isaac, the leader of the band, who steps in and cuts him with an upward thrust as his arms are raised, coming in through the armpit and slicing into the chest. The other man, older, in his fifties with a beard of pepper and salt, fights well and honourably. He backs himself into a corner of the room when he sees the numbers, forcing them to come at him one at a time. He manages to take an arm off one of the Edomeans – Haron – before they bring him down, bubbling blood from his mouth, falling to his knees and then on to his face.

There are more deaths. Six guards in the inner gatehouse. A dozen priests asleep in their beds – they surround them in the dormitory with raised swords and bring the blades down at the same moment so that all twelve die without waking. A man returning in the night from the privy dies with his head half in a dream he'd had of a woman – not his wife – bearing a garland of flowers. They give him a red necklace before he even knows who they are.

When they have taken the inner courtyard, they send for their eminent leaders – the men who are too old now to fight but will wish to see the glorious victory. They slit the throats of two guards posted at the door to the High Priest's house in the Temple when one of the men goes to take a piss and the other comes to see where he went.

They think that the High Priest will have escaped into the Temple building. But he is waiting there in the upper chamber of his small house. Perhaps he did not think it could come to this. Or perhaps, like his father, he believes so strongly in the power of the office that he knows no harm will come to him. Who would hurt the High Priest? And perhaps he can still reason with them. Perhaps it is not too late for peace.

It is then that Bar-Avo comes, a warm fur robe around him and four strong men by his side. They have saved this for him. He is an old man, but still commands the respect he did in the prime of his life

– Av-Raham taught him how to do that. He comes wrapped in layers of warm clothes and with one of his men holding a hood above his head to keep him dry.

As they cross the threshold of the Temple, through the gates that are now thrown open, Bar-Avo finds himself thinking again of that man who was crucified in his place by Pilate, half a lifetime ago. Of how certain he was that the world was coming to an end, and how perhaps it is coming to an end, perhaps it has always been his place to make it come to pass.

They enter the chamber of Ananus. He has been the son most like his father, the one most fit to take Annas's mantle as far as the business of accommodating to Rome goes. He has tried to keep this worthless peace, he has apologized for Rome and made excuses for her. He has made the daily sacrifices to Rome in the holy Temple. Bar-Avo has already had his elder brother Jonathan killed. Ananus does not know Bar-Avo's name, but he knows whom to fear.

When he sees who is there, his body tenses. He begins to shake. His lips become pale. He tries to call out for the guards, then stops himself, saying, 'No, no, they're dead already, aren't they? Dead, for you have killed them, haven't you? Yes, I know you have.'

Bar-Avo hits him across the face. It is not a hard blow. But no one has struck the High Priest in quite some time, probably since he was a little boy. He turns very white. Does he begin to understand now the seriousness of his situation?

'What do you want?' says Ananus.

Bar-Avo smiles. 'Just to talk, High Priest. For now, only to talk.'

'I have nothing to say to a man like you.'

Bar-Avo strikes him again. It is like a game between them. Bar-Avo's composure does not alter as he hits the High Priest, or as he sits back in his chair and says, 'Very well, then. I shall say a few things to you.'

He reminds himself suddenly of another interview, where he was the one standing, and his interlocutor was sitting just so, composed, behind a desk. Is he Pilate now? Is any man with enough swords at his disposal Pilate?

They have the usual dance.

Bar-Avo requests information about the strongholds of the city, about the weapons in the Temple. Ananus refuses to answer.

Bar-Avo flatters, suggesting that the High Priest has a great deal of influence with the people and that a speech from him could convince them to fight against the Romans.

'If every man in this nation took up swords against them,' says Bar-Avo, 'they could not stand against us. United, we cannot be defeated.'

'You will kill us all like this,' says Ananus. 'You and your fucking faction, you and your army of five thousand men – don't you know there are fifty thousand who serve the Temple? Don't you think they're more important than you? Them alone. Not even beginning to count all the others.'

'Traitors,' says Bar-Avo, 'collaborators. Rome would control Jerusalem for ten thousand years if they had their way. The land must be free. The people thirst for freedom!'

'The people don't care!' Ananus is shouting now. 'They support you because you bring them bread and water and willow bark for their fevers.'

'It's more than you do.'

Ananus inclines his head, a little.

'We distribute bread also. And we give them a place to talk with the Lord. Most people . . . listen, ordinary people –' and Ananus has never sounded more patrician than now – 'out of a thousand men, do you know what nine hundred and ninety want? A good price for their crops, a good husband for their daughter, good rain in its season and good sun in its time. They don't care who rules. They don't care about who controls holy Jerusalem as long as they can still go to their Temple and worship in peace. Most people want us to find a way to live peacefully with Rome.'

'Rome who slaughtered their sons? Rome who raped their daughters?'

'Even so. There will be more daughters and more sons, thank

God. And shall they also be sacrificed to fight an unwinnable war?'

'We shall win,' says Bar-Avo, 'for God is with us.'

Ananus shakes his head. He is so old now, though his eyes are still sharp and his mind is not clouded. Once he had been as tall and as strong as his father. The best of the brothers, people said, the best of the five of them, with those muscles in his shoulders like hard knots of old rope. But the power in his mind is not in his body now. He could not fight these men off.

'God is with the victor,' he says, 'that is all God has ever done. Listen –' he places his hand palm-down on the table, as if he concealed a trick underneath it – 'it is not too late to make your peace. People remember my father. The men who were his friends are my friends now. I have a great deal of influence. I could speak on your behalf. Perhaps some arrangement can even be brokered. Your forces are strongest in the east, are they not? Perhaps we can make an agreement with the Roman captains in the east to give you some control of that region –'

Bar-Avo slams the heel of his hand on to the table.

'We do not negotiate,' says Bar-Avo, 'with the occupying force. The whole of the land is ours.'

Ananus will not give up. No one who longs for peace can ever give up. Not even now, with the knife on the table before him.

'There will come a better day than this,' he says, 'there will come a better way. God has promised us this land. Don't you think it's for Him to fulfil His promises in the time and in the way He sees fit?'

The storm whips up again and around Ananus's little chamber the wind moans and the great gouts of rain like the blood of the lamb scattered to the four corners of the altar splatter in through the open window and the thunder crashes and the lightning cracks because God is angry with the land though Ananus does not know how he could have done differently.

He has lived his whole life under the words of his father, the same words the whole family lived to: keep the peace, keep the Temple working, keep the sacrifices which allow us to speak to God every day. It is he who has oiled the relationship between the new governor and the Temple, who has maintained his father's old relationships with Syria and Egypt, with informants in Rome and along the coast. Every man must choose what to dedicate his life to and he has chosen this: only peace. Not justice, because peace and justice are enemies. Not vengeance, not loyalty, not pride, not family, not friends, not – on occasion – dignity. Only ever peace, which demands the full load of a man's life. But his life has not been enough.

He is calling out loudly for his guards as they approach, although he knows his guards are dead, although the wind whips his words away and the thunder drowns them out.

He is making a point, rather than hoping to escape.

Bar-Avo touches the spot on the man's forehead, between the eyes, but it does not calm him. He places a restraining hand on the forehead and their eyes meet.

'I dedicate your death to God,' says Bar-Avo.

'You condemn all of us to bloody war,' says Ananus.

'Rather everlasting war,' says Bar-Avo, 'rather everlasting flight and battle and flight again, than surrender now.'

And he remembers the crowd shouting, 'Barabbas! Barabbas! Barabbas!'

There is that Roman game called 'one of two will die, and the crowd will decide which'. If that game had fallen out the other way round, he would not be here now to complete this task, and that other man, Yehoshuah, would have continued his own curious work. And everything would have been different. But the world continues as it is and it is not given to us to see the contrary outcome. And Bar-Avo does not play that Roman game. It is he who decides who will live and who will die.

Ananus begins to say, 'You are wrong . . .' but he does not complete the sentence.

And Bar-Avo puts the knife to Ananus's throat and bleeds him like a lamb.

Epilogue

'I should not mistake if I said that the death of Ananus was the beginning of the destruction of the city, and that from this very day may be dated the overthrow of her wall, and the ruin of her affairs.'

Josephus, *The Jewish War*, V, 2

There is a way to break a city, if a city needs to be broken. It is not a magnificent spectacle. It is no swift victory with an easy triumph to be taken in Rome before proceeding to greater glory in other lands. The people will be so ruined that they will have little worth even as slaves. The treasures of the city may be destroyed before you can parade them in glory. Nonetheless, sometimes there is no other way.

First, encircle the city with a great host of men – this kind of victory is expensive, also. One should attempt it only on a city, like Jerusalem, which has rebelled so flagrantly and with the spilling of such a quantity of Roman blood that no other option is available.

The people of Jerusalem had killed the High Priest whom Rome had set over them. They had appointed their own High Priests and minted their own currency and made every appearance of becoming again a sovereign nation with her capital in Jerusalem. Titus, the son of the Emperor Vespasian, was dispatched to deal with Jerusalem, along with four legions – that is, twenty-four thousand men – and in addition double that number of auxiliaries.

The honour of Rome must be preserved. Once Rome owns a city, that city cannot simply declare that it is free. It has to be retaken with such force that the news will echo around the world. Titus, the son of the Emperor, therefore, with a force of seventy-two thousand men.

Second, see that no man can leave or come into the city. Even if the city is encircled by men, you must take care to guard the high mountain passes and the places that seem impassable. It is these people's native land. They know its secret passageways.

Allow no food in, no wagons delivering grain, no fresh-pressed oil from the northern olive groves. Take those wagons to feed your own soldiers with. It will be a slow process. Stocks take a long time to run down. Hunger takes a long time to build. Be sure to keep your soldiers occupied, well fed and entertained. You would not want them to think of mutiny. Remind them often of the treasure that awaits them inside the holy city.

Then it is wise to build a high wall around the city. It will be your sentry if your lookouts are overwhelmed by attackers. Hunger makes men desperate and mad. They say that during the siege of Jerusalem women stole food from their children, men killed each other over a handful of barley. Stop up the watercourses into the city. The siege of Jerusalem lasted from March to September, the hottest months of the year. When hunger comes, it is without mercy. They say that men ate the dead. They say that a woman's house was found by the smell of roasting flesh and they discovered that she had cooked her baby in an oven and was eating its leg daintily.

If you are lucky, wise heads will prevail, urging surrender on the people before destruction comes. The zealots of Jerusalem had killed their wisest heads. Men attempting to desert were killed. Some flung themselves off the walls, preferring to die quickly rather than suffer the agonizing slow torture of starvation.

Your soldiers will be bored. Allow them their head a little, to release their energies. Soldiers building the platforms which would allow them, in time, to scale the walls of Jerusalem used to enjoy showing their food to the starving prisoners of the city. They allowed the sweet scent of roasted lamb to drift across the walls, so that every person in the city looked hungrily at every other one.

Titus, a wise leader, also gave his soldiers captured escapees from the city to crucify in a variety of amusing positions. This one upside-down. That one as if dancing. Another two nailed together as if locked in an embrace. Such simple entertainment will occupy them usefully.

Do not underestimate your enemy, however. The Jews were cunning. They dug tunnels under the wall surrounding them and hollowed out the earth under the soldiers' platforms, propping them up with timber. When the works were complete, they sent men in with bitumen torches to set the timber struts on fire and the first the Romans knew of the whole operation was when their platforms suddenly collapsed into the tunnels and pure flames burst through the ground and consumed them utterly. This lengthened the siege considerably.

Do not be concerned about setbacks, however. Hunger will eventually destroy the people. In Jerusalem, after a few months, they ate even the sacred wheat set aside for the Holy of Holies, and the sacred oil for the holy lamps. When they asked people to swear they had not a handful of barley, they used the very name of their God, Yahaveh, as the binding seal of the oath, that same name which had been so sacred to them that any who uttered it was put to death. Very few men, it turns out, love God more than they love their own aching hungry belly. They will sink to such degradation of themselves that you will scarcely believe it possible.

As time goes on, more and more people will attempt to desert the city. Use them where you can – for information, or to take as slaves. Do not hesitate to kill them if they seem useless.

Batter the walls, of course, night and day. Attempt to lever out stones. Build up your platforms again. There will come a time to invade. You will be fighting against weakened, sickly, hungry men. You will prevail, for Rome always prevails. This is the whole of the law.

There is nothing new under the sun, says Solomon, son of David, that selfsame David who stormed the walls of Jerusalem and took her from the Jebusites, who perhaps themselves had taken her from someone else.

So it goes the same way. The battering of the walls had not ceased for six days and six nights. The inexorable platforms rose level with the city walls and the commander, Titus, had them test the ground under the struts with long blades ceaselessly. The people in the city knew the end was coming.

They were different then from the way they had been one hundred and thirty years earlier, when Pompey first let a stone tumble from the wall in the glittering air. The services in the Temple continued, but what did they have to sacrifice? They had eaten the sacred oil and the sacred grain. There were no lambs left to slaughter. The priests circled the sanctuary with pale skin and dark hungry eyes and a gnawing sense within them that God was angry and His wrath could not be quenched.

Titus knew that the wall would fall the day he stood in the morning on the highest platform and addressed the citizens of Jerusalem. The stench of the place rose to his nostrils even as his generals helped him up the wooden structure. There were rotting bodies in Jerusalem, unburied. It was silent, apart from the birds circling overhead. He spoke loudly. The dark-eyed people on the ramparts could hear him.

'People of Jerusalem,' he said, 'you Jews have been in constant rebellion since Pompey first conquered you. Not just rebellion – open war with Rome. And why did you think you had any hope at all?

'Did you think you'd win because of your numbers? A tiny proportion of the Roman armies has been strong enough to defeat you. Did you think you'd win because of the loyalty of your allies? We are in the empire of Rome and no nation would support you over us. Did you think you'd win because you're so muscular and strong? Even the Germans are our slaves. Did you think you'd win because of your strong walls? There are no walls stronger than the ocean that encircles Britain and yet they kneel down and worship our swords.

'No. Do you know why you thought you'd win? It was because

we were kind to you. We gave you too much. We crowned your own people as kings, we let you observe your religious laws, we even let you take collections for your Temple. We treated you well, and you have taken our kindness as a sign of weakness.

'Jews, surrender now. We will kill only the men and take the women and children as slaves. Surrender now or understand what it means for Rome to be unkind.'

Titus is even now regretting the generosity of Pompey when he stood in his sandals in the Holy of Holies and said, 'Let them keep their ritual, why not? They have fought bravely.' Pompey should have crushed them, and then Titus would not have had to undertake this long and boring siege.

The people of Jerusalem sent back a message that if he would only let them leave, they would depart, every man, woman and child, into the desert and leave the empty city to Titus. Titus angrily replied that they should understand their position: they had been conquered, they could not bargain. He prepared his troops for the final assault.

The Jews say that at this precise moment a tiny beetle flew into Titus's ear and laid an egg which grew into a grub. And they say that over time that grub bored into his brain and lived there as a full-grown beetle, eating more and more of the matter of his head every year so that the pain and the sensation of being battered from the inside were utterly intolerable to him and when he died and they opened his head they found that the beetle had grown to the size of a bird. But no commentators other than the Jews mention this, so one may doubt the accuracy of these reports.

And the first stone fell, brought down by the battering engines. The soldiers swarmed into the city and began to kill, for they had waited a long time and many of their fellows had been killed by Jewish missiles and Jewish fire across those many months. Titus was no Pompey, and this siege had been no swift and well-managed affair. In any case, the purpose was not to secure the city for the good of Rome but to punish. To send a message.

The soldiers pulled down the buildings stone from stone. They slew anyone they met. They set fires in the colonnades of the Temple and the other public buildings, so that the silver and gold covering the timbers melted into shining puddles on the floor of the great plaza.

And they came at last to the Holy of Holies in the very heart of the Temple, where, they had been promised, the richest prizes of gold would be. They stopped then, amazed. Not just by the precious metals but by the workmanship, the rich decoration on every surface, the finely turned candelabrum, the beautiful silver trumpets whose metal was as thin as a blade of grass. Jerusalem's riches were here, indeed, her most precious things entirely inward.

The soldiers milled around the outer sanctuary, collecting the golden goblets and ewers. And one man, seeing the veil across the inner sanctuary ripped away and the space within revealed, jumped up on his friend's back to get a better view. And yes, the strange little sanctuary was empty. And, laughing, he pulled a burning timber from the hand of his friend and positioned himself just so and pulled back his arm, straining at the shoulder, and threw it like a javelin into the holiest place in the world.

The old wood and the dry cloth caught fire almost at once. And in the whole of Jerusalem there was a wailing, keening cry as of a woman who has woken in the morning to find her child dead.

There were other brutalities. The Romans set fire to one of the remaining colonnades of the outer court even though six thousand women and children were sheltering there, having been told by a false prophet that God had promised him that this place alone would be spared. The corpses were piled up so high on the altar of the Temple that blood flowed in a constant river down the steps.

They set fire to all the large buildings of the city: the council chamber, the tax office, the citadel, the palaces, the dwelling places of men of high rank, even the building that had once been the Prefect's home. By the eighth day of the August moon those who still lived woke to see the dawn blood red, for the whole city was on fire.

The fires burned for days. And when they finally burned them-selves out, the soldiers went through the city and if any stone was sitting on top of any other they pulled them down. Except for one wall, the Western Wall of the outer courtyard of the Temple, which had remained standing and which it pleased Titus to leave in place to show what a mighty feat he had accomplished by destroying this city.

Titus took his troops back to Rome and there he celebrated a great triumph, parading through the streets of the city the holy ves-sels he had won in battle from the Temple in razed Jerusalem. They constructed a triumphal arch of marble depicting the spoils of war, Titus's Arch, which stands in Rome to this day, just west of the Col-osseum. And they minted a special commemorative coin in honour of the victory: Judea Capta, it read, Judea is captured. They struck more and more of them, for twenty-five years. And all across the Empire, from Britain to Egypt, from Spain to Turkey, when men paid for a loaf of bread or a side of pork or a turn at the whore, they paid with a coin showing a Jew bound with his hands behind his back or a woman weeping under a Judean date palm.

'How deserted sits the city that once was full of people!
How like a widow she is, who was great among the nations.
The princess among all provinces has become a slave.'

The Book of Lamentations

Time continued, of course. The Jews did not cease to rebel, nor did the Romans cease to smite them. The Emperor Hadrian, crushing a rebellion sixty-five years later and attempting to forestall another, renamed the city and forbade the Jews from entering it at all. His soldiers brought in new populations to Judea and chased the Jews out into other lands, to arrive in Antioch or Syria or Gaul or Kush or Rome herself and mourn their Temple and conduct their little rites of remembrance.

And in time, a new god rose in Rome. A small cult, grown slowly mighty. And although one might say: this was the triumph of the

Jews, this Jew-god risen to a high place in Roman esteem, nonetheless by the time he arrived there he was no longer a Jew at all, quite the reverse in a sense.

For the new god was welcomed for one thing at least: it was evident to all that the destruction of Jerusalem must be a message from the God of the Jews. The wisest men sought for prophecies that could make the thing comprehensible. They thought of signs they had seen – perhaps a comet, perhaps a cow giving birth to a lamb. The new god, the Crucified King, provided an explanation: the Jews had angered their God by rejecting his true emissary. The people fingered their coins, rubbing their thumbs over that weeping Jewish woman, the figure of a man with his sword raised against her. It needed an explanation. If the Jews had rejected their God's true emissary, that was why Jerusalem, one of the greatest and most famous and most prosperous and most beautiful cities on the earth, had been destroyed. Blame could not, this explanation made abundantly clear, in any way attach to Rome.

Storytellers know that every story is at least partly a lie. Every story could be told in four different ways, or forty or four thousand. Every emphasis or omission is a kind of lie, shaping a moment to make a point. So when, between thirty-five and seventy years after Yehoshuah's death, Mark and then Matthew and then Luke the compiler and then John the theologian came to tell their stories it was as well for them to exonerate the Romans, who ruled the empire they lived in, and to blame the Jews, whose wickedness had clearly caused the destruction of their holy city. It was as well for them to add in perhaps a line here or there in which Yehoshuah had predicted that the Temple would fall, that the city would fall. This made him look wiser, as it made the Jews look worse for not believing, even in face of such clear evidence. Nothing happened without a reason.

Storytellers know that people enjoy tales that explain to them the origin of things, the way things come to be the way they are. This story is no different. Every story has an author, some teller of lies. Do not imagine that a storyteller is unaware of the effect of every word they choose. Do not suppose for a moment that an impartial observer exists.

Once upon a time there was a man, Yehoshuah, whose name the Romans changed to Jesus, for that sat more easily on their tongues. There may well indeed have been such a man, or several men whose sayings are united under that one name. Tales accreted to him, and theories grew up around and over him. He became, like Caesar, the son of a god. Like the god Tammuz, or the god Ba'al, or the god Orpheus, it was said he died and rose again. Like Perseus, he was born of a woman who had never known a man. He was turned into a god and certain things were lost and certain things were added.

And when one peels away the gilding and the plaster and the paint that were applied to him, what remains? So much of what he said, he took from the Torah of the Jews. 'Love your neighbour as yourself' is an old Jewish ideal. But Yehoshuah was unique, in his time and place, for saying, 'Love your enemy.'

It is a dreamer's doctrine. Visionary, astonishing. And a hard road, in times of war and occupation. If all involved had listened to those words, matters would have fallen out quite differently. And if those who claimed to follow him later had dedicated themselves to that one thing – 'Love your enemy' – much bloodshed might have been avoided. But perhaps the idea was too difficult, for it is not much observed, even to this day. Easier to prefer one's friend to one's enemy. Easier to destroy than to build or to keep a thing standing.

And so the Temple burned. The walls of Jerusalem fell. The people were scattered into exile in ten lands and ten times ten. And they took with them their unusual stubbornness and their distinct ways. And a book walked those same paths, from synagogue to synagogue at first, telling a tale of how miraculous one man had been and how evil those who rejected him were, and therefore bringing good news for some and bad for others.

This was how it ended. And all the sorrow that came after followed from this.

Notes on Sources

This is, of course, a work of fiction. Much of it is made up, especially the personal lives of public figures, which tend not to be recorded. However, many of the most surprising parts of this book are based in fact. So, a few brief notes on some of the things that are true. In so far as we know what is true. My main sources have been the works of Josephus, the Talmud and the Gospels themselves.

Miryam

'When his family heard about it, they went out to lay hold on him, for they said: "He is out of his mind"' – Gospel of Mark 3:21

'Then his mother and brothers came to see him and, standing outside, sent someone in to call him . . . And he answered them saying, "Who is my mother, or my brothers?" And he looked about on those who sat around him and said, "These are my mother and brothers!"' – Gospel of Mark 3:31–35

Josephus, *Antiquities of the Jews*, XVII, 10, contains an account of the rebellion at the festival of Shavuot (The Feast of Weeks, or Pentecost) in around 4 BCE, along with the result: 'The number of those that were crucified on this account was two thousand.'

Iehuda from Queriot

'A follower said to him: "Lord, let me first go and bury my father." But Jesus said to him: "Follow me, and let the dead bury their dead"' – Gospel of Matthew 8:21–22

'And in Bethany, in the house of Simon the leper, as he sat at table there came a woman with an alabaster flask of pure spikenard, very precious. And she broke the flask and poured it on his head. And some disciples were angry and said, "Why waste this perfume? It could have been sold for a very high price and the money given to the poor." . . . Then Judas Iscariot, one of the twelve apostles, went to the priests to betray him' – Gospel of Mark 14:3–10

Caiaphas

'Seven days before Yom Kippur [the Day of Atonement] we sequester the High Priest from his house . . . we even make sure there's another wife for him, because what would happen if his own wife died?' – Talmud Yoma 1, 1

'And the priest shall write these curses in a scroll, and he shall wash them out in the bitter waters. And he shall make the woman drink the bitter waters that cause the curse' – Numbers 5:23–24 (the whole ritual is recounted in Numbers 5 throughout)

The massacre in the square by plain-clothes soldiers is recounted in Josephus, *The Jewish War*, II, 9.

Bar-Avo

Sicarii mingle with the crowd and kill people with daggers concealed in their cloaks in Josephus, *The Jewish War*, II, 13.

Epilogue

'[Titus's soldiers] caught every day five hundred Jews; some days they caught more . . . they nailed those they caught one one way and another a different way, to the crosses for a joke. Their multitude was so great that there was no room for all the crosses' – Josephus, *The Jewish War*, V, 11 (Titus's speech here is also largely taken from Josephus)

Acknowledgements

First of all, I must thank my mother, Marion, who passed on an interest in the history of this period to me, and my father, Geoffrey, an historian himself, who taught me the value of rigorous research, in so far as it is possible. The interest in lies I probably came to myself. I am grateful to my Hebrew teachers, who may not want their names associated with a book that is quite so visceral as this, and to Mrs Louise Pavey, who taught me Latin and, more importantly, taught me to love it.

Thanks to my agent, Veronique Baxter, and my editor, Mary Mount, for support, faith and courage. Thank you.

Thanks to Giles Foden, who told me it was time to write it, and to Jacqueline Nicholls, Dr Raphael Zarum, Daniel Harbour, Dr Lindsay Taylor-Guthartz, my research assistant, Rebecca Tay, and Francesca Simon for pointing me in good directions to get to grips with this complicated period. Thanks to the friends and colleagues who have read it and discussed it with me: Andrea Phillips, David Varela, Miki Shaw, Dr Benjamin Ellis, Natalie Gold, Susanna Basso and Daniel Hahn. Thanks to Seb Emina for the word 'tallest' and other creative wonders and to Rebecca Levene for title inspiration. Thanks to the North London Writers' Group, especially Emily Benet, Neil Blackmore, Alix Christie and Ben Walker for wonderful, firm, thoughtful suggestions. Thanks to Esther Donoff, Russell Donoff, Daniella, Benjy and Zara Donoff, and to Leigh Caldwell, Bob Grahame, Yoz Grahame, Tilly Gregory, Rivka Isaacson, Ewan Kirkland, Margaret Maitland, Rhianna Pratchett, Robin Ray, Poppy Sebag-Montefiore and Nicole Taylor. Thanks to Adrian Hon, Alex Macmillan and Matt Wieteska for staying strong and holding the (besieged) fort.

Particular thanks to Professor Martin Goodman and Professor Amy-Jill Levine, who graciously took time to read and comment on the manuscript and picked up scores of errors. All errors that remain are, of course, my own. For those who want to start learning about the Jewish history of this time, I can't recommend better than Professor Goodman's *Rome and Jerusalem* and Professor Levine's *The Misunderstood Jew*.

And finally. All books, when one looks at it, have wide roots, fumbling out in search of help and inspiration. This one has a longer taproot than many, perhaps.

This is a true story: after I had mostly finished researching this novel my mother, Marion, happened to find her father's Victorian copies of Josephus. Eliezer Freed, my grandfather, who died when I was two years old, was a novelist and short-story writer, fluent in ancient languages, a self-taught musician, inventor and scholar. I flicked through his Josephus with mild curiosity about differences in translation. And there, in his own handwriting, I found that my grandfather had marked up precisely the passages that I'd been looking at: the ones about Jesus. He had the same question mark in the margin, the same part bracketed where we both, I imagine, made the same frown at the same moment.

So it seems as though my family has been after this hare for a while. I suspect that if my pious and kind grandfather had written a novel about Jesus his might have been a bit more gentle.

Jews aren't encouraged to think a lot about the afterlife. There's some reward, they say, for a life lived well, but better to focus on the world we can see, better not to spend your years on earth obsessed with the world to come. The life after death we should mostly anticipate is twofold: the continuation of our ideas and our studies, and the continued life of our children and grandchildren. So it feels fitting to end the book on this note, in my discovery that I have produced a very Jewish kind of resurrection.